THIS SONG WILL SAVE YOUR LIFE

leila sales

 SQUARE FISH · FARRAR STRAUS GIROUX · NEW YORK

DISCARD

To Katherine Deutch Tatlock:
steadfast friend, brilliant artist, and world's best godmother

SQUARE
FISH

An Imprint of Macmillan
175 Fifth Avenue
New York, NY 10010
macteenbooks.com

Square Fish and the Square Fish logo are trademarks of Macmillan and
are used by Farrar Straus Giroux under license from Macmillan.

Square Fish books may be purchased for business or promotional use. For information
on bulk purchases, please contact the Macmillan Corporate and Premium Sales
Department at (800) 221-7945 x5442 or by e-mail at specialmarkets@macmillan.com.

Library of Congress Cataloging-in-Publication Data
Sales, Leila.
    This song will save your life / Leila Sales.
        pages cm
    Summary: Nearly a year after a failed suicide attempt, sixteen-year-old
Elise discovers that she has the passion, and the talent, to be a disc jockey.
    ISBN 978-1-250-05074-8 (paperback)
    ISBN 978-0-374-35139-7 (e-book)
    [1. Interpersonal relations—Fiction.   2. Popularity—Fiction.
3. High schools—Fiction.   4. Schools—Fiction.   5. Disc jockeys—Fiction.
6. Suicide—Fiction.]   I. Title.

PZ7.S15215Thi 2013   [Fic]—dc23   2012050408

Originally published in the United States by Farrar Straus Giroux
First Square Fish Edition: 2015
Book designed by Elizabeth H. Clark
Square Fish logo designed by Filomena Tuosto

10 9 8 7 6 5 4 3 2 1

AR: 4.8 / LEXILE: HL720L

Lyrics from "Never Be Alone" by Simian, which were rerecorded as
"We Are Your Friends" by Justice vs. Simian, used by permission
of Oli Isaacs (This Is Music Ltd).

We go down to the indie disco every Thursday night.
Dance to our favorite indie hits until the morning light.
—The Divine Comedy

1

YOU THINK IT'S SO EASY TO CHANGE YOURSELF.

You think it's so easy, but it's not.

What do you think it takes to reinvent yourself as an all-new person, a person who makes sense, who belongs? Do you change your clothes, your hair, your face? Go on, then. Do it. Pierce your ears, trim your bangs, buy a new purse. They will still see past that, see *you*, the girl who is still too scared, still too smart for her own good, still a beat behind, still, always, wrong. Change all you want; you can't change that.

I know because I tried.

I was born to be unpopular. There was no other way it could have gone. If there were just one place where it first fell apart, I could dream of going back in time and finding myself and saying, "Listen, ten-year-old Elise, just don't wear that oversize bright red sweater with the tufts of yarn sticking out of it like pom-poms. I know it is your favorite, because it looks so special, but don't do it. Don't be special."

That's what I would say to my younger self if I could pinpoint the moment when I went astray. But there was no one moment. I was always astray.

I've gone to school with the same kids since kindergarten. And they knew what I was long before I did. I was uncool by *fourth grade*. How is it even possible to be an uncool fourth grader? Didn't we all just string together friendship bracelets and daydream about horses and pretend to solve mysteries back then?

But somehow, even in fourth grade, they knew. A new girl moved to our town that year, from Michigan. She and I used to sit outside together during recess while the other girls played don't-touch-the-ground tag, and we'd talk about the witches' coven I wanted to form, because I'd read a chapter book about a witches' coven and my dad had given me some incense that I thought we could use. And then one day on the playground, Lizzie Reardon came over and casually said to my new friend, "Don't spend too much time with Elise. She might rub off on you." I was sitting right there. It wasn't a secret. I was a social liability.

This was *fourth grade*.

We went to a middle school twice the size of our elementary school, and then we went to a high school twice the size of our middle school. But somehow all those new kids, every one of them, immediately found out about me. Somehow it was that obvious.

When I was little my mom used to schedule my playdates with different girls: Kelly, Raquel, Bernadette. Then in fifth grade, Kelly moved to Delaware, Raquel invited every girl except me to her roller-skating birthday party, and Bernadette sent me a note to let me know that she only hung out with me because her parents said she had to.

I used to hang out with the neighborhood boys, too, when I was a kid. We would build forts in the summer and snowmen in the winter. But around the time we went to middle school, everyone started thinking about *dating*, which meant that no boy would be caught dead playing in the snow with me anymore lest someone see us and think he had a *crush* on me. Because obviously, having a crush on Elise Dembowski would be just about the lamest thing an eleven-year-old boy could do.

So by the end of seventh grade, I had no one. Okay, I still had kids who I splashed around with at my mom's summer lake house. I had my parents' friends' children, none of them quite my age, who would sometimes come over for family dinners. But I had no one who was really *mine.*

Last summer, after freshman year, I decided I couldn't go on like this anymore. I just could not. It's not like I wanted to be Lizzie Reardon, captain of the soccer team; or Emily Wallace, part-time teen model; or Brooke Feldstein, who could (and did) hook up with every guy in school. I didn't need to be the most exciting, beautiful, beloved girl in the world. I just needed not to be me anymore.

You think it's so easy to change yourself. It would be just like a movie makeover montage, pop music scoring the ugly girl's transformation from bespectacled duckling to cheerleader swan. You think it's so easy, but it was a whole summer's worth of work. It was watching TV constantly, like I was doing homework, taking notes on who all these characters were, making charts of who came from which shows. It was reading gossip magazines and women's magazines every week, testing myself when I was in the drugstore checkout line: "Who is that woman pictured on the cover of *Marie Claire*? Which reality TV show was she in?" It was hours of sunshine every day thrown away in favor of hunching over a computer, reading fashion blogs and celebrity blogs and perfume blogs. Did you even know that perfume Web sites exist? What is the point?

The one thing I couldn't bring myself to do was listen to the music. I tried, for nearly an hour. Then I gave up. It was *bad*. Not even interesting-bad, like the movies I went to see alone, taking note of which lines in a romantic comedy made the audience laugh. The popular music wasn't interesting-bad, it was *bad*-bad. Auto-Tuned vocalists who couldn't really sing; offensively simplistic instrumentation; grating melodies. Like they thought we were stupid.

I would have given almost anything to change myself, but I wouldn't give in to that. I hated that music more than I hated having to be myself every day. So I just read about popular musicians online and made flash cards about them until I felt prepared to talk about them. But not to listen to them.

All summer I spent on this. Ten weeks, uninterrupted, except for the time I spent record shopping, and the weekend I spent trying to repair my dad's computer, and a week that I had to spend at the lake house, where there is no TV or Internet. So, okay, I guess there were some interruptions, but still, you have to believe me when I tell you that the rest of the time I was working really hard on becoming cool.

This should have been a red flag, I realize in retrospect. Working really hard on anything is, by definition, not cool.

The week before school began, I went shopping. Not only did I go shopping, I went to the *mall*. I was ready. I knew what I was supposed to wear—I had read so many issues of *Seventeen* by that point, I could rattle off the five best mascara brands without even thinking about it.

So I knew what I was supposed to do, but I couldn't bring myself to do it. I wasn't going to spend $150 on a pair of jeans. I wasn't going to drop $300 on a purse. Come on, Kate Spade, you can't fool me—it's a *bag*. The Sierra Club regularly mails me bags for *free*. Or, okay, for a $25 donation, but really, that pays for saving forests, not for manufacturing tote bags, which I can't imagine costs more than a dollar or two.

Both my parents gave me some money for back-to-school clothes, and I had some money saved up, but I resented spending it all on clothes that I didn't really *want*. I mean, yes, I wanted to look like a cool person, but I didn't want to become impoverished in the process.

It's probably different for girls who have always been cool. Probably when they go shopping, they just have to fill in with a new pair of sneakers here or a new belt there. But I was inventing myself from scratch.

I went through every item in my closet. Which of these could I bring with me into my new life? Not the sweatpants, not the sweatshirts. These jeans, maybe, though the cuffs are wrong. This sweater, maybe, if it had a different neckline.

I thought all my clothes were fine. I liked them, even. They made a statement. The Indian sari that I had tailored into a summer dress. The Ramones shirt I got at a thrift store on Thayer Street, so threadbare that it just had to be an authentic relic of the seventies. The white boots with unicorns printed on them because, even though I'm fifteen, I still think the unicorn would be the world's greatest animal.

But that is the problem with me. That, right there. Not just that I owned these clothes but that I *liked* them. That after ten weeks of learning what real people did, I still liked my wrong, wrong clothes.

So I threw my wrong, wrong clothes into garbage bags and tied them shut as tight as I could, as if my unicorn boots might try to stage an escape. I hid the bags in the attic of my mom's house. Then I went on a shopping spree at Target for every knockoff *Seventeen*-style garment that I could find. Even then, the total wound up being way more than I had ever spent on clothes in any one of my thrift-store trips. It made me sick to look at the receipt.

But can you put a price on happiness? Really, if that's what it costs to make you glad to be yourself, then isn't it worth it?

On the first day of sophomore year, a Thursday, I sprang out of bed at six a.m. It takes time to make yourself look like a cool person. You can't just roll out of bed looking cool, or at least I can't.

So I got up. I washed and conditioned my hair. I shaved my legs, which is something I didn't know you were supposed to do until an ill-fated all-class pool party at the end of eighth grade. I put on my first-day-of-school outfit, which I had tried on a zillion times already: loafers, fitted jeans, a T-shirt without any writing or patterns on it, a headband. Headbands are back, you know. I read it in a magazine.

"I'm going to school," I announced to Dad.

He blinked at me over his newspaper. "No breakfast?"

"No breakfast." My stomach felt tight and jittery; breakfast was the last thing I wanted.

Dad's gaze drifted to the table, which was piled high with bread rolls, jam, bananas, milk, a pitcher of orange juice, and boxes of cereal that he had obviously set out for me. "You want breakfast like a monkey?"

"Dad, please." I never have to go through this routine at my mom's house.

He picked up a banana. "What do monkeys say?"

When I was a kid, I was really into bananas. I still like them, but when I was in elementary school I basically *subsisted* on them. My dad thought it was hilarious to make me ask for them by scratching at my armpits, jumping up and down, and saying, "Ooh ooh ahh ahh." You know. Like a monkey. So I thought it was hilarious as well. Anything that was proven to make my dad laugh made me laugh, too.

Sometime during middle school, it occurred to me that the monkey act might be stupid. But my dad never got over it.

"Ooh ooh ahh ahh?" He tossed the banana from hand to hand.

"I have to go, Dad." I opened the door.

"All right, kiddo. Knock 'em dead." He put down the banana and stood up to give me a hug. "You look great."

And I guess that should have been a warning sign, too,

because dads do not have the same taste as teenagers in what looks great.

I walked to the corner to wait for the school bus. Usually I'm running to catch the bus just before it pulls away because I'm cherishing every last moment in my house, where it's safe, before I have to go face the next eight hours.

But that morning, I made it to the bus stop with minutes to spare. I'm never early to anything, so I didn't know what to do with myself. I watched cars driving past and people coming out of their duplexes in business suits, off to work. I fought the pounding urge to put on my headphones. All I wanted was to listen to music, but wearing headphones makes you look cut off from the rest of the world, antisocial. I wasn't going to be antisocial this year. I was decidedly pro-social.

A few other kids showed up at the bus stop, too, but none of them spoke to me. It was so early, though. Who wants to have a conversation so early in the morning?

The school bus finally pulled up, and we all got on. I did not sit in the front. The front is where the losers sit, and I was not a loser anymore. Instead I sat in the middle of the bus, which is a relatively cool place to sit, even though I didn't feel cool about it. I felt panicked and nauseated about it, but I did it anyway. The bus drove off, while I sat on the peeling olive-green upholstery, taking deep breaths and trying not to think about what happened the other time I sat in the middle of the school bus.

It was last April, and for whatever reason I wasn't sitting in the very first row, like usual. Chuck Boening and Jordan Di-Cecca suddenly sat down next to me, and I had been so excited, even though I had to press my body against the window to make room for them both.

It's not like I was so excited because they are so hot, even though they are. It was just because they were talking to me, looking at me, like I was a real person. They were asking me what I was listening to on my iPod. They seemed genuinely interested. And I lost my head.

"I always see you with your headphones on," Jordan said, leaning in close, and that was flattering, that anyone cared about me enough to recognize that I *always* did something.

"Yes," I said, and did not elaborate that I always had my headphones on so I wouldn't always have to hear the world around me.

"What are you listening to?" Chuck asked.

"The Cure," I said.

Jordan nodded. "Oh, cool. I like them."

And that was exciting, too, that this suntanned soccer champ and I liked the same eighties goth band. I believe that a person's taste in music tells you a lot about them. In some cases, it tells you everything you need to know. I thought, in that moment, that if Jordan liked the Cure, then he wasn't the cookie-cutter preppy boy I'd always assumed. And I imagined that he thought, in that moment, that if I liked the Cure, then I wasn't the tragic loser he had always assumed. We were both more than our labels, and maybe we could be friends and go to concerts together.

So when Jordan went on to say, "Let me see," I handed him my iPod.

Why? Why did I believe he had to *see* my iPod to know what

I was listening to? I told you, it's the Cure! You want to know more, I'll tell you the title of the song! You want to know more, I'll tell you how many minutes and seconds into it I am! But shouldn't I have wondered why he needed to actually *hold* my iPod?

I handed it to him, and he grabbed it and ran off to the back of the bus with it, and with Chuck, and with everyone else on the bus cheering them on.

Was it really *everyone* else on the bus? Or was that just how I recalled it now, five months later? Some people on that bus must have had something else going on in their lives. Some girl must have recently broken up with her boyfriend. Someone must have been worrying about his bio test. Really, could every single person on that bus have just been caught up in the thrill of seeing my iPod stolen? Really?

It seemed like it, yes.

So what do you think I did? Did I go charging down the aisle of that bus, eyes ablaze, and *demand* that Jordan and Chuck return my iPod, because it did not belong to them, because they did not deserve to listen to the Cure under any circumstances, let alone under these? Did I use my righteous indignation to reclaim my iPod, and did I emerge from this struggle triumphant, with everyone else on the bus now cheering for *me*?

No. Instead, I let them run to the back of the bus with my iPod. I let them go. And then I leaned my head against the window and I cried.

Does this seem weak to you? Could you have done better? Fine, by all means, do better. But you don't understand this: sometimes when you are worn down, day after day, relentlessly, with no reprieve for years piled on years, sometimes you lose everything but the ability to cry.

I got my iPod back eventually. I told my homeroom teacher, and she told the vice principal, Mr. Witt, and he made the boys return my iPod and write letters of apology. Mr. Witt also told the bus driver, who somehow didn't know—or acted like he didn't know—what had happened on his bus, captured in his rearview mirror. The bus driver was annoyed with me, because it was my fault he got in trouble, and he barked at me, "From now on, sit up front, where I can keep an eye on you." Which I did for the last month and a half of freshman year.

So now, on the first day of sophomore year, when I sat near the middle of the bus—to the front of the middle, but still—I felt my whole body trembling, because I knew how big a risk I was taking. The knot in my stomach had tightened, and as the school bus rounded a corner, I seriously worried that I might throw up. Fortunately, I swallowed it down, which is good because vomiting on the first day of school is not cool. Also not cool is rocking back and forth as you sit in a school bus, breathing loudly, and wiping your sweaty palms on your new knockoff designer jeans. But even that is cooler than vomit.

Because my stop is one of the first on the bus's route, nearly all the seats were empty. They filled up fast, though. New kids got on at every stop, shrieking with excitement over new haircuts, new book bags, new manicures. Chuck and Jordan and their crew were nowhere to be seen, thank God, which implied to me that either they had all been expelled or their families had been relocated to prison camps. Or they just knew someone who had gotten a license and a car.

You might think that the absence of the iPod thieves would have made this a delightful bus ride, but it wasn't enough. My goal this year was not "see if I can get through a single hour without being tortured." It was "be normal. Have a few friends. Be happy."

I wanted someone to sit with me. I could even picture what she would be like. She would be cool, but casually cool. Artistic, with an embroidered shoulder bag and long, messy hair. Maybe she would wear glasses. She would see right through this horrible charade of high school.

But this imaginary girl did not sit down next to me. No one sat down next to me. The bus filled up, stop by stop, until eventually all the seats were taken and three girls were crowded together across the aisle from me, while I was still alone. We're not allowed to sit three to a seat, and I hoped the bus driver would yell at one of them to move to the empty space next to me. Sometimes he yells about stuff like that. But he didn't yell, and no one moved, and I sat alone the entire ride to school.

But that's okay, right? It was early in the morning, remember. It was practically the middle of the night. Who wants to have long, involved conversations with new friends at that hour? No one.

The bus pulled up in front of Glendale High School, and everyone immediately began jostling to get off. You know, because school is just so amazing for them. They can't wait to get off the bus so they can start passing notes and planning parties and making out with one another.

I got off the bus alone, and I went to homeroom alone, and I got my schedule for the year and didn't compare it with anyone.

The bell rang and I went to Spanish alone, and when the bell rang again I went to Geometry alone. And, again, "alone" is preferable to "molested," but I wanted more this year. I had spent all summer gearing up for this, and *I wanted more.*

In American Lit, Amelia Kindl asked to borrow my pen. She used my name, too. She leaned over from the desk next to mine and whispered, "Hey, Elise, could I borrow a pen?"

I said, "Sure," and smiled at her, because I read in a psychology study that people like you more when you smile.

She said, "Thanks," and smiled back. Then we both turned our attention to the teacher, so it's not like that was the beginning of a lengthy and fulfilling conversation, but it was something. It was an acknowledgment that I existed. If I didn't exist, why would I have pens?

I liked Amelia. I always had, ever since I first met her, in middle school. She was smart but not nerdy, artistic but not weird, and friendly to everyone. Amelia wasn't popular in the Lizzie Reardon sense of the word, but she had a core group of girl friends, and I imagined them having slumber parties every weekend, making popcorn and doing craft projects and watching movies. I would like to be someone like Amelia.

After American Lit, I made the mistake of passing Lizzie Reardon in the hallway. Last year I knew Lizzie's entire schedule and would follow incredibly byzantine routes, or hide in the bathroom until I was late to class, just to avoid her. This was a new year, with new schedules, so there was no accounting for Lizzie yet. She could be anywhere. Like in the hallway between American Lit and Chem.

I stared straight in front of me, using the ostrich approach: *If you can't see her, she can't see you.* But Lizzie is more wily than an ostrich.

"Elise!" She got directly in front of my face. I tried to ignore her, to keep walking. *"Elise!"* she called out again, in a singsongy way. "Don't be rude. I'm *talking* to you."

I stopped walking and stood very still. That's the rabbit approach: *If you don't move, she can't see you.*

Lizzie looked me up and down and then up again, to stare directly into my eyes as she said, "Wow, you look like a ghost. Did you go outside once this *entire* summer?"

This was not, by any stretch of imagination, the worst thing Lizzie had ever said to me. By some stretches of the imagination, this was the kindest thing she had ever said to me.

But it cut me, the same way Lizzie always knew how to cut me. I realized now that for every moment I had spent inside, watching popular movies and reading celebrity gossip blogs, I should have been outside, tanning. For everything I had done, there was something just as important that I had never thought to do.

Aloud I said nothing, and in a fit of mercy or boredom, Lizzie left me to go on to class.

Soon it was lunchtime. Still no one had directly addressed me, other than Lizzie, and Amelia, that time she asked for a pen. Maybe my clothes were wrong. Maybe my haircut was wrong. Maybe my headband was wrong.

Or maybe, I reasoned, everyone was still getting caught up from their summers apart. Maybe no one was thinking about making new friends yet.

I went to the cafeteria, which is easily the worst place in the entire world. Like the rest of Glendale High, the cafeteria is dirty, loud, and low-ceilinged. It has almost no windows. Presumably this is because they don't want you to be able to look outside and remember that there is a real world that isn't always like this.

I walked into that cafeteria clutching my brown-bag lunch so tightly that my knuckles turned white. I faced a room filled with people who either hated me or didn't know who I was. Those are the only two options. If you know me, then you hate me.

But I was not going to be intimidated. I was not going to give up. This was a new year, I was a new girl, and I was going to use the next thirty-five minutes to make new friends.

I saw Amelia sitting at the same table as last year. She was one of ten shiny-haired girls, all in sweaters and no makeup. One of them took photos for the *Glendale High Herald*. A couple of them were in the school a cappella group. Another one of them always got to sit out gym class because she had a note saying that she did yoga three evenings each week. I felt like if anyone in this room could be my group of friends, it would be them.

So I put one foot in front of the other and, step by step, approached Amelia's table. I stood there for a moment, towering over the seated girls. I forced myself to speak, for one of the first times since leaving home that morning. My voice came out squeaky, like a wheel in need of grease. "Would it be okay if I sat here?" is what I said.

All the girls at the table stopped what they were doing—stopped talking, stopped chewing, stopped wiping up spilled Diet Coke. No one said anything for a long moment.

"Sure," Amelia said finally. Had she waited an instant longer, I would have dropped my lunch and fled. Instead, she and four of her friends scooched down, and I sat on the end of the bench next to them.

So it's that easy, then? I thought, staring around the table. *It's that easy to make friends?*

Of course it's not that easy, you idiot. Nothing is that easy for you.

The girls immediately returned to their conversation, ignoring me. "Lisa swore she'd never been there before," one of them said.

"Well, she was lying," said another. "She'd been there *with me.*"

"Then why would she say she hadn't?" countered the first girl.

"Because she's *Lisa*," explained a third girl.

"Remember that time she told us she'd hooked up with her stepbrother at that party?" said one of the girls. "At, um . . ."

"At Casey's graduation party," supplied another.

"Wait, you mean she didn't?" the first girl asked.

"*No,*" they all groaned.

And I hung on their every word, and I laughed a beat after they laughed, and I rolled my eyes just as soon as they rolled their eyes—but I realized that somehow I hadn't prepared for this situation. In all my studies of celebrities and fashion and pop stars, it had never occurred to me that my potential friends might just be talking about people I didn't know and things I hadn't done. And I couldn't research that. That was just their lives.

The weight of this truth settled onto me until I felt like I was suffocating from it. How do you suddenly make friends with people? It's ridiculous. They have years and years of shared memories and experiences. You can't drop into that midway through and expect to know what's going on. They wouldn't have been able to explain it all to me if they had tried. And they weren't trying.

The girl sitting across from me picked a bean sprout out of her front teeth and said something that sounded like, "We sent rappers to the gallows on Friday."

I giggled, then stopped when she pursed her lips and raised her eyebrows at me.

"Sorry," I said. "You just said . . . I mean, what are the gallows?"

People also like you more when you ask questions about them, by the way. They like it when you smile, and when you ask them to talk about themselves.

"The Gallos Prize for the best student-made documentary film," the girl explained.

"Oh, I see. Cool. And what's rappers?"

"Wrappers," she said. "It's my film about people who go to mummy conventions."

The sheer amount of things I didn't know about these girls, that they were never going to tell me, was overwhelming. It was like the time my mom and I went to Spain on vacation and I'd thought I knew how to communicate in Spanish because I'd studied it in school for three years, but I didn't know. I didn't know at all.

But you can see, can't you, how these are the sorts of girls I would want to be friends with? If that were at all possible? They did things like film documentaries about mummy conventions! I wanted to do that, too!

Well, not *that*, per se. I didn't know anything about film-making, and the idea of mummy conventions was honestly a little creepy to me. But I wanted to do stuff *like* that.

I was so caught up in trying to follow the conversation, in trying to look like I belonged, that I didn't even notice that the lunch period was nearly over until everyone at the table touched her finger to her nose.

"You," said a girl in a bright flowered scarf, pointing at me.

"Yes?" I said, smiling at her. *Remember, smiling makes people like you more.*

She looked directly into my eyes, and I felt that same excitement as when Jordan and Chuck had asked me what music I was listening to. Like, *Hey, she's looking at me! She sees me!*

When will I learn that this feeling of excitement is not ever a good sign? That no one ever sees me?

"You," she said again. "Clean up."

Then the first bell rang, and everyone at the table stood up, together, and walked away, together, leaving all their soda cans and plastic bags and gobs of egg salad littering the table.

I stayed seated as the cafeteria emptied around me. Amelia hovered for one moment, letting her friends get a head start. "We always do that," she said to me, her eyebrows pulled together with a little bit of worry. "You know, the last one to put her finger on her nose has to clean up. That's our rule. So, today that was you."

Amelia smiled at me apologetically, and I guess that study was right, because her smile did make me like her more. I could have said, *That's a messed-up rule.* Or I could have said, *But I didn't know.* Or I could have said, *Do you honestly always do that? Or did you just do that* to me? Or I could have said, *Why don't you stay and help me?*

I could have said anything, but instead I said, "Okay."

And Amelia walked away, and I started throwing eleven girls' trash into the garbage can.

As I scooped up potato chip crumbs, I realized this, this most important truth: there are thousands, millions, countless rules like the one Amelia just told me. You have to touch your finger to your nose at the end of lunch. You have to wear shoes with this sort of heel. You have to do your homework on this sort of paper. You have to listen to this band. You have to sit in this certain way. There are so many rules that you don't know, and no matter how much you study, you can't learn them all. Your ignorance will betray you again and again.

Picking up soggy paper napkins, thick with milk, I realized, too: this year wasn't going to be any different. I had worked so hard, wished so hard, for things to get better. But it hadn't happened, and it wasn't going to happen. I could buy new jeans, I could put on or take off a headband, but this was who I was. You think it's so easy to change yourself, but it's impossible.

So I decided on the next logical step: to kill myself.

2

DOES THIS SOUND RIDICULOUS AND DRAMATIC, to decide in the middle of a totally average school day that this life has gone on for long enough? Was I overreacting? Well, I'm sorry, but that is what I decided. You can't tell me my feelings are overwrought or absurd. You don't know. They are *my* feelings.

I had considered suicide before, but it seemed so played out, so classic angsty teen crying out for attention, that I had never done anything about it. Today I was going to do something about it.

But I want you to know, it wasn't because I had to pick up other people's trash that I decided my life wasn't worth living anymore. It wasn't because of that. It was because of everything.

I left school right then and walked the five miles home, having no other mode of transportation. The weather was warm and breezy, and the sun shone brightly overhead. I listened to my iPod and thought about how there are good things in life, like fresh air and sun and music. Basically anything that doesn't involve other people. And it would be sad to leave all that behind forever, to never again see a cloud moving across the sky, to never again listen to the Stone Roses on my iPod as I walked in the sunshine. But at this point, having blown off half of my first day of sophomore year, I felt like I had pretty well committed myself to the suicide thing.

I came home to an empty house. My father works in a music store, and he wouldn't be home until six p.m. That gave me a few hours to address some logistical questions.

First, how to die? My dad doesn't own a gun, and even if he did I wouldn't know how to shoot it, and even if I did I wouldn't, since I am staunchly pro–gun control. I wasn't going to hang myself because that seemed to require a lot of engineering skills that I didn't have. And maybe I could ask the Internet "how do I make a noose," but that creeped me out. I figured that if it creeped me out that much, I probably didn't want to do it.

I'd once heard a rumor about a girl in New York City who tried to step off the roof of her apartment building and fall to her death. I guess that might work in New York City, but my dad's apartment building is only two stories tall, so I discounted that idea as well.

I could overdose on pills, but I remembered, as I went through the bathroom cabinets, that my dad doesn't keep many pills in the house. Dad is very into holistic remedies, and I don't think you can overdose on echinacea and neti pots. I could go to the drugstore and buy more pills, but that would take another half hour at least, and I wanted to get cracking. Furthermore, if I tried to overdose but didn't succeed, then I would run the risk of living, but being severely brain damaged. I am already socially disabled; I don't need to be mentally disabled on top of that.

So I settled on cutting myself until I bled to death. I wandered around the house, looking for something sharp enough to kill me. I know, I know: razor blades. But do you keep razor blades just lying around your house? Why? Are you doing a lot of woodworking projects?

I found my dad's X-Acto knife in the kitchen, buried under the front section of yesterday's newspaper. That's what my dad uses his X-Acto for: cutting out interesting articles without messing up the rest of the paper in the process. I picked up his X-Acto, and for some reason this overwhelmed me with sadness, but I didn't know whether I was feeling sad about my father's pathetic, unnecessary commitment to keeping his newspapers in good condition or whether I felt sad because I knew that, once I was dead, he would never want to cut articles out of the newspaper again.

I took the X-Acto blade upstairs to my room, where I sat down at my computer to make a suicide playlist. I didn't really want to die to MP3s. I wanted to die to records. The sound quality is better. But each side of a record lasts for only about twenty minutes, and I couldn't handle the idea of slipping out of consciousness for the very last time to the *click . . . click . . . click . . .* of a record that had reached the end and needed to be flipped over.

So I made a long playlist of songs that I thought I wouldn't mind dying to. It wasn't like making a road-trip playlist or a running playlist—I had never killed myself before, so I had no idea what I would want to listen to when it was too late for me to skip to the next song. Like, maybe when you're dying, you actually want to hear something really upbeat. Maybe when the moment came, I'd want to die to ABBA.

I spent a long time tweaking the playlist, sometimes listening to songs all the way through because I knew I would never hear them again. My playlist wound up being two hours long because I didn't know how long this would take, and I didn't want to run out of music and die in silence.

Again, I knew I could look this up. *How long does it take between the time you cut yourself and the time you die?* The Internet would know. But I wouldn't ask, because that made everything seem so clichéd. Another teenage suicide attempt, another cry for attention. It's all been done before.

Only mine wasn't going to be a cry for attention. Mine was going to be punishment. Punishment for Jordan DiCecca and Lizzie Reardon and those girls at lunch and everyone who had ever tortured me or turned their backs while I was tortured. And punishment for myself, too, of course. Punishment for being wrong.

But when I started thinking about punishment, I realized that I really wanted to leave a note, explaining why I had done it. What if Dad found me dead, and no one ever knew why, so none of the right people ever blamed themselves? Then what would be the point?

But a note was going to take me a while to write. I couldn't just scribble off something like, "Goodbye, cruel world," and stab myself through the heart. I wanted to explain it all, so everyone understood I wasn't being crazy and melodramatic. I wanted to start from the beginning, so they understood why I did this. I wanted to name names.

And as I thought more about Dad finding my dead body and suicide note, I realized also that this would make things even worse between him and Mom. I knew exactly how she was, and she would blame him for my death, even though it wasn't his fault. She would blame him because I was at his house, and she blamed him for everything that happened to me at his house, even things he couldn't control, like the time I was staying with him and got strep throat.

So, okay. Look. This was getting complicated. I wanted to die, but I wanted to make sure Dad didn't get in trouble for it, and I wanted to make sure all those bitches at school *did* get in trouble for it, and this was going to require a detailed suicide note and also probably a location that wasn't Dad's house. Plus I had spent so long on my playlist that it was already nearly five o'clock. So, realistically, this wasn't a great day for dying. Which was a disappointment, but also sort of a relief.

Since I already had the X-Acto knife, though, and I already had the playlist, I decided to go into the bathroom to practice a little. To practice cutting myself, I mean. Just a little, so that when the time came to do it for real, it wouldn't be scary. It would just be the logical next step.

I brought my laptop into the bathroom with me. I set it down on the floor and turned on "Hallelujah," the Jeff Buckley version. I pulled a bottle of rubbing alcohol out of the cabinet and poured it over the X-Acto, to sterilize the blade. I wanted to hurt myself, yes, but I didn't want to get an infection, too.

I sat down on the lid of the toilet. I held the X-Acto blade to the inside of my left arm. I stood up, walked out of the bathroom and back to my bedroom, and I picked up my teddy bear from my unmade bed. I carried him back down the hall to the bathroom, locked the door behind me, sat back down on the toilet seat, put my teddy in my lap, and started the song over from the beginning.

I again placed the X-Acto against the inside of my left forearm, but this time I pressed down. I drew a line straight across.

It didn't hurt. It just felt numb.

So I cut a second line, just a little bit closer to my wrist. That didn't hurt either. So I pressed down harder the third time, and I held it.

That hurt.

For a moment, I watched the blood bubble out of those thin slits through my arm. In Bio last year, I learned that blood is actually a dark maroon when it's inside your body. It's the exposure to oxygen that turns it bright red. And there must have been a lot of oxygen in my bathroom, because that blood was bright, bright red.

I stood up and turned the sink faucet on high. I held my arm under it to wash away the blood, but more blood kept coming out and kept coming out. Every time I tried to take it out from under the faucet, it just started bleeding harder.

You need to apply pressure in this sort of situation. Everyone knows that. So I kept my left arm still under the spray of the faucet while, with my right hand, I rooted around in the medicine cabinet for a bandage that would be big enough to cover my forearm. I finally found one wedged behind the bottles of rose hips and garlic pills.

I took my arm out from the sink and immediately pressed the bandage onto it. So that was good. That looked fine. I would wear long-sleeved shirts for a couple days and no one would ever know.

I grabbed my laptop in my right hand and my teddy in my left, and I unlocked the bathroom door and walked back to my bedroom. "Hallelujah" was just drawing to a close. That hadn't taken long at all. I felt like I had been in the bathroom forever, but "Hallelujah" isn't that long of a song.

I sat down at my desk and pulled out the Glendale High directory. It was in pristine condition. Because I never called anyone. Who would I have called?

I looked down at my arms, resting on my desk. Both of my hands were shaking. And blood was starting to seep through the bandage, dyeing it from gauzy white to bruised-apple red.

I stood up from my desk chair and carried my teddy bear and school directory into the corner of my room. I sat on the floor, pressing my back flush against the wall, all the way from my head to the base of my spine.

It turns out that I had been lying. I hadn't thought I was lying, but I was. When I said that I really wanted to die, that I wasn't a teen cliché, that I wasn't doing this for attention, that I, for one, *meant* it. I hadn't known it but I was lying, lying, lying. Because the next thing that I did was pick up my phone, with my right hand, and call Amelia Kindl to tell her that I had just cut myself. On purpose.

That's what I discovered about myself on the first day of my sophomore year of high school: I didn't really want to die. I never had. All I ever wanted was attention.

3

HERE WE ARE NOW. HERE WE ARE, THE FIRST
Thursday evening in April, a full seven months after I slit my
wrist and then called Amelia Kindl to tell her all about it. The
sun has just gone down, and it's dinnertime in the Myers
household.

Members of the Myers household include my mom; her
husband, Steve; their five-year-old son, Neil; their seven-year-
old daughter, Alex; their dogs, Bone and Chew-Toy; and, sometimes, me.

I am part of the Myers household every Saturday to
Wednesday, one month out of the summer, Christmas Day, and
Thanksgiving evening. The rest of the time I'm at my dad's, on
the other side of town. Except for sometimes, like this particular
Thursday, we have to move things around because my dad's
away. This time I believe his band was playing a show at the Six
Flags in Florida. When I was a kid, I would have begged and

pleaded to skip school to travel with him, but by this point in my life I have been to so many Six Flags and Busch Gardens with my dad and his band that they just don't excite me like they used to.

My parents' schedule for me may sound confusing, but it doesn't feel it. We've been doing the joint custody thing since I was six, so we got the hang of it a long time ago. At this point, everyone in my family has a smartphone with a synced-up Elise Calendar, and we just go wherever our phones tell us to.

Dinnertime in the Myers household requires everyone sitting in the dining room together, eating two different meals (mac and cheese or chicken fingers for Alex and Neil, real food for the rest of us), and having Dinnertime Conversation. Mom and Steve are the founders and copresidents of an environmental nonprofit called Bravely Opposing Oil Over International Lines, known to us insiders as BOO OIL. The idea is that if we have Dinnertime Conversation as a family, then the three of us kids will develop a more nuanced understanding of the world around us, so we will grow up to become educated members of a working democracy.

I would say there's a 15 percent chance that, if I hadn't been raised to be an educated member of a working democracy, I would have turned out cool. I'm not completely blaming my mother for my social problems or anything. I'm just saying that Lizzie Reardon clearly has no interest in being an educated member of a working democracy, and, so far, that seems to have served her well.

Here is what the Myers household's Dinnertime Conversation sounded like on this particular Thursday:

Mom: "I have some good news: we've finally decided what sofa we're getting."

Alex: "WHAT?! We have to get a new *sofa*?"

Neil: "Whhhhyyyyy?"

You see that? Educated members of a working democracy in action. Everyone participates in the democratic process. All our voices are heard.

Mom: "Because the old sofa is disgusting."

Steve: "The dogs have thrown up on it so many times, it's vomit-colored."

Alex: "I *like* the color of vomit."

Neil: "Me, too."

Mom: "Fine, then we'll get a new couch that's the same color, since you like it so much."

Alex: "But if it's the same color, then why can't we just keep the old one?"

Mom: "Because, I told you, it's disgusting."

Neil: *(inaudible comment)*

Steve: "What's that, champ?"

Neil: *(eyes brimming with tears)* "I love our sofa."

Alex: "It's okay, Neil. We're going to save it."

Neil: *(sniffling)* "Ho-o-o-ow?"

Steve: "Yeah, how?"

Alex: "Elise, how are we going to save the sofa?"

Me: "A sit-in."

Alex: "Yeah, a sit-in."

Neil: "What's a sit-in?"

Alex: *"Duh."*

Neil: "What's a sit-in, Alex?"

Alex: "It's a . . . It's not a thing you can just *describe*."

Mom: "It's when a group of people decide that they want something to happen, so they sit in one place and refuse to move until their requests have been met."

My mother can't help herself: if anyone asks her a question about civil disobedience, she feels obligated to reply.

Alex: "That's what we're going to do. Who's going to sit in at our sit-in?"

(Alex, Neil, and I raise our hands.)

Mom: "Really, Elise?"

Me: "I support young activists."

Neil: "Let's go now! Let's go sit in now!"

Alex: "Quick, before the new couch comes!"

(Neil and Alex each grab one of my arms and try to pull me out of my chair.)

Me: "After dinner, okay? I'm going to stage a sit-in at the dinner table for a while. Then I'll go join your sit-in in the living room."

After Alex and Neil run off to protest our parents' injustices, Dinnertime Conversation turns to the news of the world. Technically Dinnertime Conversation is always supposed to be about the news of the world, but sometimes we get sidetracked by other topics, like how much we love sofas, or whether Steve tried to sneak tofu into Alex's macaroni again.

The big news story of today was that a boy in Arizona had brought a gun to school and opened fire on his homeroom class, killing three and wounding eight before turning the gun on himself.

"It's a tragedy," Mom said, which is the most blatantly true statement ever, but I guess that's what you say when you can't think of anything else.

"This is why we need stricter gun control." I tore off a chunk of baguette. "I say this all the time. But does anyone ever listen? No."

"You could stage a sit-in," Steve said. "I hear you like sit-ins."

"Love 'em," I agreed. "Can't get enough of them."

"You wouldn't do anything like that, would you, Elise?" Mom asked supercasually.

I knew what she was asking. I knew, but that didn't mean I was going to make it easy for her. "I wouldn't do anything like stage a sit-in advocating harsher restrictions on handguns?" I said. "I might."

She frowned and stared down into her water glass. "I mean, you wouldn't . . . do anything like what that boy did."

This is what happens, by the way, when you cut yourself and then tell an oversensitive girl who does the oversensitive thing of immediately alerting 911. What happens is that, more than half a year later, your mother will ask you, in all seriousness, whether you would take a gun to school and shoot up the place. Because you are suspect now. You are a wild card.

Mom and Steve were silent, waiting for my answer. I stabbed my fork into my quinoa salad, then realized that stabbing probably made me look violent. "No," I said. "I wouldn't kill anyone."

We've been over this before. Whether or not I would kill anyone, I mean. No, I wouldn't.

I think that's a boy thing anyway. Or, I don't know, not necessarily just boys, but people who aren't like me. I may *hate*

Lizzie Reardon and Chuck Boening and now Amelia Kindl most of all, but I would never try to hurt them directly. I wanted to hurt myself. I blamed them, yes, but I blamed myself more.

After dinner, I joined Alex and Neil in the living room. We sat purposefully on the couch and took turns saying what we loved about it.

"I love that the pillows look kind of like faces so you can hold them up and make them talk to each other," said Neil. He held up two couch pillows and demonstrated.

"Huh." I looked at the pillows. They did have some dents and wrinkles that could possibly be mistaken for eyes and a mouth. "Good point, Neil."

"*I* love that there's this hole between these two cushions and it's the perfect place to put my Barbies when they've been captured by the evil sea witch because it looks just like a whirlpool. And then the evil sea witch turns them all evil, too, because she gets inside their heads and they can't think their own thoughts anymore, they can only follow her evil commands."

I looked silently at Alex as she slid her arm in and out of the gap between couch cushions. I used to play make-believe games like that when I was her age, with the same hole on this same couch.

"You shouldn't play that game, Alex," I said finally.

"What? Underwater Capture?" she asked.

"Yeah. Other kids don't play games like that."

"Yes, they do," she said, and even her eyes reminded me of myself, gray-blue and too big for her face.

"They don't. They play games with other kids. Like School. Or House. Or soccer."

"I hate soccer," Alex said.

"I know. I hate soccer, too. But you should play it anyway."

"Elise?" Neil had lain down on the couch and was resting his head on my lap. It was past his school-night bedtime, but my mom and Steve have never been ones to interrupt a sit-in. "Elise, it's your turn to say a thing you love about the couch."

"I love . . ." I absentmindedly rubbed my hand across the ragged, stained fabric. I supported young activists, but Mom was right; this couch was a piece of shit. "I love that this couch has never judged me."

"Yeah," Neil agreed sleepily.

"Yeah," said Alex. "Good couches don't do that."

I sat there and did my American Lit reading until both of them fell asleep. Then Mom and Steve came in and picked them up to carry them upstairs to their bedrooms.

"You realize this is a sit-in, right?" I asked. "That means you two are scabs."

"It *was* a sit-in," Mom said, wrapping her arms around Neil. "Now it's just a sleep-in." She kissed me on the top of my head. "Good night, Elise. Don't stay up too late."

I waited for a while after the rest of my family went upstairs. Then, once all was silent and dark, I put on my sneakers and I snuck out of the house.

This is something that I started to do after I cut myself. Not right away; for the first few months, my parents were so freaked out that they basically kept me under house arrest. But half a year later, we were back to normal. It's not like they *forgot* that their daughter had torn up her wrist with an X-Acto knife. I don't think you can forget something like that. I just don't think you can think about it every day without driving yourself crazy.

So in March, as spring was starting to peek through the cold, I began to walk at night. I'd wait until midnight or so, once everyone in the house was asleep, and then I'd put on my shoes, grab my iPod, and head out into the night.

It's surprisingly easy to sneak out of my house. It's an old building, built by some rich merchant family in the 1800s, so it doesn't have a normal house layout. Mom and Steve's bedroom is on the third floor, Neil's and Alex's are on the second, and I alone live on the first floor, in what had once been the maid's quarters. If I were a different sort of person, I could have taken advantage of this situation to sneak out to something cool. Like keg parties. (I assumed some kids in my town had keg parties, though maybe I only got that idea from movies.) But, since I was just me, I just snuck out to walk alone.

I never knew how many miles I traveled. Something about that first day, when I walked five miles home from school, made me realize: five miles is nothing. So now I wandered around town, sometimes just for half an hour, sometimes until the sun was starting to rise, however long it took for me to get tired. No one saw me and no one knew, and for this reason, these nighttime walks were the only times that I didn't feel trapped in my life.

Walking at night is like walking in a dream. It's dark, so I don't notice much of the scenery. I don't wear my watch, so time becomes meaningless. I'm not carrying a tote bag or a backpack or whatever usually weighs me down in the daytime, so I feel light and bouncy. I listen to music as loud as I can, and I don't think about anything.

I know some people would get scared walking alone when it's so late, but I am not one of those people. I just don't see anything to be scared of. For one thing, *Forbes* has declared Glendale to be America's number-one safest city every year since I was a kid. (Except for one year, when there was a small rash of car break-ins. Glendale dropped to America's number-two safest city, and there was a lot of outcry about how we needed to "reclaim our crown.")

For another thing, I've never been scared of the dark or silence. When I was younger, my dad and I used to walk around his neighborhood together before I went to bed. He said he liked looking at the stars because it cleared his head. It clears mine, too.

Tonight I walked vaguely in the direction of my school, out of the residential area with its parks and big single-family houses, and into the bordering neighborhood, where mostly college students lived and hung out. I passed by their blocky four-story apartment buildings, then headed down the hill, bypassing shuttered coffee shops, boutiques, and restaurants. A few cars drove by. I saw a woman letting herself into an apartment, and a couple strolling along, pausing occasionally to peer in darkened shop windows. Nobody my age, of course.

At the end of the hill, I turned left onto a wider, grayer street that mostly housed warehouses and storage units. This was the route my school bus took in the mornings. There were no trees in sight, only a few spread-out streetlights, and two girls across the street. Standing still. Watching me.

My heart immediately started beating faster, and I snuck my hand inside my jacket pocket to click off my iPod so I could hear what was going on. In my experience, when people noticed me, it never led to anything good.

"Hey, you!" one of them shouted across the road.

Just keep walking, I told myself. *It's like when Lizzie Reardon calls your name in the hallway. Just keep walking. Think invisible, and if you're lucky maybe you will become invisible.*

"Girl over there!" she yelled again. "You're going in the wrong direction!"

I stopped when she said that. For some reason, this statement really threw me. I wasn't going *anywhere,* so how could I be going in the wrong direction?

"Come here!" she called.

I obey direct orders. That's why I cleaned up a full lunchroom table, that's why I gave Jordan my iPod, and that's why I crossed the street now. Because someone told me to.

The two girls were leaning against a graffitied wall. The one who had shouted was a little taller than me, heavyset, and smoking a cigarette. She wore a black-and-white polka-dot dress with a bright yellow cardigan, and she had feathers in her hair.

"Start's in there," she said, cocking her finger at the building behind her.

This was like *I'm sending* Wrappers *to the Gallos* all over again. *Start's in there.* Why did people always have to speak in code?

"Okay," I said.

"Have you been here before?" she asked me.

I shrugged in a way that probably meant yes, but could have meant no.

"We haven't been here since it was over in Pawtucket," the polka-dot-dress girl went on, gesturing west with her cigarette, even though Pawtucket was roughly nine miles north of where we stood now. Also, how could they not have been somewhere since it was somewhere else? This whole thing was very *Alice in Wonderland*.

"Do you want a cigarette?" she offered me.

"No, thank you," I said, then added, "I don't smoke."

She nodded. "That's good. These can kill you." She took a long drag on her cigarette, as if to prove the point.

Her friend spoke up for the first time. She was petite and had a blond pixie haircut. She reminded me a little of a foal, all gangly legs and round eyes. She spoke with an accent that made her words just a little hard to understand as she said, "Vicks, it sounds like you were offering her a cigarette because you were trying to kill her."

The first girl's mouth dropped open in faux horror, her bright red lipstick forming a big O. "I was being *generous*."

The friend shrugged her bony shoulders. "Well, she doesn't know us. For all she knows, you were trying to infect her with cancer." She adjusted her short, fringed leather jacket over her gold sequined dress.

"You're from England?" I asked the skinny friend, dissecting her accent.

"Originally," she said. "I grew up in Manchester."

"Manchester!" I exclaimed.

"You've been there?" She sounded surprised.

"No, but I've always wanted to go."

"Don't. Manchester is a shithole," she said decisively. "The whole town looks like this." She swung her arm out to encompass the blank street of warehouses.

"The Smiths are from Manchester, though," I said.

"And New Order," she added, sounding proud. "And Oasis."

"Okay, blah blah, we get it, all the world's greatest bands come from your hometown," the polka-dot-dress girl threw in. "Thanks for rubbing it in."

"Only because it's such a shithole," the British girl said. "People have to create some kind of art so they have something to think about other than their shitty lives."

"Yeah, but Glendale's a shithole, too, and how many world-class musicians come from *here*?" countered her friend.

"You. For example."

The polka-dot-dress girl snorted and stubbed out her cigarette on the wall. "Yeah, right. Come on, let's go back in before I smoke another one and give us all cancer."

They walked a few feet away from me, then turned around when they noticed I wasn't with them. "Are you coming or what?" demanded the polka-dot-dress girl.

And something about feeling like I was in a dream, or a Lewis Carroll hallucination, made me feel okay about answering, "I'm coming."

I scampered after them as they turned a corner, down a small alleyway between warehouses. I was probably about to get kidnapped. But, honestly, I would have rather been kidnapped by these girls than remained un-kidnapped among my class-mates. If getting kidnapped meant a trip to Manchester, I was all for it.

"What's your name anyway?" the bigger girl called over her shoulder.

"Elise."

She turned around to look me up and down. "Like the Cure song?"

"Yes," I said.

She nodded her approval. "This skinny bitch here is Pippa. I'm Vicky, short for Victoria, of course."

"Like the Kinks song?" I blurted out. Then I blushed. That sounded dumb coming out of my mouth. I sounded overeager, juvenile. Uncool.

But she gave me a broad, beaming smile. "Yeah," she said. "Like the Kinks song."

At the end of the alleyway stood a large black man with a shaved head and pierced ears, guarding a closed door.

"Hi, Mel," chirped Vicky.

"Heya, Mel," said Pippa, standing on tiptoe to kiss him on both cheeks.

"Who's this?" he said gruffly. He squinted down at me.

"Elise," I said. I stuck out my hand to shake his, but he kept his firm arms crossed over his chest.

"You got ID?" he asked.

All I had was my iPod. "Not on me," I answered. "But I promise my name is Elise."

"She's twenty-one today," Vicky butted in. "Isn't that exciting? Happy birthday to you, happy birthday to you, happy birthday, dear Elise—"

"If this girl's twenty-one, then so am I," Mel said with an eye roll.

"You mean you're *not* twenty-one?" Vicky feigned surprise. "I swear, Mel, you can't be any older than that. Your skin is baby-soft."

41

The corners of Mel's mouth twitched like he was fighting a smile. "I'm old enough to be your father, Vicks."

"No way!" Vicky said. "My dad is *old*. You know that magazine old people get?"

"No," said Mel.

"Well, there's a magazine, and my dad has been getting it since I was six years old. Plus he goes to bed every night at nine. Mel, you have *never* been in bed at nine."

Mel shrugged his broad shoulders. "Age is more than just a number. It's a lifestyle."

"So what you're telling me here," Vicky said, "is that Elise really *is* twenty-one, even if she doesn't have the ID to prove it."

Mel groaned and began to reply, but Pippa stepped forward. "Come on, Mel," she said quietly, and I couldn't tell what it was, if it was her posture, or the expression on her face, or her voice, or the halting way she touched her tiny fingers to her hair, but I couldn't imagine anyone in the world saying no to her. "Be a gentleman. Elise is with us."

And Mel stepped back and opened the door for us.

As we walked past him and into the building, I marveled at this. Not at Vicky's banter or at Pippa's feminine wiles, but at their willingness to say, unprompted, *Elise is with us.*

Why are you being nice to me? I wanted to know. But I didn't ask. If I asked that, they might realize their mistake. Instead I just lightly pressed the inside of my left wrist, like I was checking for my pulse, and I followed them inside.

4

THE DOOR OPENED TO REVEAL A PACKED DANCE floor of sweaty, flailing bodies illuminated by occasional flashing lights in the otherwise dimly lit, high-ceilinged room. "Dancing in the Dark" was blasting from speakers twice my height, and most of the crowd was singing along like their lives depended on it, except for a guy who was taking photos with an expensive-looking camera, a few girls who were waiting in a bathroom line, and two guys who were hard-core making out, complete with ass-grabbing and saliva-drenched French kissing.

"This is a nightclub?" I asked, then repeated, louder, when I realized no one could hear me.

"It's Start!" Vicky replied. Her normal speaking voice was loud enough that she didn't even have to try to project over the music. "The greatest underground dance party in the world!"

Pippa shook her head, and I could see her lips moving.

"Pippa says that she once went to a better underground dance party in Sheffield. But she's full of shit. Start is it, Elise. Start is as good as it gets. You've really never been here before?"

I shook my head and admitted, "I'm not really twenty-one."

Vicky cracked up. Even Pippa almost smiled, and I could tell from the night so far that she wasn't much of a smiler. Vicky said, "Honey, none of us are really twenty-one. We're both eighteen."

"The drinking laws in this country are ridiculous," Pippa contributed.

"I don't care about drinking," Vicky said. "But I don't see why you have to be twenty-one just to have a good time."

Even at eighteen, Pippa and Vicky were both at least two years older than me. I'd just turned sixteen in January. They were probably already out of high school. Maybe they were in college. That explained why they could get dressed up in sequined dresses and feathers and go to a dance party at one a.m. on a weeknight. Because they were free.

"Speaking of drinks," said Pippa, "I'm going to get one." I watched her stride off across the room, her spindly legs balanced on high-heeled boots.

On her way to the bar, Pippa stopped by the DJ booth. She climbed two steps to the platform, where some guy with headphones around his neck was bopping in front of a computer, two turntables, and some other electronic equipment. The platform was so small that she had to stand right next to him, her elbow practically brushing against his. I could see her talking, but I couldn't tell if he was listening, since he kept his eyes focused on the equipment before him as he adjusted various dials.

"The DJ's name is Char." Vicky spoke directly into my ear. "Pippa *loooves* him."

I looked at them differently after Vicky told me that. I tried to see the love in Pippa's behavior. I tried to figure out if he loved her back.

"They look good together," I said. "Like a pair." He was a few inches taller than Pippa was, even in heels, and his dark hair perfectly complemented her platinum blond locks. Even their leather jackets looked like they'd been purchased together, a Barbie and Ken Go to the Discotheque boxed set.

Vicky grinned. "I'm going to tell her you said that. She'll love it."

Char held up a *wait a minute* finger to Pippa, then put his headphones on. Pippa hovered next to him for a moment, but when he didn't look up from his computer, she climbed down from the DJ booth and continued on to the bar.

The song transitioned into "Girls and Boys," and the crowd went wild.

"We're dancing!" Vicky shouted at me, which wasn't strictly true. *She* was dancing.

Here are all the dance floor experiences I've had so far in my life:

1. Ruining the Tiny Dancers year-end recital at the YMCA when I was six years old because I didn't know how to skip.

2. Going to a school dance in seventh grade, where they played songs like "Shake Your Ass," only with the word *ass* bleeped out, and everybody grinded up on everybody else, except nobody grinded up on me.

So, for what I think are some pretty good reasons, I don't dance.

The boys near us stopped sucking face for long enough to

scream out the chorus with everyone else. I shifted my weight from foot to foot and sang the words and tried to move my arms like Vicky did. Then I realized I looked stupid and put my arms back by my sides, where they belonged.

Pippa ran back onto the dance floor, holding a beer.

"Elise!" Pippa screamed at me, and she thrust her beer into my hands.

"Thank you," I started to say, because for a moment I thought Pippa was trying, however misguidedly, to give me a gift.

Pippa grabbed Vicky's hands in her own, and they started jumping up and down together, screaming the words straight into each other's faces. On one of their jumps, Pippa's heel landed right on my foot, but nobody seemed to notice.

I realized a beat too late that Pippa wasn't giving me a gift of a beer can. She was using me as a living, breathing cup holder. That's all. My legs slowly ground to a halt, like a wind-up toy that had run out of power.

I had this feeling suddenly. I get this feeling a lot, but I don't know if there's one word for it. It's not *nervous* or *sad* or even *lonely*. It's all of that, and then a bit more.

The feeling is *I don't belong here. I don't know how I got here, and I don't know how long I can stay before everyone else realizes that I am an impostor. I am a fraud.*

I've gotten this feeling nearly everywhere I have ever been in my life. There's nothing you can do about it except drink some water and hope that it subsides. Or you can leave.

I set Pippa's beer down on the floor. She and Vicky were still holding hands and jumping in unison, twirling each other around. A few guys nearby were watching them appreciatively. The man with the big expensive camera elbowed me out of the way to snap a photo of them. No one was looking at me. So I took option B, and I left.

Just before I slipped out the door, I paused for a moment to look at the room one more time, trying to cement this image in my mind. The darkness and the music, the sparkly headbands catching the lights, the brightly colored sneakers sliding across the dance floor.

Across the room, Char glanced up from his DJ equipment. He held one headphone to his ear but left the other side free as he surveyed the crowd. He moved his mouth slightly, as if talking or singing to himself. His eyes scanned the room and rested, briefly, on me.

I held his gaze with mine for a long moment. He didn't smile, but his expression was friendly, I think, or maybe just curious.

Then he looked back down at his computer, and I walked out.

When my alarm went off at 6:35 the next morning, I felt discombobulated. Even though I stayed up too late all the time, I didn't usually feel so groggy. I had trained myself to get through days on minimal sleep. In fact, school felt better when I felt out of it. It's like getting anesthetized before a surgical procedure.

After turning off the alarm, I stared at my ceiling and tried to figure out what was going on. Had I actually uncovered a secret warehouse dance party? Or had I dreamed up the whole thing as some kind of pathetic wish-fulfillment fantasy?

Then Alex came running into my room, screaming, "Mom says I'm supposed to tell you to get up! And she says it's going to rain! And she says what do you want for breakfast!"

That's the problem with life. You never get enough time to stare at your ceiling and try to figure out what's going on.

At breakfast, not one member of the Myers household said anything to me like, "So, did you stumble across any nightclubs at one o'clock in the morning while you were pacing the back roads of Glendale?" Instead, people at breakfast said things like, "I have a five o'clock call with the funder, so can you pick up the kids from afterschool?" (Mom), and "Champ, I promise that is the same sort of Eggo we get every week. It just looks browner, but if you closed your eyes, it would taste exactly the same" (Steve), and "I'm not going to go to school, I'm going to sit on the couch all day, and you can't stop me, 'cause I'll be participating in the democratic process" (Alex), and "It looks like it's whole wheat. You *know* I don't eat whole wheat Eggos" (Neil).

So, clearly, nightclubbing was not at the top of anyone else's mind this Friday morning.

I caught my school bus with seconds to spare and sat in the front row. After the first day of this year, I had given up on trying for the middle of the bus. What, you think that if you sit six rows back from the driver instead of one row back, people will be fooled into thinking you're cool and join you? I tried that. That did not work. My classmates may be idiots, but even they are not so easily fooled.

I pressed my face to the smudged bus window and watched warehouse after warehouse roll past us as I looked for Start. And what I found was this: in the rain and in the morning, they all looked exactly the same.

I took my face away from the window and leaned back against my seat as the bus rounded the corner. If I hadn't been there to see where the party had once been, I never would have known it was there at all.

School was normal, which is to say soul-crushingly depressing. I sat in class and wrote the lyrics to "Dancing in the Dark" in my best cursive handwriting in the margins of my notebook. I imagined Vicky sweeping into the room, with Pippa stalking in behind her on four-inch heels, and announcing to the class, "Elise is with us! None of you appreciate her, and you don't even deserve her. Elise, it's time. We are here to take you to your real life. You have suffered long enough through this one, but this was only a test, and the test is over now." And then I would rise to my feet and join hands with them, and together we would run off into the sunset.

I drew a picture of all of this in my notebook. But that was as close as it was going to come to reality. Not least because it was only eleven thirty, so the sun wasn't setting, and, even if it were, I wouldn't have been able to tell, because it was raining.

Eventually it was time for lunch. Sophomores are *not* allowed off campus, and they are *not* allowed to wander the halls. Therefore, here were my options for how to spend my lunch period:

Option one: Sit in the library and read a book and listen to my iPod, which is basically the perfect way to spend thirty-five minutes of a school day, except that you are *not* allowed to eat in the library—nor are you allowed to eat in the halls or classrooms—so when I go this route, I am ready to faint from hunger by the time school lets out for the day.

Option two: Sit in Ms. Wu's classroom and discuss math with her. This is actually a great bargain, since she doesn't seem to know or care that we are *not* allowed to eat in classrooms. When I'm with Ms. Wu I get to eat my sandwich without running into any of the popular kids, because a defining characteristic of popular kids is that they do not like to hang out with math teachers. Furthermore, Ms. Wu tells me interesting math stuff, some of which might even prove useful when I take the SATs next year, and good SAT scores are my best hope for getting into a good college and therefore escaping this hellhole.

Unfortunately, Ms. Wu teaches during my Friday lunch period. Ms. Wu's classroom is a good option on Tuesdays. But not on Fridays.

Option three: Sit in the cafeteria, at a table with my friends.

Oh, did I not mention that I have friends now? Did I somehow leave that out? I have friends now. Surprise!

My friends are named Sally and Chava. They are both less popular than me, and I don't know why, but I hope it's because they are unbelievably boring. They have only one interest, and that is: what the popular kids are doing.

Sally and Chava follow the popular kids' lives like soap operas. Brooke Feldstein cannot give one blow job to one member of the school basketball team without Sally and Chava knowing about it, discussing it on the phone, following up on it with an in-person conversation, soliciting eyewitness testimony from any-one else who might have been within a two-mile radius, googling it, and placing bets on what brand of lip gloss Brooke was wear-ing at the time.

I must note that Sally and Chava are not friends with Brooke Feldstein. I don't think they have ever talked to her. They just follow her antics from afar. They are Brooke Feldstein's silent but adoring fan base.

Today I was hungry enough from walking all night that starving in the library wasn't an option, and Ms. Wu's Friday class ruled out that one, so I was stuck with my dear friends in the cafeteria.

The big news of the week was that Jordan DiCecca had bro-ken up with his girlfriend, Laura, for this other girl, Leah. Everyone knew this. But had he *cheated* on Laura with Leah *before* breaking up with her? That was the real question.

"He definitely did," said Sally over lunch. "There is no way Jordan would have broken up with Laura if he hadn't already tried out Leah to make sure that she'd, you know, put out."

Chava chewed on her lip, looking doubtful. "He could have just asked her. Like, 'Hey, Leah, if I break up with Laura, would you have sex with me?'"

"Come on, you know Jordan," Sally said. We didn't. "He would want some sort of guarantee on his investment." Sally bit into a stick of celery. Sally and Chava eat only raw vegetables for lunch because they are trying to lose weight. Then they split a pack of Entenmann's donuts for dessert. They have explicitly stated that they believe that if they were seven pounds lighter (Sally) or thirteen pounds lighter (Chava), then they would have popular friends and not have to sit at the loser table with each other and me. This sounds pathetic and delusional, but I let them continue to believe it because, after all, it's no more pathetic and delusional than believing that you can make friends by sitting in the middle instead of the front of the school bus.

"Laura and Jordan were together for more than a year," Chava said thoughtfully.

Sally nodded. "It was a year in February."

"That's forever. This is such a huge change. It's really sad, you know?"

I could tell she wasn't kidding. Chava looked like Neil and Alex hearing that we were getting a new sofa. I guess nobody takes change that well.

"You could stage a sit-in about it," I offered.

Blank looks from my friends.

"You know. 'We won't budge from this cafeteria table unless Jordan and Laura get back together!' "

Sally and Chava looked way less enthusiastic about this idea than Alex and Neil had.

"I'll make protest signs for you to carry," I went on. "If that would help you any."

Sally leaned forward, lowered her voice, and said, "I wonder how long he and *Leah* will last."

You may wonder how I managed to make these friends. Well, I will tell you: making friends is actually not that hard when you drop every single one of your standards.

Our cafeteria tables are unofficially arranged with the most popular kids sitting in the center. As you work your way out to the edges of the room, the tables become filled with less and less desirable people. Amelia Kindl's table, for example, is four rows in from the back row. Sally and Chava's table is in the very outer rim of the cafeteria, directly in front of the bathrooms. In every regard, it is the worst table.

I was out of school for a couple weeks after I cut myself. Which wasn't even as enjoyable as you might expect, since I spent the entire time worrying about going back to school. When I finally did, and I entered the cafeteria for the first time, I looked for a table where no one would have any clout to order me to move, or to ask questions that I didn't want to answer, or to make me clean up after them. I sat down at Sally and Chava's table, and they didn't tell me to leave, so now they are my friends, apparently.

"I wonder what she'll wear to the dance tonight?" Chava mused.

"Probably something new," Sally said wisely. "Leah always gets a new dress for dances." She turned to me. "Hey, do you want to come over to get ready for the dance together?"

"Um." I swallowed a bite of my PB&J. "Is there a school dance tonight?"

"The Spring Fling," Chava replied, and she didn't even add anything like *"Obviously"* onto her answer. Chava is a little dumb and impossibly boring, but she is doggedly nice.

"How did you miss all the posters and the announcements and the ads in the *Herald*?" Sally asked. "Honestly, Elise, sometimes it seems like you don't even go to this school."

"Well, that is the goal," I said.

"Anyway, will you come over before so we can get ready together?" Sally asked. "My mother said I'm allowed to wear body glitter, just for tonight."

"Ooh," Chava contributed.

Sally has the sort of parents who evaluate her every time she leaves the house to make sure she doesn't look like a "streetwalker" (Sally's dad's word, not mine). This sounds like child abuse to me, yet Chava thinks Sally is the lucky one because *Chava's* family is so religious that she's not allowed to go out on Friday nights at all, regardless of what she's wearing.

"I'm not allowed to drive, though," Sally added. "Just in case someone spikes the punch." Sally has her driver's license, but her parents constantly come up with reasons why she's not allowed to use it. That still puts her ahead of Chava and me, since neither of us can drive at all.

Mostly I feel bad for Sally and Chava, but sometimes I'm jealous of them. Their parents clearly screwed them up for life, or at least for high school, so they have someone to blame for their uncoolness. I don't have that luxury. I can only blame myself.

I picked apart my sandwich crust and tried to figure out how to reply to Sally without hurting her feelings. I recognized her invitation as a sign of friendship—honestly, I did. This was Sally's way of being friends with me. But the thought of going over to her house and dressing up in whatever teenagers are supposed to wear to school dances, and being given permission to wear a certain amount of body glitter, and getting a ride with Sally's parents back to this same building, where we could stand near these same people who would continue not to talk to us, only this time my least favorite music would be blaring in the background . . . I mean, you could not pay me enough money. And,

54

in fact, no one would be paying me any money. On the contrary, I would have to pay five dollars at the door.

"Thanks, Sally," I said, "but I'm not going tonight."

"Oh, no!" Chava said, like something really bad had happened.

Sally wrinkled up her nose. "Don't you like to dance?"

I thought about last night, about the flashing lights and the thrumming music and Vicky and Pippa, jumping up and down, their feet always hitting the floor at the exact same time. "Dancing is okay," I said.

"So, you should come then," Sally determined.

"No," I said again. "But you have fun. Hey, I wonder who will ask you to dance tonight?"

And that distracted them. No one ever asks Sally to dance at these things, but that doesn't stop her and Chava from thinking that someone might, someday. Tonight could be the night. The body glitter could make all the difference.

Maybe I should feel worse for Sally and Chava than I do for myself, but I am not that generous. Okay, they live in a fantasy world, but at least their fantasies give them a nice protective cushion. I have fantasies, too, like the one about Pippa and Vicky appearing in the middle of my history class to rescue me from my life. But, unlike Sally and Chava, I know that my fantasies are not going to come true.

That night, while Sally and Jordan and his new girlfriend and his ex-girlfriend were all at school, partying it up, I sat at home, making a springtime playlist in honor of the Spring Fling. I called it "Get Out of the City and into the Sunshine." I left the window open, so my room smelled like fresh air, and I felt happy. I felt happy because everyone else was at school, while I, for the next fifty-eight hours, could be wherever I wanted to be.

At midnight, I laced up my sneakers and headed out, retracing my steps from the night before. Following my path back to Start. In addition to my iPod, I stuck a comb into my back pocket. You know, just in case I ran into any of them again— Pippa or Vicky or Char—I might want to fix my hair.

But I didn't run into any of them. I reached the block where Start had been twenty-four hours earlier, and it was nothing, just an empty, ugly street. After walking back and forth and back again, I managed to identify the alleyway where I had trotted behind Pippa and Vicky. But it was just an alleyway. No Mel at the end of it, no party to guard.

I stood uncertainly in the middle of the silent street, dwarfed by warehouses. The school party had ended hours ago. And Start had never even begun. The nighttime offered nothing for me.

So I turned my back on where Start should have been, I turned up the volume on my headphones, and I returned to my home, alone.

5

I DIDN'T SEE PIPPA OR VICKY AGAIN FOR TWO
weeks. If Start wasn't on Friday nights (or Sunday nights either,
as I discovered when I walked over there again, just to check), I
thought it might happen again on another Thursday. But the
next week I was staying at my dad's, which is what the Elise
Calendar says to do pretty much every single Thursday. My dad
lives on the other side of town from Start. Even for me, that
would be way too long a walk.

But the Thursday after that, Dad had to stay at work late to
staff an in-store concert, so I was back at Mom's house, where
everything was the same except for the couch. So much for the
power of civil disobedience. After Dinnertime Conversation
(topic of the day: fossil fuels. Fossil fuels is always Mom and
Steve's default topic), and after finishing my homework, I walked
over to Start.

And it was back. The street was as deserted and dark as always, but Start was happening behind those windowless concrete walls. I could sense it.

Sure enough, when I turned down the alleyway between the warehouses, there was Mel, looming in front of the door. He was talking to some girl in a fur shrug.

"Honey," I heard him saying to her, "did you kill that thing yourself?"

She muttered a reply.

"Listen. Here's when it's okay to wear a dead animal: When you killed it yourself. Or when you are a drag queen and it's wintertime. Neither of those situations apply here."

The girl sighed and removed her shrug. Mel stepped aside to let her into the club. "Meat is murder!" he called after her.

I stepped forward. "You're a Smiths fan?" I asked him. *Meat Is Murder* is one of my favorite Smiths albums.

"That's my generation," he said. "I was going out to parties like this one back when the Smiths were still releasing new material. Yes, I am *that* old."

"So, wait," I said, "do you actually not allow fur coats?"

Mel leaned down to be on eye level with me. "To be honest, we don't have a dress code here. That doesn't stop me from enforcing the standards I want to see, but it's not an official rule. The flyer just says 'fix up, look sharp.'"

I looked down at my tennis shoes, jeans, and long-sleeved shirt, already a little sweaty from my brisk walk. "I didn't do that," I said.

"No," Mel agreed. "You could stand to fix up and look a little sharper. But I'll let it go this time. ID, please."

Shit. This thing again.

"I . . . don't have my ID on me."

Mel shrugged. "No ID, no entry, honey."

I stared at him. He stared back at me. This had been so easy when I was with Pippa and Vicky that I hadn't thought about how hard it could actually be. Of course you need an ID. Of course, as always, there is an arbitrary, invisible fence in place. You can't see it, but it will always keep you out. It will always encircle happiness and keep you out.

"Are you crying?" Mel asked, his eyebrows knitting together.

"No." My voice came out higher and more nasal than it was supposed to. "I'm just . . . Do you remember me, Mel? I was here a couple weeks ago?"

He looked at me for another long moment before his eyes lit up with recognition. "You're friends with Pippa and Vicks."

"Yes." My knees felt weak with relief, and I didn't tell him that "friends" wasn't quite accurate.

"Why didn't you just say that? They're already inside. You can go on in to meet them." He went to open the door, then turned back to me. "How well do you know those girls?" he asked.

"Not well," I admitted.

He nodded. "Then I'll tell you this: Vicky's got talent, and Pippa's got issues."

"Okay." I didn't know what he meant, and I made a move for the door.

"Which do you have?" Mel asked, blocking the entry with his body. "Talent or issues?"

I paused for a moment, thought about this. "Both," I said at last.

Mel laughed and opened the door for me. "Good answer."

Inside, "Blue Monday" was blasting from the speakers, and the dance floor was even more crowded than last time. I tried to figure out how many people were packed in there. A hundred, maybe? Two hundred? It was impossible to tell through the flashing lights and everyone constantly moving around and around.

I scanned the crowd and eventually spotted Vicky and Pippa—my friends! Mel called them my friends, so it's just like they're my friends!—next to the DJ booth. Vicky was wearing a colorful, flowery dress that looked like a really stylish muumuu, and pink boots that made me briefly long for my unicorn boots. My horribly, horribly uncool unicorn boots.

Pippa was dressed all in black, and her legs went on for miles between her improbably high heels and her improbably short dress. She was clutching a tumbler filled with ice and a brownish liquid. The two of them were posing with their hands in the air for the photographer guy with the big camera.

I pushed my way through the dancing crowd until I reached them. "Hi!" I said, then wondered if maybe they had forgotten me, just as Mel did. Isn't that funny, to think that the people who have lived in your daydreams for the past two weeks, the people whom you've drawn in your chemistry notebook, to think that those people might not even know who you are?

But I needn't have worried. Vicky recognized me immediately. "Elise!" she shrieked. She even gave me a hug, like she was my mother or Alex.

Basically what I'm saying here is, the only people who ever hug me are the people who share 50 percent of my genetic code.

"Where did you *go* last time?" Vicky demanded, holding me by the shoulders. "We turned around and you were just gone!"

I brushed my fingers across the inside of my left arm and tried to think of a way to answer Vicky, other than just saying, *Sometimes I get overwhelmed.*

"You totally pulled an Irish goodbye," Vicky went on.

"What's an Irish goodbye?" I asked.

"It's when you just take off suddenly and don't tell anyone you're leaving," Pippa spoke up. "And it's a racist thing to say."

Vicky rolled her eyes. "One, no it's not. Two, you're not even Irish, Pippa. You're English."

Pippa shrugged. "They're still part of the empire."

"The *empire*?" Vicky screeched. "Now *that* is racist!"

"Hey," I interrupted, "who is that guy who was taking your photo a minute ago? With the camera that looks like it's worth more than my life?"

Vicky laughed. "That's Flash Tommy."

"Not his real name," Pippa contributed.

"I think *Tommy* is his real name," Vicky said.

"Tommy isn't a real name," Pippa said. "It's a *nickname*."

Vicky turned back to me. "Flash Tommy is a nightlife photographer. He goes out and takes photos of parties and then posts them to his Web site."

"Why?" I asked.

"Because that's his job," Pippa said, like this was a real thing, like, "Oh, yeah, any functioning society has got to have its doctors, its teachers, and its nightlife photographers."

"It's because somebody has to document our glory days," Vicky said.

61

The DJ transitioned into a Strokes song.

"I told him to play this," Pippa said. "I did this. That's the best part about being friends with the DJ. You always have somewhere to stash your coat, and sometimes he'll play songs for you."

The DJ hopped down from the booth to join the three of us. "Hey," he addressed me. "You were here a couple weeks ago, right? You look familiar. What's your name?"

"Elise," Pippa answered for me. "Like the Cure song."

I totally saw what Vicky meant when she told me that Pippa *loooved* the DJ. The way she had jumped in to reply to his question, even though it wasn't directed at her. The way she fluffed her hair. The way she smiled at him. Maybe Pippa read the same study that I did, about how people like you more if you smile at them.

"Hi, Elise-like-the-Cure-song." The DJ grinned and stuck out his hand. "I'm Char-like-the-Smiths-song."

I stared at him blankly.

"You don't know the Smiths?" he asked.

"I know the Smiths," I snapped, because lord knows you can launch any kind of criticism at me, lord knows I've heard it all before, but don't you *dare* doubt my musical knowledge. There's not much I can do right, just this one thing, but you cannot take this one thing from me. "I love the Smiths," I went on. "I just don't know a Smiths song called 'Char.'"

"It's his DJ name," Vicky explained, rolling her eyes. "DJ This Charming Man."

"But that's such a long name," Pippa continued. "We just call him Char. Short for Charming." She batted her eyelashes at him.

"Huh." I narrowed my eyes at him. He was wearing a fitted, unbuttoned sport coat and a skinny blue-and-white-striped tie with dark washed jeans and spiffy white sneakers.

He nodded. "I know what you're thinking, and I agree. *Charming* is a bit of an overstatement. But at least it gives me something to aim for."

Pippa giggled. "Who wants to go up for a drink?" she asked, but she wasn't asking me or Vicky.

Char shook his head. "I have to change the song. Sorry."

He climbed back into his booth and put his enormous headphones back on. Pippa stayed where she was, like she had changed her mind about the drink. A second later, Char transitioned out of the Strokes and into Whitney Houston, "I Wanna Dance with Somebody (Who Loves Me)."

Pippa and Vicky squealed at the same time and started madly dancing. It was obvious to me that Pippa was putting on a show for Char, but when he climbed down from the DJ booth, he made eye contact with me, not Pippa.

"Do you want to dance?" he asked, holding out his hand to me.

"I wanna dance with somebody," Whitney sang, *"with somebody who loves me."*

I shook my head, feeling myself blush. "I don't really dance."

Char furrowed his brow. "Why not?"

"I . . . I don't really know how."

Char started dancing then, making weird jerking motions with his arms and stomping his feel at awkward intervals, like a spasmodic soldier. "Can you do better than this?" he shouted over the music.

I nodded, smiling despite myself.

"Great! Then you know how to dance." He stopped doing the soldier moves and grabbed my hand in his. "Just follow my lead."

"But I don't know—"

He just shook his head and sang along in a loud falsetto: "So when the night falls, my lonely heart calls."

He bent his elbow to pull me in toward him, then pushed me back with his arm. It was so fast that I didn't have time to say anything before, suddenly, we were dancing. He twirled me in toward him, then switched hands and spun me back out the other way. He passed our arms over my head and then around my side. And the whole time he was doing some crazy, complicated footwork. His legs looked like spider legs.

"Watch my face!" he shouted over the music. "Not the floor!"

"I can't help it!" I shrieked. "I don't want to fall."

"You're not going to fall!" he shouted.

"I feel like I'm on a roller coaster!"

Char stopped spinning me around and pulled me in to him. "I need to change the song," he said into my ear. "Playtime is over. Come with me into the booth for a sec."

He led me into the DJ booth. It was only a few feet off the ground, but I felt suddenly like a god, looking down at the party from on high. The wall behind the booth was covered with Post-its on which people had written song requests or notes. *Play some Sabbath! Something with a beat. Do you have anything by the Bluetones? DJ This Charming Man ROCKS!* I watched Pippa and Vicky, just below us, still dancing like maniacs. Vicky was jumping up and down and punching the air, while Pippa swayed on her heels, rolling her shoulders and head around. Pippa stared at me for a moment, narrowing her eyes as if sizing me up for something—though for what, I could not have said. Then she tossed her hair and returned to ignoring me.

"I can dance!" I exclaimed as Char bent over his laptop.

"I told you," Char said. "Everyone can dance."

"Well, really it's that *you* can dance. I just followed. Where did you learn to dance like that, by the way?"

"Church youth group," Char replied without looking up.

"I don't believe you."

"That's good. That's a good policy. Try never to believe me unless you absolutely have to."

"So, where did you learn to dance?"

"My wedding," Char replied. He transitioned into a Primal Scream song. "I had to take a lot of dance classes before my wedding. You know, for our first dance to Elton John."

For some reason this gave me a weird pang, which lingered even after I glanced at his ring finger and reassured myself that he was just kidding again. It was like the *I don't belong here* feeling, sort of. It hit that same place in my stomach.

"Char," I said, and asked for a third time: "Where did you learn to dance?"

He looked up at me then, though his hand was still fiddling with dials. "I taught myself," he said finally. "I go out a lot."

I nodded like I was very wise and knew all about going out a lot.

"How old are you?" he asked me suddenly.

"Sixteen."

Char hung his headphones around his neck. "I like that."

"What?" I felt self-conscious all of a sudden, and I crossed my arms across my chest. "That I'm only sixteen?"

He laughed. "That sounds creepy. No, I like that you're honest. Some girls might claim to be older, you know, so they seem more mature or whatever. You're not pretending to be anything you're not."

"I suck at pretending to be anything I'm not," I told him, leaning against the booth's railing. "It's not for lack of trying."

He laughed again.

"Your turn," I said. "How old are you?"

"Nineteen. Twenty in June."

"How long have you been doing this?" I gestured out at the room.

"I've been DJing at Start for a year and a half now. I'm precocious," he confided.

"Oh, me, too."

"Really?" He raised an eyebrow. "At what?"

"Pretty much everything. I started speaking in sentences when I was a year old. I could read chapter books by the time I was six. During fourth grade math class, I just sat in the back of the room with my own middle school pre-algebra textbook. My favorite band in kindergarten was the Cure, because I liked their lyrics."

Why are you telling him this? Do you think this will make him like you more? In all your life, telling people these things about you has never once made them like you more. Don't you know this by now?

"Wow." Char pursed his lips. "So you're, like, a genius?"

"No," I said. "I'm precocious, and I work hard. It's not the same."

"All of that was in the past," he said. "The middle school textbooks and all that. What precocious things are you up to these days, Elise?"

I tried to think of my answer to his question. The last thing I had really studied with that sort of vigor, the last thing I had thrown myself into so wholeheartedly and whole-mindedly, thrown myself into until I was covered in it, breathing it in until I almost drowned. The last thing was *how to be normal.*

"I'm not really doing that anymore," I told Char. "I'm too old to be precocious."

"Pshh. You're a baby," he said, and I felt that same pang again, deep in my stomach. "*I* am too old to be precocious. But I'll keep claiming it anyway." He turned back to his computer and clicked around some more. "All right, if you're so smart, help me out here. What should I play next?"

"Well, what do you have?" I asked, trying to peer at his song list over his shoulder.

"I have everything," he told me.

"'Cannonball,'" I suggested. That had been the last song I was listening to on my headphones as I walked over here.

"The Breeders? Sure." I watched as he pulled up the song on his computer, then put on his headphones and fiddled with the turntables in front of him.

Pippa came over and tugged on Char's pant leg. He bent down to speak with her briefly, then stood up and said to me, "Hey, can you do me a favor? I'm going outside with Pippa for a sec. Take these"—he plopped his headphones around my neck—"and then, when this song ends, take this slider here and push it over to the other side."

"What?" I said.

"It's really easy. It's already cued up. Just move this thing here, and it will transition into the next song. I'll be back before you have to do anything else." Char laughed. "Don't look so panicked, Elise."

I looked out at the room of dancing, kissing, drinking people and asked, "But what if I screw up?"

Char placed his hands on my shoulders and looked into my eyes. "You won't screw up. I believe in you."

Then he hopped down from the booth, linked hands with Pippa, and ran out of the room with her. It was just me, standing alone, overlooking the party.

Anyone who said *I believe in you* obviously didn't know me very well.

The Primal Scream song was nearing its end. I could hear the music beginning to fade out, and I could see on Char's computer program that only twenty seconds remained. I took a deep breath, and then I shoved the slider over, as fast and as far as it would go.

The response from the crowd was instantaneous. As soon as the opening chords of "Cannonball" came out, everyone in the room screamed as one. People raised their hands and their drinks to the ceiling. A big group of boys in the center of the room started jumping up and down like they were on a trampoline.

The disco ball overhead scattered a million little lights over me, and I felt like I was sparkling from every inch of my body.

"Oh my God," Vicky said right into my ear. I had been so focused on the crowd, I hadn't even noticed her climbing into the DJ booth next to me. "Not you, too!"

"Not me, too, what?"

"You're smiling," Vicky said accusingly. "You're smiling like a crazy person. Are you in love with Char now, *too*? Does everyone just have to go and fall in love with him on sight?"

I was smiling like a crazy person because I had just made a hundred people dance, I had just made a hundred people scream, I had just made a hundred people happy. I, Elise, using my own power, had made people happy. But I didn't try to explain this to Vicky. All I said was, "I'm not in love with Char. I don't even know him."

"You see why they call him This Charming Man now, though, don't you?" Vicky demanded.

I thought about Char for a moment as I stared out over the party. I thought about the way he smiled at me, the way he touched me when we were dancing, the way he said *I believe in you*. "I guess he could be kind of charming," I conceded.

"Oh, ha," Vicky replied sarcastically. "Ha, ha, ha."

My entire childhood, I embarked on projects. Big, all-encompassing projects. When I was eight years old, my project was a dollhouse. I was everything to this dollhouse: contractor, architect, carpenter, electrician, furniture maker, and, once it was ready for dolls to live in it, I also played the roles of Mother, Father, and Baby.

When I was eleven I became fascinated by collages. My bedroom was filled floor to ceiling with catalogs, magazines, and fabric samples. I spent hours every day gluing paper to paper, and I was very happy.

When I was thirteen my big project was stop-motion animation. I spent most of my time writing scripts, crafting characters and scenery, filming them, editing the film, and uploading them to the Internet, where roughly three people watched them—my dad, my mom, and Steve.

My last big project was becoming cool. That one didn't work so well. I don't know why, exactly. I put as much effort into becoming cool as I ever put into my collages, but my collages turned out beautiful, while becoming cool turned out ugly and warped. Since then I focused on smaller projects. Waking up in the morning. Doing my homework. Walking around at night. Breathing.

I liked projects where I could take things apart and figure out exactly how they worked. The problem is, you can't do that with people.

Even though it had been months since my last big project, my parents were still accustomed to them. So when I asked my father for DJ equipment, he didn't ask why.

Because Dad works at a music store, he was able to get me turntables and a mixer for cheap. He brought them home for me on Friday evening, and I immediately ran up to my room and spent the rest of the night trying to figure out how to work the equipment. I didn't even go downstairs for dinner.

That's one of the nice things about my dad's house: there is no official Dinnertime Conversation. If my mother's house is filled with chatter and arguments and dog barks, my father's house is filled with music and newspapers and books. Other people's words, not our own. If I want to spend all night trying to transition between songs without leaving a gap in the music, then my dad spends all night alphabetizing his record collection, and we are both content.

The *problem* with my dad's house, of course, is that it's miles and miles away from Start. Which meant I had to come up with a way out of there for next Thursday night. Already some of the shininess I'd felt was disappearing from memory, my sparkle flaking off me like chipped nail polish. Friday morning, six hours after I'd left Start, I strode into Glendale High like no one could touch me. I saw Amelia Kindl looking at me out of the corner of her eye all through English class, and I didn't even flinch. I thought about that moment of power, playing "Cannonball" for a room of strangers, and I thought, *Amelia Kindl, you cannot hurt me.*

That was the morning. But by noon, my armor had already started to wear away. At lunch, Emily Wallace paused at my table next to the bathroom and said, "You know you're wearing my vest, right?"

I said, "Excuse me?"

She smirked and pointed. "That vest. It's mine. I donated it to Goodwill last year."

"Oh," I said. I looked down and touched the buttons on my vest, which had looked so pretty and normal when I put it on earlier. I wanted to say to Emily, *So what?* I tried to call upon the power of Start, to remind myself of that moment when it was just me and the music and a roomful of people loving me and the music.

But that seemed so far away from me and Emily in this fluorescent-lit cafeteria right now. So I said only, "Oh," while my friends, Chava and Sally, stared at their celery sticks and said nothing at all.

So, no, I couldn't wait to go to Start again.

On Wednesday evening, as I prepared myself a mug of hot chocolate, I asked my father, "Is it okay for me to spend tomorrow night at Mom's this week?"

Dad looked up from his newspaper. "Why?"

I'd been hoping he wouldn't ask *why*. I didn't mind lying by omission. Like how I'd just never gotten around to mentioning that I spent hours every night roaming the streets of Glendale. But I preferred not to lie directly.

"Because I have a big history project that I need to finish working on and hand in on Friday," I answered. "It's at Mom's, and it would be a huge hassle to bring it over here." Dad didn't respond for a moment. "It's a diorama," I offered.

Dad nodded at that. He knows from experience how big my dioramas can get. "All right," he said. "I hope Mr. Hendricks appreciates it." He pulled out his phone and switched the dates on the Elise Calendar, and that was that.

And it's a good thing he did, too, because Thursday . . . Thursday was bad. Thursday, I really needed Start.

6

SOMETIMES YOU JUST HAVE THOSE DAYS. WHEN you know, from the moment you wake up, that everything you touch you will break, so the less you touch, the better.

Thursday was one of those days.

My alarm didn't go off, so I didn't have time to shower before school. Dad was in a grumpy mood because his band's show the next week had been canceled, and then he was in an even grumpier mood after I missed the bus and he had to drive me all the way to school. In Chem I realized I had forgotten my lab report, even though I had been working on it until midnight, so that was an automatic ten-point deduction. And *then* we had scoliosis testing.

For scoliosis testing, all the girls had to line up in the gym and then go behind a screen, one by one. It was unclear what happened once you went behind the screen. Presumably the nurse checked you for scoliosis, but it was equally possible that she made you recite the alphabet backward or perform an interpretive dance.

I wound up standing in the scoliosis line directly in front of Amelia Kindl. I could hear her sighing over and over, even though I didn't look at her. Finally I couldn't take it anymore, so I put on my iPod headphones, but I could still *feel* her sighing.

I was prepared to ignore Amelia for the entirety of fourth period, but Amelia, apparently, had other ideas, and eventually she tapped me on the shoulder.

I took off my headphones and turned around. "Yes, Amelia?"

"Why are you doing this to me?" she demanded.

I stared at her. The last conversation that Amelia and I had had was on the phone, the night after the first day of school. Over the past seven and a half months, I had imagined her saying many things to me. All of them started with *sorry. Sorry I made you clean up our lunch table and possibly drove you to self-mutilation* would have worked. *Sorry I freaked out and told 911 that you tried to kill yourself* also would have done the trick. *Sorry I couldn't be the friend that you wanted me to be* was what I was really holding out for. *Why are you doing this to me?* was not actually an option.

"Why am I doing *what* to you?" I asked.

"Acting like I'm some sort of *criminal*," Amelia replied.

"I'm not," I said.

Amelia played with the ends of her honey-brown hair and adjusted her glasses on the bridge of her nose. She took a deep breath and went on. "You've spent the entire year ignoring me or glaring at me like I'm a serial killer."

I thought, for the zillionth time, about what a nice girl

Amelia was. She was a nice girl with a nice life, so people were nice to her. In Amelia's world, nobody ever ignores you or glares at you just for kicks.

If Amelia had to be me for even one day, I think she would just fall to pieces.

"And, you know, if that's how you want to act, well, that's fine. But now *this*?" she said. "Don't do this to me, Elise."

"I don't know what *this* is," I told her honestly.

"Oh, please." Her voice cracked. I had no idea what I'd done to hurt her. Part of me felt bad about it, whatever it was, but then another part of me said, very smugly, *Good*. She cleared her throat and continued, "If you want to give me mean looks all through English class and cross to the other side of the hallway whenever you see me coming, that's, you know, whatever. But stop spreading rumors about me."

"I'm not spreading rumors about you," I said, as the line moved forward. "I don't know what you're talking about. But I don't actually care. Because you, Amelia . . . you betrayed me."

I thought that this might be it—this might be the moment when Amelia said sorry—but instead she said, "That's not true. We weren't even friends; I can't have betrayed you. I saved your life."

I flashed back in time, and all of a sudden it was like I was right back in my bedroom in my dad's house, "Hallelujah" playing on my computer, my left arm bandaged and pulled in close to my chest as I dialed Amelia's phone number for the first and only time in my life.

I saved your life, she had said, and she kept looking at me now, blinking her soft brown eyes nervously.

"No," I told her. "You didn't."

Then I went in to get scoliosis-tested, and it turns out I don't have scoliosis, so that was one success. But also I wasn't wearing a bra today, which Lizzie Reardon noticed as I was putting my shirt back on after the scoliosis test, so by the end of the day, everyone at school had heard that I was probably a lesbian. Because if there's one thing we know about lesbians, it's that none of them wear bras.

Anyway. I've had worse days in my life. But not many.

I needed Start that night more than I'd ever needed anything. I needed excruciatingly loud music, I needed strangers, I needed darkness.

It felt like it took my family forever to fall asleep that night. Neil woke up crying from a nightmare, and then right when I was about to leave the house, Steve came all the way downstairs to double-check that he'd remembered to turn off the oven. (He had.) I'd already put on my shoes and was standing by the front door, so when Steve saw me, I had to immediately pretend that I was double-checking to make sure the door was locked. (It was.)

By the time everyone was tucked away in bed, it was twelve thirty, and I was fighting to keep my eyes open. I thought about not going out at all. But that wasn't really an option.

At the last moment before I left the house, I went up to the attic and pulled my unicorn boots out of the garbage bag where they had lived since September. I knew that I wasn't supposed to wear them. But I needed a little bit of magic tonight.

When I arrived at Start, Mel was standing outside, as usual.

"Hi," I said brightly.

He frowned and looked me up and down, and I felt my heart sink. Was he going to ask again for my ID?

But all Mel said was, "Elise, honey. Did we or did we not already discuss fixing up and looking sharp?"

I tugged my hair elastic out of my ponytail and shook my hair out so it fell into tangled waves down my shoulders. "Better?" I asked.

Mel rolled his eyes. "Here we put in all this effort to provide you with a life-changing experience, week after week, and you can't even put in the effort to change out of your Old Navy henley shirt? Come on. Meet me halfway."

I kicked my foot out so that he could see it under the door light. "Unicorns?" I said.

Mel nodded slowly. "You look like a five-year-old, but at least you're trying." He opened the door for me.

"How's it going tonight, by the way?" I asked, in what was meant to be a friendly way.

Mel rolled his eyes. "It's a shitshow."

I saw what Mel meant as soon as I found Vicky, hovering near the bar. "Thank God you're here," she said, grabbing both my arms.

"I know." I laughed. "I feel the same way."

"No, I mean, I *need* you."

"That," I said, "is amazing to me." I looked around. "Where's Pippa?"

"Where do you *think* Pippa is?" Vicky asked.

"Uh, I have no idea. With Char?"

"Char!" Vicky hooted like this was the most ridiculous idea ever. "Please. Pippa is there." She jerked her thumb to point across the room, and when the lights flashed, I could see Pippa's tiny figure crumpled on a bench against the wall.

"Is she asleep?" I asked.

"That would be fantastic," Vicky replied. "If Pippa were asleep in the corner of Start, that would honestly be ideal. I dream of that day."

"Vicky—" I began.

"She's drunk," Vicky snapped. "She passed out."

"Oh." I looked across the room again. I guess that made more sense; Pippa's half-upright position didn't seem to be that comfortable for sleeping.

I didn't know much about drunk people. Neither Mom nor Steve drank at all. Dad usually had a six-pack of beer in the fridge, and some nights he'd have one when he got home from work, but some nights he wouldn't. I knew that kids at my school went to parties and got drunk and sometimes passed out, because Chava and Sally talked about this a lot. But obviously I had never seen that behavior in action, since no one had ever invited me to a party.

"Shouldn't you take her home?" I ventured.

"Absolutely." Vicky adjusted her big feathered earrings. "A good friend would unquestionably take Pippa home right now. Actually, a good friend would have taken her home an hour ago, and would have held back her hair as she puked, and would have made her drink a big glass of water, and would have tucked her into bed, and would have sent an e-mail to her prof to explain why she won't be in class tomorrow."

"But you're not doing that," I ventured.

"Correct. Because, Elise, do you see that guy there at the bar? The one who's paying for his drinks?"

I followed her gaze to see a guy who looked to be in his thirties, wearing a button-down shirt and big sunglasses. He was holding a soda can in one hand and a pink drink in the other.

"He is a booking agent," Vicky went on. "He books Start, and he books rooftop parties all over town in the summer, and he books bands for two of the big clubs downtown. And he wants to talk to me about the Dirty Curtains. That's my band. And I am not leaving here until that has happened. Do you think this makes me a bad friend, Elise?"

I shrugged. I didn't know enough about friendship to answer Vicky's question with any degree of expertise.

"I know how to be a good friend," Vicky went on. "And I know how to be a good musician. I don't always know how to be both at once."

"It'll be fine," I said. "Pippa's awake again, so I'm sure you have nothing to worry about. See?"

Vicky glanced across the room. Pippa had roused herself enough to talk to two guys. They were a lot taller than her, and she was standing up to speak with them, but she kept swaying and having to grab on to their arms to stay upright.

"Swell," Vicky said.

The booking agent approached us then. He held out the pink beverage to Vicky, and she took it.

"Hello," he said to me, holding out his now-empty hand to shake. "I'm Pete. Welcome to my club."

"Elise." I shook his hand and tried to avoid his gaze, like he would see in my eyes that I was only sixteen.

"Hey, Elise, I'm sorry to ask," Vicky said, "but would you mind just giving us a minute?"

I smiled and moved away, but I didn't really know where to go. I tried to dance by myself for a song or two, but it wasn't as fun alone. I did a slow pass around the room. Char was up in the DJ booth, but he looked too busy to talk, and, anyway, I felt too shy to just go up there and start a conversation. I didn't know how Pippa managed to do that.

Thinking of Pippa, I glanced over at her. One of the tall guys who had been talking to her now had her pressed up against the wall. He was grinding into her, holding her head upright.

I went back to the bar to find Vicky. She was with Pete still, but they'd been joined by another guy and girl, and Pete seemed busier talking to them than to Vicky. She stood a little bit apart, like she was waiting her turn.

"Vicky?" I said.

She gave me a quick smile. "Sorry to banish you earlier. I'm just trying to . . . I don't know, if he would just *talk* to me . . ."

I shook my head. "I'm fine. It's Pippa."

Vicky looked over to where Pippa's rag-doll body was stuffed between a wall and a guy groping her chest. "Shit," she said, and in about two seconds she was across the room grabbing the guy, pulling him off of Pippa. I stayed a step behind her.

"Get your hands off of her!" Vicky screamed over the music.

The guy stepped back and Pippa sagged to the ground, un-balanced without his support.

"Whoa!" He put up his hands. "What's your problem? She was fine with it. Right?" he said to Pippa. Pippa did not reply.

"This is not what 'fine with it' looks like," Vicky retorted. "Girls who are 'fine with it' are able to keep their eyes open without help, and they can speak in full sentences. I guess you haven't had much success with that kind of girl, and I can see why. You're a pervert."

Vicky hauled Pippa to her feet. "Help me, okay?" she said to me. Together we dragged Pippa over to the DJ booth.

"Char, I need to talk to you," Vicky called up to him, shaking his leg.

"I'm kind of busy, Vicks," he called back. "I'm working. Write it on a Post-it, okay?" He gestured at the pad of stickies near us.

Vicky adjusted herself so more of Pippa's dead weight was leaning against me, and then she shouted to Char, "Put on a goddamn long song and *come talk to us.*"

Char must have been able to tell that Vicky wasn't kidding, because he transitioned into "A Quick One, While He's Away," a song by the Who which is about eight and a half minutes long. He jumped down from the DJ booth. "Is everything okay?" he asked us.

Vicky shook Pippa's body at him. "Does everything *look* okay?"

Pippa's eyes fluttered. "Chaaaaarrr," she slurred. "I ffffancy you."

"You should take her home," he told Vicky.

"I have brought her home so many times," Vicky said. "I just want this one shot, Char."

"You're talking to Pete?" Char asked.

"I was. Until this happened. Will you take her?"

"No way," Char said. "I'm *working*. If you need to stay with Pete, just call a taxi and send her home in it."

"Great idea," Vicky said sarcastically. "Last time I did that, she paid the taxi driver three hundred dollars in cash and passed out in her elevator. Someone needs to go with her, and it should be you."

"No," Char said.

"It should be you," Vicky repeated. "Don't act dumb; it doesn't suit you. She wouldn't be like this right now if it weren't for you."

They stared at each other for a long moment. Finally Char sighed and said, "You know I'd take her, Vicky. But I have to DJ until two o'clock. What do you want me to do, just throw on a mix CD and walk out the door? This is my *job*. And of all nights, Pete's here. How fast do you think I'd get dropped if he saw me just put my iTunes on shuffle and take off?"

"I could DJ," I offered.

They both looked at me.

"Thanks, Elise," Char said, running his hand through his hair, "but you don't . . . I mean, you did a great job playing that one song last week, but that doesn't mean you can DJ an entire party for an hour, or however long it takes me to get Pippa home and get back here."

"I can do it," I said again. I felt my heart slamming against my chest. "I got turntables and everything. I've been practicing."

"Come on, Char," Vicky said. "She'll be fine. Start can handle itself for an hour. Pippa cannot."

Char kept shaking his head.

"Remember how you believe in me?" I said.

"Fine," he said. "Get up there. When this song is over, transition out of this and into something else. If you can do that, then *maybe* I will accompany Pippa home."

"No problem," I said. I climbed up into the DJ booth, which felt so much farther from the ground than it had last week. I could feel Char's eyes on me. *Focus, Elise.*

I lightly touched the dials and the knobs on Char's mixer, acquainting myself with each of them. I brushed my hand against the turntables. I looked at the computer. A minute and a half left of "A Quick One, While He's Away." A minute and a half to cue up the next song.

I had practiced this for three nights in my bedroom. That's not a lot of practice. Char had been doing this for years. Still, I'm not precocious for nothing. As "A Quick One, While He's Away" came to an end, I crossfaded into "It's the End of the World As We Know It (And I Feel Fine)." Suddenly everyone in the room was pogoing up and down and speeding through the lyrics as one.

"See?" I called down to Char, trying to catch my breath.

He heaved a sigh. "Fine. I'll be back as soon as I can." He gave me a look that clearly said *Don't screw this up,* then put an arm around Pippa's narrow shoulders and guided her out of the room.

"Yes!" Vicky pumped her arm. She turned to go back to the bar, but then she looked back to ask me, "Are you actually okay up there?"

"Um . . ." I was scrolling through Char's song list as fast as I could. "Hard to say."

Vicky nodded, gave me a little salute, and went back to find Pete.

Time from there passed not in minutes, but in songs. I didn't look up from the DJ equipment once, and I barely ever took off Char's enormous headphones. I didn't think about Char, or Vicky, or Pippa, or Amelia, or Lizzie—I thought only one song to the next.

Fifteen, twenty songs later, I felt a hand on my back. I spun around to see Char. "You're back," I said.

I took off the headphones and held them out to him, but he waved his hand. "You might as well finish up," he said.

I rubbed my eyes. "Finish up? What time is it?"

"Nearly two."

I didn't know what answer I had been expecting. I had lost track of the night a long time ago. I played a couple more songs, all the while aware of Char standing right behind me. At five minutes to two o'clock, I put on "Wonderwall" and I took off the headphones and set them down on the table. I leaned against the railing and massaged a crick in my neck.

"Shall we dance?" Char asked me.

I shook my head. "I'm tired."

"That's not a good reason." He held out his hand.

I took it, and we climbed down from the booth. We danced together, but it wasn't like dancing to "I Wanna Dance with Somebody." Less fancy footwork, more swaying. The song was slower, the night was almost over. Around us I saw people gathering up their jackets and bags. Char grabbed both my hands and leaned back, and we spun around and around until I could see nothing but Char's face framed against a blur of colors.

When the song ended, the lights came up on a mostly empty room. The few people left were finishing up their drinks and moving toward the door. Char let go of my hands and went back to the DJ booth to pack up his equipment.

"If you can wait a few minutes, I'll give you a ride home," he said to me.

I could have walked, but I had to wake up for school in four and a half hours, and it had been a very long day. I slumped on a bench, pulled my knees up to my chest, and watched Char. In the full light, he looked paler than I had expected. Paler and plainer. I probably looked paler and plainer in the light, too.

I looked around for Vicky but didn't see her anywhere. An Irish goodbye, no doubt. I just saw the bartenders counting money and a couple still making out against a wall, until Mel came in and shooed them out the door.

"Ready?" Char asked. His equipment was packed in a big messenger bag slung over his shoulder.

We walked out of the lights of the club and down the moonlit, empty street until we reached his car. It was small, almost too small for Char to fit his long legs into.

"Where to?" he asked, starting the motor.

"Harrison and President. I'll direct you." We drove down the street in silence for a moment. "How's Pippa?" I asked at last.

"She'll live."

I watched the shadows flashing across his face as he watched the road. "Why did Vicky say that Pippa wouldn't be like this right now if it weren't for you?"

"Because Vicky likes to blame other people for her best friend's drinking problem."

"Seriously, Char."

"Oh, you were asking *seriously*? Well, in that case, there is a possibility that Pippa might be . . . mad at me."

"Why?"

"She has rage issues. Just flies off the handle. It's really quite sad."

I rolled my eyes. "Do I have to ask you every question twice in order to get a straight answer out of you?"

"Yes."

"Okay, then, for the second time, *why* is Pippa mad at you?"

Char leaned back against his seat and kept his eyes on the road. "Because I slept with her."

I blushed. I'd never heard anyone say something like that so casually before. More than anything else tonight, it made Char seem older than me. "Why did that make her mad?" I asked. "I thought she liked you."

"She did. It's complicated."

"Just try me," I said. "I love complications."

He laughed. "Okay, look. Pippa and I hooked up after Start last week. This week she showed up expecting me to . . . I have no idea. Ask her out? Be her boyfriend? Play 'Chapel of Love' and get down on one knee in my DJ booth and propose to her? Needless to say, I didn't do any of that. And I made it pretty clear to her that I don't intend to. So then she got mad. And *then* she got drunk."

"Do you like her?" I asked.

"Has anyone ever told you that you ask a lot of questions?" he said back.

"You know, it's possible that one or two people have mentioned that to me over the course of my life. Do you *like* her?"

"Of course I like Pippa. But I don't like her like that."

I thought of Pippa, her high heels and stunning dresses and adorable haircut and winning dance moves and charming accent. "Why not?" I asked.

"Because she's not . . ." He paused, searching for the reason, then shook his head. "I just don't want to be tied down like that."

"So then why did you have *sex* with her?"

"Because she's hot."

There was a long silence. I stared out my window.

"I told you it was complicated," Char said at last.

"It's no worse than trigonometry," I muttered.

Char cleared his throat. "In other news, I don't think I thanked you for taking over the turntables tonight. Thank you."

"It was fun. Well, it was hard. But it was fun, too."

"You were good."

It was a very small compliment, but it came from someone who mattered, about something that mattered. I felt a smile spread across my face. "Really?"

"Yeah. It was cute. How did you learn to play?"

"I just taught myself last weekend."

Char choked a little. "You're joking."

"I'm sorry; I can teach myself anything. Well," I corrected myself, "*almost* anything."

He glanced at me. "That's a weird thing to be sorry for."

"No, it's not. Take this right here, and then it's two lights on."

"Your transitions could use some work, though," Char went on. "You don't know how to beat match at all. And you looked kind of freaked out the entire time."

"Hey!" I exclaimed. "I've had, like, eight hours of practice. Give a girl a break."

"If you want, I could teach you."

"Really?" I said.

"Of course really. It's probably more interesting than teaching yourself. Let me give you my number. Just text me over the weekend if you want to come over to my place and practice."

I programmed his number into my cell, and then I stared at it for a long moment. Char had a phone number. He had a home. He probably had a job or a college and a last name and parents and all of that, too. He didn't just spring into existence late on Thursday night and then blink out again at two a.m. He was a *real person*.

I wasn't sure I liked that.

"Is it this turn here?" he asked.

"Oh, you can just leave me at the corner. I'll walk the rest of the way."

"Don't be ridiculous. I'm not going to let you wander the streets alone at this hour."

I considered telling him, *It would not be the first time*. But all I said aloud was, "Fine, then take this left. It's that white Colonial across the street. Number 77."

Char coasted to a stop and stared out the window at my house. I was glad to see that it was as dark and quiet as I'd left it. Although my parents had never yet caught me sneaking out, that didn't mean they never would.

I tried to see the house through Char's eyes. The gingham curtains in the living room. The welcome mat. The swing set in the yard. The two low-emissions cars parked in the driveway.

"This is a nice house," he said.

"Thank you."

He looked at me then like he was really seeing me for the first time. "What's a nice girl like you doing at a warehouse night-club at two a.m. on a school night?"

"It's complicated," I said. And then I got out of his car and went inside.

Sometimes you just have those days where everything goes wrong. But sometimes, and totally unexpectedly, something can go right.

7

MY HANDS WERE SHAKING WHEN I ARRIVED AT
Char's home on Sunday afternoon. I had texted him earlier in
the day to ask if he was free to teach me about DJing, and he
wrote back, SURE! COME OVER @ 3 AND WE'LL MAKE MUSIC :) So
he had *invited* me here, I reminded myself.

But still. That didn't mean he actually *wanted* me here. As I
rang the buzzer to his apartment building, I imagined him,
maybe with a bunch of his friends, hiding behind a parked car,
watching me, laughing, and saying, "Oh my God, I can't believe she actually showed up. Like she believed I was serious!"

That wasn't what happened. What happened was that Char
answered the door, looking like he had just woken up, but nonetheless happy to see me. "Hello!" he said. "If it isn't Elise, the
precocious DJ."

I gave him a silent glare. I don't need to take a bus all the way across town on a weekend for someone to make fun of me. I can do that just by going to school.

I had told my mom that I was spending the afternoon at Sally's house. I briefly considered telling her that I'd made a new friend and I was going to hang out with him, figuring she would be delighted to hear that my social life was blossoming. Then I decided that, because my new friend was a nearly-twenty-year-old male whom I'd never seen in daylight before, maybe my mom didn't need to know.

"Did you bring your laptop?" Char asked.

I held it up for him to see.

"Excellent. Let's do this."

I followed Char as he bounded up four flights of stairs and then down a short hallway. He was wearing cutoff jeans and a plain red tee with a small rip in the back, and he had a Chicago Cubs baseball cap jammed down over his unruly hair. In this outfit, he still looked like the Char I knew, but he also looked like somebody else. Like he could have been any of the guys at my school—a little older, but no more special. I suddenly understood why Mel kept telling me to "fix up, look sharp." The everyday Char didn't wear fitted suits or leather jackets. Maybe the everyday Pippa didn't wear four-inch heels or sequined dresses either. The everyday me didn't play music at late-night dance parties. I couldn't tell which was the way Char actually was: Char at Start, or Char at home.

He unlocked the door to his apartment. Actually, *apartment* would be a compliment. It was a room. A big room, with a bed at one end and a kitchenette at the other, but still just a room.

There were a bunch of boxes stacked up in the middle of the floor, and Char's DJ setup rested on top of them: a turntable, a mixer, a laptop, and speakers on either side.

Char looked around the room, his lips pursed, like he was seeing it through my eyes. "Right," he said. "I just moved in, is why there are all these boxes still."

"Oh, when did you move?" I asked politely.

"October."

I squinted at him. "You know it's April, right?"

He shrugged.

I looked around at his unswept floor, unmade bed, and white walls—blank except for that *Trainspotting* poster about "choose life" and an enormous Smiths poster that said GIRLFRIEND IN A COMA on it.

Then I shrugged, too, set down my computer, and said, "Okay, so teach me something I don't know."

He laughed and sat down on his bed. "I've never taught anyone to DJ before. I don't want to sound like your bio teacher."

"I don't take bio," I told him. "I'm in chem now. I'm a sophomore."

He rolled his eyes. "I guess the thing to know about DJing is that it's not just playing one song after another song, like you were doing on Thursday. That's good, and it takes practice to do that using the equipment. But that's not enough, because, at the end of the day, anyone can put together an iPod playlist and press play, but not just anyone can have my job.

"There are two things that make someone a great DJ. One is technical skills. Not leaving gaps between the songs, not accidentally playing two songs at once, starting songs from the point that you want—that kind of thing. One of the most important things to master is beat matching. Do you know what that is?"

"It's when you fade in one song while you're still fading out the other," I answered, while looking around the room for a place to sit down. Nothing. No chairs, no couches, no rug. The only place to sit was on the bed, next to Char. But the idea of that made my hands feel shaky again. Did he have sex with Pippa here, in this bed?

"Right," Char said, like he was answering my unspoken question. "If there's a pause between songs, people will use that as an opportunity to go to the bathroom, or get another drink, or for whatever other reason leave the dance floor. Your goal, as DJ, is to make them stay *on* the dance floor. So when you match the beats from one song to the next, there's an overlap, but it sounds harmonious, not cacophonous, and no one even notices that they're dancing to the next song until they're already in it. Give it a shot."

So I hooked up my laptop to Char's mixer, and he talked me through transitioning from "Love Will Tear Us Apart" to "Young Folks." But it did not sound, as he had suggested, harmonious. It sounded like a headache.

Char leaned back against his pillows and watched me, a smile playing on his lips.

"Okay, what am I doing wrong?" I asked after the third time that I completely failed to align the two songs.

"It's just hard," Char said. "For starters, you've picked two songs that happen to be really tricky to beat match. Start with something more straightforward. I learned to do this by transitioning from 'This Must Be the Place' into 'This Must Be the Place.' It's easier to figure out how songs match up when they're the same song."

So I tried doing that for a while, but still I couldn't get the beats to hit at the same time.

"I think I've ruined this song for myself," I told Char. "Have I ruined it for you, too? I'm sorry. It used to be so enjoyable."

"It takes more than ten minutes of repeating the same song for me to grow sick of it," Char said. "But there are definitely songs that I've ruined for myself. Like 'Girls and Boys.'"

"The Blur song?" I said, resting the headphones around my neck for a moment. "But it's so good!"

"Ah, that just means you don't go out enough. I've been going out three or four nights a week for the past three years. That means I've gone out roughly five hundred times. And *every single time*, I have heard that song. Now, the word *girls* appears in that song thirty-two times. That means that I have heard Damon Albarn say the word *girls* more than *sixteen thousand times*. What percentage of my life do you think I have spent listening to that song?"

I shrugged. "Math."

"Algebra?" he asked.

"Geometry. Algebra was last year. I'm a *sophomore*, Char." I put the headphones back on and tried again for the "This Must Be the Place" into "This Must Be the Place" transition. No luck.

Char hopped off the bed and came over to stand next to me. He reached across me to press pause on my computer. Then he gently removed the headphones from my head and flipped them so that one side was pressed against his ear and the other was pressed to mine. His head was just a few inches away from my own. "Okay," he said, and he started the song from the beginning again. Then he took my free hand and pressed it to the turntable. He rocked our hands back and forth on the record so that I could hear the same beat of the song repeat over and over in the headphones. "You hear that?" he asked. "That's the kick. You want it to match the downbeat on the other song."

He gestured at me to start the other song, and then in my free ear I heard him start to count measures, while in the headphones I heard only the kick of the first song as we kept rocking our hands forward and backward together. "And *one*-two-three-four, *one*-two-three-four, *one*—"

He pulled my hand off the record, and the two songs took off together, perfectly in sync.

He let go of my hand but didn't move away. "Now slowly take that slider from one side to the other," he instructed, and I did. "And that, Elise," he concluded, turning to face me straight on, "is how to beat match like a DJ."

Suddenly, "This Must Be the Place" wasn't ruined for me anymore. Suddenly it was the greatest song I had ever heard.

"You know," he said, studying me, "you actually have a fantastic smile."

"Three years of braces," I explained.

"No, seriously," he said.

"They also pulled four teeth. Before the braces. That probably helped."

"Why don't you smile more often?" he asked.

"I smile about as often as I feel like smiling," I answered. "Sometimes more, because I read this study that said people like you better when you smile."

Char laughed. "Does that work? Are people really that easy to trick?"

"In my experience," I said, "no."

"Bummer." He returned to his bed.

"So how's Pippa?" I asked, switching over to an old Smokey Robinson. The transition sounded messy again, but a little better this time.

Char sighed.

"You know," I said, "just speaking of people who want people to like them better. It's a natural transition."

"No offense, but your transition from 'This Must Be the Place' to 'This Must Be the Place' worked better."

"How is Pippa?" I repeated.

"Pippa texted me on Friday with a million apologies and thanks, since Vicky told her that I was the one who carried her home from Start. So that seemed good, because if she could text, then at least we knew that she was alive."

"And how did you respond?" I asked, scrolling through songs on my computer.

"I didn't."

"You just didn't text her back?"

"Yeah."

"Seems a little rude, Char."

He leaned his head against the wall. "I just don't want to lead her on, you know?"

"So that's the last that we've heard from Pippa?" I asked. "A text acknowledging that she's alive?"

Char looked shamefaced. "Not exactly."

I sighed. "What did you do?"

"Well, I ran into Pippa and Vicky at Roosevelt's last night." I must have looked blank, because he added, "It's a bar. They have this amazing monthly soul night. The DJ spins only forty-fives, and his collection is out of this world. Last night he was playing this Lee Dorsey song I'd never even *heard* before—"

"Pippa," I reminded him.

"Pippa. Right. I brought her home with me."

I stopped the song with a screech. "You're telling me you didn't want to lead her on, so you *brought her home with you?*"

He rested the back of his hand against his forehead. "I hear what you're saying. I don't know. It made sense at the time."

"When did she leave here?"

"About an hour ago."

I looked around Char's room again, seeing it now with fresh eyes. Pippa was *just* here.

"Vicky is going to kill you," I said.

Char gave his pillow a shove. "Vicky is overprotective. It's not like I'm some pariah, preying on Pippa's naïveté. She knows how I feel. She wasn't drunk last night, or at least not as drunk as she usually is. She made her own rational, adult decision to come home with me. She wanted to."

I thought about Pippa on Thursday, passed out on a bench. "I think Pippa wants a lot of things that aren't good for her."

Char shrugged. "Don't we all?"

I rubbed my thumb across the inside of my left wrist and didn't reply.

"This is a downer," Char said abruptly. "I shouldn't be burdening your young mind with my old-man problems."

"Once again, if you missed it, *I am a sophomore.* And furthermore? It's not like you have to be a legal adult to have problems."

"Oh, really?" Char laughed. "What are your problems? Chem class is that hard?"

I kept my thumb on my wrist and said nothing.

"Anyway," Char replied, "you came all the way over here to learn to DJ, not to hear about all the ways that I've screwed up with girls."

"Go on, then."

"Okay, like I said, there are two things every great DJ needs to be able to do. One is to master the technical skills. Which you're doing. Good job. Unfortunately, that's about ten percent of what it takes to DJ right.

"The other part, the part that really matters, is that you need to be able to read a crowd. You can't just play whatever songs you like. You have to figure out what people are responding to, what they want to dance to, which songs they already know and like and which songs they're going to like once you have introduced them. Every crowd is different, and even at Start, every week is different. *That* is why I still play 'Girls and Boys' sometimes. It doesn't matter that I've heard Damon Albarn sing the word *girls* more than sixteen thousand times. As long as people still want to dance to it, it is still worth playing."

"Okay," I said. "So how do I do that? How do I figure out what people want?"

"You watch them," Char said. "You stand in the DJ booth, so you're near them but not part of them. And whenever you can, you look up from what you're doing and you see how they're reacting."

Char's words made me think of all the magazines I had read, all the movies I had watched, all the blogs I had studied, trying to figure out what it is that people want me to do. "I don't think I'm very good at reading the crowd," I said.

"That's because it's an acquired skill," he said. "It takes practice, sometimes years of practice. And sometimes even the best DJs get it wrong. I think it's natural to just want to play your favorite songs and force everyone to love them as much as you do. And sometimes, in the right context, they will. Over the past two years, I have turned everyone at Start into a huge fan of this random oldies song called 'Quarter to Three.'"

"I don't know it," I said.

"Exactly. And the kids at Start *beg* me for it now. But it took a while. Most people don't immediately like new things. They want to dance to the songs they know. As DJ, you obviously know more songs, and better songs. That's why it's your job. But you can't always be teaching them. Sometimes you have to play along with them. It's a balance."

"So you just stand up there and look around the room and figure out what will make people happy?" I asked.

"Pretty much. So, go on. Give it a shot."

"Okay." I looked down at my computer, then back up at Char. "Wait, who is my pretend crowd?"

"Me."

"Oh." I frowned around his room for a moment, then put on "Born Slippy NUXX."

"I *do* like this song," Char said. "What tipped you off?"

I pointed to the *Trainspotting* poster taped to his wall.

"Great movie," he said. "Great sound track. Okay, let me have a turn. Pass me my laptop, will you?"

So I did, and then when "Born Slippy NUXX" was over, he put on an upbeat song. "This is 'Quarter to Three' that I was telling you about," he said. "It's good, right? I found it on some oldies compilation. It's only, like, two and a half minutes long. You can play something once it's through."

I started searching through my music collection again.

"You know, you can sit down," Char said.

"Where?" I asked, looking around in case he had hidden a couch somewhere in this twenty-square-foot room.

"Here." He patted the bed beside him.

I hesitated, then picked up my laptop, carried it over, and sat down next to him. I thought it might feel different because it was a boy's bed, or because it was Char's bed, but it just felt like a bed.

"Hey," Char said abruptly, looking over my shoulder at the thousands and thousands of songs on my computer, "do you want to DJ at Start? I mean for real, not just because I'm dealing with a Pippa crisis. You could have, like, a half-hour guest DJ slot every Thursday, and you could play whatever you wanted. Except for 'Girls and Boys.' Okay, fine, you could sometimes play 'Girls and Boys' if you really wanted to."

"Are you serious?"

"I'm totally serious," Char said. "I saw you on Thursday, and you're a natural. Plus," he said with a grin, "I'm your teacher."

"But don't you need, like, permission? From Pete or someone? Can you just do that?"

"Hell yeah, I can do that." Char leaned back on his elbows. "I'm the DJ. It's my night. I can do whatever I want."

I thought about it for a moment. I thought about how tired I had been, waking up Friday morning after only a couple hours of sleep. I thought about how my back hurt from standing and my ears rang. But I also thought about how exciting it had been. How powerful I had felt, knowing that I alone had the ability to make people dance, the ability to make them happy.

"You're smiling again," Char noted. "You can't make me like you that way, now that I know your tricks."

"Char," I said, "I would *love* to DJ at Start."

"Then it's settled," he said. "You only have four days until your first gig, so you better start practicing." He nudged me with his shoulder and nodded toward my computer.

I played a Cat Power song, and Char said, "This is good. It's kind of sad, but I like it." And then he played a song that I didn't recognize, and he said, "I can't *believe* you've never heard Big Audio Dynamite. You'll love them." And then I played a song, and he played a song, and we kept going like that for the rest of the afternoon, just playing each other music that we liked. The sun was streaming in through his curtainless windows, and his bed was soft and comfortable, and I would pinpoint this day, afterward, as one of the last times that things were as perfect as they seemed, before everything came tumbling down.

8

WHEN I AGREED TO DJ AT START, I FORGOT ONE
important thing: my parents.

It's not that I was going to ask for their permission to walk
alone down abandoned streets to DJ a warehouse dance party at
one a.m. on a weeknight. I didn't feel like that was any of their
business. However, I did need permission to stay at my mom's
house on Thursday night. And not just this Thursday night.
Every Thursday night.

I asked my mom first, since I figured she would be an easier
sell than my dad.

"Why?" she asked.

It was later on Sunday, after my magical afternoon at Char's.
Alex and Neil were in their pajamas, watching half an hour of
educational television before bedtime. My mom was in the study
she shares with Steve, clicking away on her computer.

"I just want to spend more time with you," I said.

You know how manipulative you are. You always know. I love my mother fiercely, and some days I even love spending time with her, but in no way did I have so powerful an urge to spend *more* time with her that I would request to change the custody schedule that we all agreed on when I was a kid.

Plus, time with my mom is never just time with my mom. It invariably means time with Steve, Alex, Neil, Bone, and Chew-Toy, as well. We had exactly seven minutes left in this one-on-one conversation before she would go into the family room, snap off the television, and send my little brother and sister to bed. Otherwise they might accidentally be exposed to more than half an hour of television, which would presumably turn their brains to Silly Putty on the spot.

I knew that getting more quality time with my mom was not my goal. But *she* did not know that. I saw her cheeks glow as she raised her eyes from her computer to look at me. "But then your father only gets you Wednesdays and Fridays," she said. "I'm not sure that's fair."

My mother is very, very into fairness. Like, to the point where she will kennel Bone while Chew-Toy gets fed dinner and vice versa. She doesn't think it's *fair* for one dog to eat some of the other dog's kibble. She also lets Alex stay up exactly twenty minutes later than Neil, because Alex is two years older than Neil, and that is *fair*; however, she will not let Alex watch any more television in her extra twenty minutes because that is *not fair*. Whenever Steve denies them dessert, and Alex wails, "That's not *fair*!" I can practically see Mom's brain whirring, trying to determine whether Alex is or is not correct.

"I'm sure Dad will understand," I told my mother, even

though 1) I was not at all sure of this, and 2) that completely did not address her question.

But Mom said, "Well, it's all right with me if it's all right with him. We'll be glad to have you around more often, sweetie."

And that's the thing about my mother and fairness. She really wants to be fair to everybody. But if she can't be fair to one person, then she wants that person to be my father.

My parents separated when I was four years old, and Mom blames the dissolution of their marriage entirely on Dad. At her lake house last summer, I guess she felt that I was now old enough to understand what went wrong between them—which is reprehensible, by the way. You are never old enough to hear details about your parents' marital problems.

Regardless, Mom told me, "We weren't happy together. We both knew we weren't happy, but he was the one who brought it to that breaking point. I was so ambitious, and he was so . . . well, he was content with what he'd already done. He was happy to rest on his laurels. When I wanted to create more, build more, start BOO OIL, have more kids, renovate the house, he wouldn't get behind it. He wouldn't get behind *me*. I would have done anything to make our marriage work. But your dad has never liked anything that requires *work*. I'm telling you, never fall for a music man. It only ends in heartbreak."

Her whole story made it sound to me like Dad had done her a favor. Why would she have *wanted* to stay with him if they were that unhappy? But that is not how my mother sees it.

So even though Mom got Steve, and two adorable new kids, and two adorable new dogs, and a way bigger house, and a lake house, too, even so, she has never felt fully compensated for the way my dad treated her twelve years ago.

And I think that's why she didn't protest now, when I told her that I wanted to spend more time with her. Instead she said, "Just check with your father, and then I'll tell the rest of the family the happy news."

So later that night, after I knew he would be home from work, I closed myself into my bedroom to call Dad.

"Elise!" he answered. "Good to hear from you, honey. How was your weekend?"

"It was fine," I said. "Hey, have you heard of a band called Big Audio Dynamite?"

"Sure," he replied. "That was Mick Jones's band after the Clash. Good stuff. Why?"

"I heard one of their songs today," I said. "I liked it." That was about all I felt like telling my dad about my afternoon at Char's apartment. Then I took a deep breath. "Daddy," I began, which is not something I've regularly called my father since I was Alex's age, "would you mind if I started staying at Mom's house on Thursday nights?"

There was a brief moment of silence on Dad's end of the line.

"Maybe I could switch it for another night at your house? Like Tuesdays?" But even as I said this, I knew it wouldn't work. Dad has to work at the store until closing every night of the week except Wednesdays, Thursdays, and Fridays. That's why those are my nights with him. The rest of the time he comes home so late, and sleeps so late, that I could stay with him and never see him at all. And my parents are not okay with that, especially not since I cut myself. After that, I haven't been allowed to stay at either parent's house if there aren't going to be adults home at a reasonable hour. I don't understand that rule, since the time when I cut myself was the middle of the afternoon, but whatever.

As predicted, Dad said, "No, Tuesdays wouldn't work, I have to be at the store until late."

There was another pause.

"It's just that there's this new extracurricular activity I want to do," I tried to explain. I stared out my bedroom window. "But it's on Mom's side of town, so—"

"Was this your mother's suggestion?" Dad broke in.

"That I stay with her on Thursdays?" I asked, surprised. "No. She had nothing to do with it. It was my idea."

"Oh," my father said. "Well, if it was your idea, then that's fine."

"Really?" I squealed.

"This is what you want?" he asked.

"Yes! Thank you so much, Daddy. I'll see you Wednesday. Love you!"

And that is how I got a weekly guest DJ slot at Start. It wasn't pretty. But that's how I did it.

There are some people who want to win at whatever they do, even if the things they do are not the sort of things one wins at.

I am one of those people.

When we had a gardening section in fifth grade science class, I wanted to be the *best* gardener. When I learned how to do embroidery at day camp, I wanted to be the *best* at embroidering. And I realized, during my second time playing music at Start, that I didn't just want to be a DJ. I wanted to be the *best* DJ.

I played a half-hour set. Char was very encouraging—he helped me plug in my laptop, and adjusted the monitors for me, and reassured me that he wouldn't leave the dance floor, not even to use the bathroom, so he would be right there if I needed him. And it went okay. I only tried to beat match twice, and both times the songs overlapped in a jarring, earsplitting way. The second time Char even climbed up to the DJ booth to help me, which was mortifying, so the rest of the time I focused on simply playing one song after another without leaving any moments of silence. I tried to read the crowd, like Char had told me, but all I could read was that the crowd did not like "Sweet Dreams (Are Made of This)." It seemed like half the room filed outside to smoke when I played it. I couldn't tell why. I had heard Char play that same song two weeks earlier, and everyone had danced.

Char relieved me at one thirty, full of compliments and encouragement. Then I packed up my computer and found Vicky, who was smoking outside, near Mel.

"Hey, lady," she called when she saw me. "You were *awesome* up there."

"I was all right."

Vicky shook out her long, thick brown hair. "Please. Give up the false modesty and just take a compliment."

With all the words I would use to describe myself, *falsely modest* had never been among them. "Thank you," I said. "But I could do better. Char is better."

"But you've been doing this for, what, a week?"

"Two weeks."

"Right, and he's been doing it for *years*. Cut yourself some slack. Anyway, Char's a dick. Don't aspire to be like him."

I didn't think Char was a dick, considering that he was not only teaching me how to DJ, but also letting me play at his party. But I could guess why Vicky might think so. "You mean because of Pippa?" I asked.

"Because of lots of things." She exhaled a ring of smoke, and we both watched it swirl up into the night sky.

"Where is Pippa, by the way?" I asked. I hoped the answer was not "passed out on a bench" again.

"Manchester," Vicky replied.

"Oh, cool. Will she be back for Start next week? I want her to see me play. I swear I'll be better at it next time."

"You were fine at it this time," Vicky reminded me. "And, no, I don't think she'll be back next week."

The way Vicky said that did not sound good.

"Her parents thought she was partying too hard," Vicky explained, crushing her cigarette butt under the heel of her gray suede boot. "Her mom freaked out because she had given Pippa, like, two hundred dollars to buy a new winter coat, and then she somehow found out that Pippa spent all the money on alcohol and basically froze all winter long. So they made her take off the rest of the semester and go back home where they can 'keep an eye on her' or something."

I wondered if Pippa felt about this the same way I felt about my parents' stupid rule that I couldn't stay in a house at night without an adult. As if that was going to help me. As if they knew exactly what my problem was and they were going to fix it.

"Do *you* think Pippa parties too much?" I asked Vicky. "I mean, you're her best friend. You would know. They're three thousand miles away."

Vicky shrugged. "We're eighteen. Everyone parties too much."

But that wasn't really an answer.

"What are you going to do without her?" I asked.

Vicky's hand reached toward her pocket, as if for another cigarette, then she shook her head and clasped her hands instead. "I have no idea," she said. "Homework?"

"Yeah . . ." I said doubtfully.

"I could clean my room," Vicky suggested. "That would take a while."

"Another great plan, sure."

"Shopping!" Vicky announced. "I will go shopping. For every day that Pippa is away, I will buy something new to make me happy in her absence."

"How many days could you keep that up for?" I asked. "Without going broke, I mean."

"I think . . . two. Maybe three, if I'm buying, like, socks. It's fine. This is what credit cards are for. Do you want to go shopping with me?"

"Um," I said, at the same time that Mel said, "Yes."

We both turned around to look at him. He stood a few feet away, blocking the doorway with his bulk. "Oh, how rude of me," Vicky said. "Mel, darling, do *you* want to go shopping with me?"

Mel snorted. "Thank you, Vicks, but I have all the dangly

earrings and studded belts that I need for this season. I was answering on Elise's behalf. Just in case you weren't sure, Elise, the correct answer is *yes*." I opened my mouth, but he just waggled his finger and admonished, "Remember, honey, fixing up and looking sharp is not optional."

"I thought you said it *was* optional," I reminded him.

Mel sighed. "For the love of God, will you just respect the wisdom of your elders for *once*?"

"Fine." I turned back to Vicky. "Yes."

"Excellent. Let's do Sunday!" Vicky jumped up and down a little. "You ready to go back in?"

Mel began to edge the door open for us, but I said, "I'm leaving, actually. I'm tired, and I have to wake up so early tomorrow. See you Sunday, Vicky!"

And I walked home.

I hadn't lied to Vicky—I *was* tired, and I *did* have to wake up so early, but that wasn't why I left early. I left because I wasn't ready to be done DJing yet. I wanted to keep doing it and doing it and never stop until I had mastered it all. When I got home, I stayed awake in my bedroom, my headphones on, practicing with my DJ equipment for hours, until the sunlight began to seep through the dark, wiping away the stars, and turning the sky from black to navy to gold.

9

TEACHERS DO NOT TALK TO ME VERY OFTEN. THEY talk to troublemakers. They talk to Chuck Boening all the goddamn time. But the last time a teacher said, "Elise, may I speak with you?" it was eighth grade and my social studies teacher wanted to know if he could submit my essay on Hitler Youth to a Facing History and Ourselves writing contest. (For the record, I said yes. For the record, I got an honorable mention. Also for the record, the principal announced this award during the next assembly, and no one looked up from their cell phones for long enough to acknowledge that this had happened, except for two boys whose names I didn't even know, who hollered, "Boo!" and then got kicked out of the assembly.)

So you can understand why I was surprised when Ms. Wu pulled me aside after math class on Friday. I tried to figure out if there was some sort of Facing History and Ourselves math essay contest that she wanted me to compete in, and if I could come up with a gentle way to tell her, "Absolutely not."

But that wasn't what she asked. What she asked was, "Elise, is everything all right?"

I blinked at her. She was sitting behind her desk, and I was standing next to her. My math class had already filed out, so we only had a few minutes before the next group of students arrived.

"Do you want to sit down?" Ms. Wu asked, pulling a chair up next to her.

"No, thank you."

Ms. Wu pressed on. "Elise, I wanted to talk to you because lately you've seemed a little . . . off. Less engaged than you used to be. Maybe even exhausted. Is there anything you want to talk about? Any problems at home?"

This woman. This horrifying woman. With her muted sweaters and her sensible heels. All those times I had eaten lunch in her classroom, watching videos of Mandelbrot sets on her computer, she was secretly, insidiously, monitoring me.

Any problems at home? Please. Sally has parents who won't let her read any books with sex in them, and everybody knows that Emily Wallace's mother made her get a boob job when she was a freshman; meanwhile, my dad buys me DJ equipment, and my mom wants only for me to be an educated member of a working democracy—yet *I* get asked if I have any problems at home?

I bet I do seem exhausted, Ms. Wu. I bet I do seem less engaged. I was up all night, doing something that *I really love*, and I'm sorry, but I just didn't reserve enough energy to fully participate in this miserable, mandatory little exercise in public education.

Since discovering Start, I had felt, for the first time in years, like good things could happen to me. I felt *happy*. Yet somehow, for the first time in years, someone was bothering to ask me what was wrong. Where were you in September, Ms. Wu? Where were you last spring? Where were you when I needed you?

"Ms. Wu," I said, "I appreciate your concern. But I'm fine. I had a late night and didn't get much sleep. I'm sure I'll feel better on Monday."

"All right," she said. "But if there's ever anything you want to talk about, you know where to find me. You're a real talent, Elise, with a bright future ahead of you, and I don't want to see you throw that away."

I looked at her sharply, wondering if this was a reference to the time I cut myself. But how could it be? Ms. Wu didn't know about that. Nobody at school knew, except for Amelia. Amelia, who now thought I had done something to hurt her, apparently. When all I had ever wanted was for her to just be my friend.

Don't think about Amelia.

"I just want you to know that I'm on your side," Ms. Wu went on. "I believe in you."

You and Char both, I thought. "Thank you," I said, and I made a mental note to stop eating lunch in Ms. Wu's classroom.

I left for my next class. Opening the door, I nearly collided with a guy who was running to beat the bell. I'd seen him before, usually recruiting people for the lacrosse team. The only other things I knew about him were that he had beautiful green eyes and seemed to wear Adidas sandals all the time, even in the winter.

"Watch it, lesbo," he snarled, lunging out of my way and down the hall.

I steadied myself on the door frame, almost bowled over by the irony. What's wrong with *me*, Ms. Wu? What's wrong with *everybody else*?

"I think we should give you a makeover," Vicky declared. It was Sunday afternoon, shortly after we had met up at Calendar Girls, a consignment shop downtown. I'd told my mother I was going shopping with my new friend, Vicky, a girl I'd met at my favorite record shop, which was plausible if not 100 percent *true*.

Now, as we pawed through cheap bracelets and belts, Vicky suggested making me over like she had just had the most brilliant and original idea in history.

I instantly snapped back, "No."

Vicky raised her eyebrows. "Why not?"

I opened my mouth to respond. Because, I wanted to explain to her, in eighth grade, Emily Wallace's friends all chipped in to split the cost of an ad in our middle school yearbook that said, ELISE DEMBOWSKI: LET US GIVE YOU A MAKEOVER! YOU DESERVE IT! Because a whole bunch of pretty girls saved up their allowances just so they could call attention to my ugliness. The yearbook adviser let the ad run because—Emily explained to me later, in her syrupy-sweet tone—he thought it was so kind that the popular girls were being generous with their beauty expertise.

Everyone saw that ad. Even Alex, who couldn't really read yet then, but who knew her letters well enough to point to my name and beam and marvel, "Look, Elise! You're in the *yearbook*!"

"Because," I said to Vicky, "I don't need a makeover. I'm happy with myself the way I am."

That's the sort of thing the psychiatrist at the hospital told me to say, even if I don't believe it. It's called an *affirmation*.

"Obviously you are," Vicky said, holding a fur coat up to herself in the mirror. "You're Glendale's hottest young DJ. I'm saying that now you can *dress* like it. That's the whole point of being a DJ, is getting to dress up like a DJ and not look like a total poseur."

"I'm not sure that's the *whole* point of being a DJ . . ."

"Fine, maybe it's, like, 30 percent of the point." She grabbed a pair of bejeweled red-and-purple pumps off the shelf. "Most of my closet is filled with rock star clothes, and I'm not a rock star yet."

"Are you really that good a singer?" I asked.

"Yes," Vicky said simply.

The way Vicky said it reminded me a little of Alex. *"Are you really a unicorn, Alex?" "Yes."* Or it reminded me of myself, before I knew better. *"Are you really going to build that entire dollhouse from scratch, Elise?" "Yes." "Are you really going to make all your own clothes by hand, Elise?" "Yes." "Are you really going to make everyone at Glendale High suddenly stop hating you?" "Yes."*

"So why *aren't* you a famous rock star?" I asked.

"Because," Vicky said, trying to shove her feet into the pumps, "it's not enough to be a really good singer. You also need a band who actually shows up for rehearsal sometimes. You need to be taken seriously. You need anyone at all to book you to play a show. You need a *break*. I cannot control everything. I can only control what my voice sounds like. And how my rock star clothes look."

"What did Pete say when you talked to him about the Dirty Curtains?" I asked. "Is he going to give you a slot sometime?"

Vicky made a face. "After about two hours of hanging around him, he told me to send him a demo and 'we'll see.' So I sent him a demo. And I guess we'll see. I'm not holding out hope."

"Could Char just invite you to play some Thursday night?" I asked. "Is he allowed to do that, or does Pete need to approve it?"

"Sure, Char could invite us," Vicky said. "But he doesn't."

"Why not?" I asked.

Vicky sighed.

"Has he heard you?" I asked. "Maybe if he heard you, and heard how good you guys are—"

"Oh, Char's heard us," Vicky said. "Pippa brought him around to band practice a month or two ago."

"He didn't like your music?" I asked quietly. "What a jackass," I added, even though I had never heard the Dirty Curtains and maybe I wouldn't like their music either.

Vicky snorted. "Please. He *loved* our music. That's why he'll never, ever invite us to play at Start. Char doesn't share his spotlight. Not with anyone who might steal it from him."

"He invited me to DJ with him," I pointed out as gently as I knew how, so Vicky wouldn't take it personally.

She nodded. "Exactly. That means he doesn't think you're a threat."

I opened my mouth to respond, but before I had the chance, Vicky handed me the shoes she'd been trying to fit into and said, "I think you should buy these."

"I don't know," I said, toying with one of the rhinestones on the toe. "They look like the eighties."

"Then they're perfect. You can play the Cure and your shoes

will match. Come on, Elise. I might not be a famous rock star yet, but you *are* a famous DJ."

"I think famous is a bit of a—"

"Shut up," Vicky said kindly. "We are going places. This is just the start. Now get in that dressing room."

So I did.

Every time I tried on something new and came out of the dressing room to model it, Vicky would sing part of a Start hit—Joy Division or the Jackson Five or Dexys Midnight Runners—and then I would say, "Yeah, I could see wearing this while that song was playing," or she would go, "Ugh, that totally clashes with the music! Take it off."

And she was good. Even just hearing her sing a couple lines here and there, I could tell: she really was that talented.

After Vicky approved a pair of lace leggings, I tried on a fluffy pleated pink dress that looked like it belonged to Madonna circa 1987. "Ta-da!" I announced as I emerged from the dressing room. I stuck one hand on my hip and the other in the air.

But Vicky was gazing into the distance and didn't respond immediately. And when she did, what she said was not "You look like an extra in *Footloose*" but "I wish Pippa were here."

I let my hands fall to my sides.

"Pippa would love today." Vicky sighed. "She'd have so much fun shopping with us. Of course, shopping with *her* could drive even a self-respecting woman to the brink of anorexia, since Pippa spends most of her time whining about how stores never have clothes small enough to fit her. It makes me want to strangle her. At least she has the shoe size of a normal person."

"What size?" I asked.

"Eight. That was how we met, actually. I saw her in the laundry room of our dorm—this was October—and she was trying to work a washing machine in, like, a sweatshirt and stripper heels." Vicky laughed. "So of course I went right over there and asked her where she got her shoes, and the next thing I knew I was trying them on. They fit me like Cinderella's glass slipper."

I watched Vicky smiling in the mirror. "So it was love at first sight?" I said.

"No way. For starters, I wasn't 'supposed' to be friends with Pippa. She lived on the sixth floor, and I was on the ninth."

"So?" I asked.

"Ah, spoken like an outsider. What you clearly overlook is that the sixth and ninth floors in Murphy Hall are locked in bitter rivalry. Because 6 is the inverse of 9, which means that the sixth floor is . . ." Vicky rolled her eyes up to the ceiling, like she was thinking about this. "Bad," she finished. "And the ninth floor is good, obviously," she added. "Very intense prank war between the two."

"I'd always kind of hoped that college would be more mature than high school," I commented.

"I do want to believe that there's some place in the world that's more mature than high school," Vicky said. "But I haven't found it yet."

"So Pippa was your sworn enemy?" I asked.

"She was definitely supposed to be. Sixth floor and all, it's like everything the ninth floor doesn't stand for. Or whatever. Plus, Pippa can be a bitch when you first get to know her. She was definitely a bitch to me at first. She's suspicious of new people. Like, she had been living with her assigned roommate for almost *two months* and she had basically never spoken to her. They would sit at desks spaced three feet apart and just not talk to each other. So Pippa was lucky to have me. She needed a friend. Then it turned out that we both like to go out dancing, and the rest is history."

"Why *do* you and Pippa like to go out so much?" I asked.

"Why do *you* like to go out so much?" Vicky replied.

"Because it's dark and no one there knows me," I answered immediately.

Vicky tilted her head. "I wouldn't get too accustomed to that, if I were you. You're the DJ now. Soon everyone is going to know you."

"Oh, please. They won't even notice me. I'm not a very *good* DJ," I reminded her.

Vicky rolled her eyes again. "Look, I don't know why Pippa likes going out. Sometimes I think she likes it just because she can drink and flirt with Char. But *I* like going out for the opposite reason as you. I feel like people there *do* know me. They see me—maybe not how I really am, but how I really want to be. They see me how I see myself. It's like I dress the part of Vicky Blanchet, rock star, and I act the part of Vicky Blanchet, rock star, and everyone at Start is willing to see me as Vicky Blanchet, rock star. And that's who I am inside, even if I don't have the record contract to prove it yet.

"No one else is willing to do that. People in the daytime see Vicky Blanchet, English major, or Vicky Blanchet, fat girl. And they're not *wrong*, but they're still somehow *overlooking* me. Is this silly? Does this make sense?"

"It's not silly," I told Vicky. And I suddenly wanted to tell her more, wanted to tell her how Amelia Kindl saw me as a crazy girl whose life needed saving, how Ms. Wu saw me as a student in trouble, how Lizzie Reardon saw me as an endless source of amusement, and how I saw myself as so much more, so much brighter. But I didn't even know how to begin, among these used cowboy boots and vintage ball gowns, how to lay out years of my life for Vicky in a way that would make sense. I didn't want to tell her how Amelia or Ms. Wu or Lizzie or anyone else saw me, because I didn't want Vicky to start agreeing with them.

So all I said was, "*I* see you as Vicky Blanchet, rock star."

"And I see *you* as Elise, DJ extraordinaire," she said, settling a big pair of sunglasses on her nose. "So buy the rhinestone pumps."

I wound up buying not only the shoes but also two new pairs of earrings, a set of bangles, a vest, two dresses, and a pair of leather pants.

"What the *hell* am I supposed to do with leather pants?" I asked Vicky as I twisted to look at my backside in the mirror.

"Wear them when you dance around your room," she explained, and I could tell from her tone that she was trying not to add *obviously*.

"But I don't dance around my room," I objected.

"Well, you should start."

The total bill was enormous, but I'd received checks from

both sets of grandparents for my sixteenth birthday, and if DJ clothing wasn't the perfect use for that money, I didn't know what was. It was still less than that bill I'd racked up on my back-to-school shopping trip, and those clothes had done nothing for me at all. But these clothes did something for me. They made me feel happy.

I went home looking for someone to share my good mood with, and the first person I saw was Alex. Actually, I just saw Alex's bare feet. The rest of her was hidden under a number of big cardboard boxes.

"Craft project?" I asked.

Alex's response came back muffled. "It's for the spring fair. Everyone is supposed to make their own building, and then we put them all together in the field so it looks like a town. And then we each sell things from our buildings, only we sell them for fake money, not real money. The fake money is called Berger Bucks."

Alex's second grade teacher is Mr. Berger.

"Doesn't that seem a little self-absorbed?" I asked her. "That he named the money after himself?"

"That's what I told him," Alex's disembodied voice replied. "But he said he was the teacher, so he makes the rules. And the money. Only he said he doesn't actually make that much money."

"Got it. So what's your building going to be?"

"A castle." Alex moved a box so her head was poking out. "A poetry castle. That's going to be the turret, right there."

I didn't see any turrets. I just saw more boxes, but I said, "It's fabulous, Alex. Very royal."

She beamed at me. Then I went upstairs, locked myself into my bedroom, and drew my curtains. I put on those ridiculous leather pants and DJed song after song, dancing with myself until I tired myself out enough to fall asleep. I didn't even need to walk that night.

10

ON THURSDAY, AFTER MOM, STEVE, ALEX, NEIL, AND the dogs went to bed for the night, I changed into one of the dresses that Vicky had helped me buy. It was short, with a tight bodice and a tutulike skirt. I put on my new bangles, too. I even ran up to the attic to get out the belt that I had painstakingly covered in multicolored sequins last year, before suffocating it in a garbage bag when I decided that I wanted to look like everybody else.

Tonight I didn't want to look like everybody else. Tonight I wanted to look like how I felt on the inside: Elise Dembowski, DJ.

"Woo-hoo!" Mel exclaimed when I showed up at Start. "Elise, honey, look at you!"

I pulled down my skirt and tried to play it cool. "I went shopping with Vicky."

"I always knew that girl was going places," Mel said. "She is a mother-loving genius, Vicks is. You are only further proof of that. Twirl for me, will you?"

I blushed. *"Mel . . ."*

"What, you'd deny me this small bit of paternal pride?" Mel stuck his hands on his waist, playing mad.

I had to smile at that, since my actual father was white, had arms about one-third as muscular as Mel's, and was probably asleep right now.

Other than right now, I had barely thought about my father all night. Yes, it felt weird to take the school bus on a Thursday afternoon to my mom's house instead of my dad's. But I got over it. Dad had called my phone after dinner, but I was too busy to talk, trying to cram in my last bit of DJ practice before taking it to the floor of Start. With my headphones on, I didn't even hear the phone ring.

When I got inside Start, I tried to beeline to the DJ booth to let Char know that I was here and ready to play whenever he wanted me to. But that guy with the big camera got in my way. Flash Tommy. He didn't introduce himself or ask permission or anything, he just snapped a bunch of photos of me in quick succession, then walked away again, his external flash leaving bright clouds in my vision.

When I finally reached the DJ booth, Char was just transitioning into the Pixies.

"Way to steal my songs," I said, climbing into the booth next to him. I edged him over a little with my hip so there would be room for us both. "Now I'll have to find something else to play tonight."

"Bummer," Char agreed. "How long is it going to take you to come up with a replacement song? You need an hour or so to think it through?"

"Oh, please. I'm ready anytime."

"All right, then, let's get this party started. Hook in."

Char kept playing while I unpacked my laptop and plugged it into his mixer. I cued up Joan Jett, "Bad Reputation," then slung my headphones around my neck and said to him, "Ready."

"Over to you, my lady," he said, gesturing grandly.

I hit play, and the room exploded.

"You seem to have things under control here." Char spoke directly into my ear as I surveyed the dancing crowd.

"You think?" I responded.

His laughter was a warm breeze on my ear. "All right, hotshot. I'll leave you to it. Can I get you a drink?"

"A water would be great, thanks," I said, looking away from my dance floor to find the next song for them. Maybe something kind of punk rock . . .

"You sure you don't want a beer or anything?"

I looked up from my computer for a moment, just long enough to raise an eyebrow at Char. "I am still sixteen, you know."

"Yeah, I've heard that."

"I might be wearing a new dress and shoes that aren't sneakers, but I'm still sixteen."

Char blinked a few times, flustered. "Some sixteen-year-olds drink beer," he said. "And all *your* beers would be free, since you're the DJ. That's one of the best reasons to become a DJ, is for the free booze."

"I thought it was for the DJ clothes," I said.

"What?"

"Never mind," I said. "I only have, like, a minute left on this song. Just bring me a cup of water. But make sure it's free. You know, 'cause I'm the DJ."

Char rolled his eyes and left me alone in the booth, and I turned my full attention to DJing.

I know that humility is a valued trait, but there's no way to be humble about this: I was on fire. It wasn't just that I had mastered the technical skills, thanks to my hours and hours of practice over the past week. It was more that something had clicked, and now I understood what Char meant about reading the crowd. They will tell you what they want. They will tell you vocally sometimes, with loud requests shouted into your ear at the least convenient times, right as you are trying to transition between songs, or with Post-its stuck to you. And they will tell you silently, by dancing or not dancing, smiling or not smiling, listening or not listening.

Tonight I had Start in the palm of my hand. They loved me, and I loved me, too.

When Char came to relieve me some time later, I said, "I can keep going. I don't mind."

"I can see that," he said, snaking his arm around me to reach his computer. "But why don't you let me have a turn, too? Just because Start is technically my night and all."

Reluctantly I transitioned over to him, then hopped down from the booth.

"*Oh* my God," Vicky said when I reached her on the dance

floor. "Do you believe me now? That you're Glendale's hottest DJ?"

I had to cover my mouth, I was smiling so wide. "I believe you now."

Vicky was standing with two guys. One of them had enough facial hair that I could have knit a scarf out of it. He was wearing a white T-shirt on which he had written in Sharpie, *I Shop at the Gap*. I couldn't tell if this was supposed to be ironic or the opposite of ironic. The other guy looked a little younger, a little heavier, and a lot less bearded.

"These are the Dirty Curtains," Vicky said. "This is Elise. Guys, am I wrong, or is Elise twice the DJ that Char is?"

"Oh, no," I quickly said. "Char's awesome!"

"I thought *you* were awesome," the younger guy said. "When you played that Buzzcocks song? That was insane! Did you see how much everyone was dancing? How did you even think to play that song?"

"I don't know," I said. "I'm the DJ, I guess."

"You were killing it up there," he went on. "Right, Dave?"

The beard guy nodded. "Killing it."

The younger guy turned back to me. "I loved it," he said earnestly.

"Aw, who's a little fangirl?" Vicky sang.

He blushed a little. "Shut up, Vicky." To me, he said, "I have this terrible habit of saying exactly what's on my mind at any point in time. Right now, what's on my mind is—how cool is it that we're hanging out with *the DJ*?"

"Char's the DJ," I said. "I'm, like . . . the guest."

"I'm Harry." He shook my hand. "And you're great."

"Oh, right," Vicky said. "How could I forget the formal introductions. This is Dave, and he's on guitar." She pointed to the guy with the beard.

"Yo." He jutted his chin upward.

"This is Harry." Here she pointed to the chatty guy. "He's on drums. His name is Harry because of his eyebrows. You know. They're hairy."

"And her name is Vicks because she smells like Vicks VapoRub all the time," Harry immediately responded.

Vicky stuck a hand on her hip. "His name is Harry because when he came out of the womb, he was so terrifyingly ugly that Mom shouted, 'Scary!' But she was crying so hard about how ugly her baby was that the doctor thought she said 'Harry,' instead."

"Her name is Victoria because she's like Queen Victoria," Harry began. "You know. A virgin."

"First of all," Vicky said. "Queen Victoria wasn't the Virgin Queen. That was Queen *Elizabeth*. Second of all, are you actually talking about my sex life? Ew. Do you want me to throw up that entire sixteen-ounce milkshake all over you?"

"Let me guess," I broke in. "You're brother and sister."

Harry and Vicky both blinked at me, like they'd forgotten they had an audience. "It's that obvious?" Harry asked.

Dave snorted.

"Okay, but here's the *real* question," Harry said. "Who's older?" He and Vicky both posed.

"Vicky is," I said without hesitation.

Harry let his arms fall to his sides. "Drat. You know all our secrets."

"Harry's sixteen months younger," Vicky added. "He's still in high school."

"Our mom liked to get pregnant a lot," Harry said.

"Ew again!" Vicky shouted.

"Everything that's on my mind," Harry said to me. "I'm telling you. It's a curse."

"He usually isn't allowed to come to Start," Vicky explained to me. "You know, because it's a weeknight, and Mom and Dad say he has to go to school in the morning and all that." She put on a high baby voice and pinched Harry's cheeks. "Don't you, my itty-bitty baby bwother?"

He jabbed her in the stomach, and she let go of his cheeks.

"So why are you here tonight?" I asked.

"Teacher training day tomorrow," Harry replied. "Thank *God*."

I had school the next day, so Harry obviously didn't go to Glendale High.

"I'm at Roosevelt," he said, before I asked.

"Oh, yeah. They're our rivals, I hear. In football."

"Boo," Harry said.

"Yeah. Boo back at you."

"Sorry to break up this pep squad interaction," Vicky said, "but can we please dance? So we're not listening to Robyn for nothing?"

So we danced. Sort of. Mostly I hopped from foot to foot, and sang along, and flailed my arms a little.

"How do you do it?" I shouted at Vicky.

"Do what?" she asked, shimmying her shoulders a minuscule amount and somehow making every guy in the room look over at her.

"Dance!" I said.

"Oh." She laughed. "First, stand up straight."

"I am."

"No, babe. You're not." She pulled my shoulders back and tipped my chin up, like I was a rag doll. Harry seemed to be trying not to laugh as he looked on. "Now," Vicky went on, "repeat after me."

"I don't want to repeat after you," I said.

"Only people who repeat after me will learn how to dance like me," Vicky announced, her nose in the air.

"I'll repeat after you," Harry volunteered.

"Thank you, Harry. Elise, feel free to join in. Repeat after me: *I deserve to be here.*"

"I deserve to be here!" Harry and Dave declared, and I mumbled along with them.

"*No one can take my dance space away from me,*" Vicky intoned, and the three of us repeated her words.

"And finally: *I don't care if anyone thinks I look stupid.*"

"But I *do* look stupid," I pointed out, as Harry yelled out his affirmations.

"So do I," Vicky said. "But *I don't care.*"

Then Vicky walked us through some of her tricks for preserving her dance space. "If someone comes up behind you, you elbow them." She demonstrated. "It looks just like a dance move, but no one likes an elbow in their kidney. Or you jump up and land right on their foot."

We all practiced jumping up and down.

"Basically, just throw your arms around a bunch and take big steps, so everyone knows which part of the dance floor belongs to you. People are not going to *make* room for you. You have to make room for yourself."

A random guy approached Vicky, but she didn't even elbow him or step on him. She just ignored him and kept dancing. After a moment, he moved away.

"I've kissed way too many boys at Start already," Vicky confided to me, sounding world-weary. "I'm over them. They're all in *bands*."

"But *you're* in a band," I pointed out.

"Exactly. So why would I need them?"

Harry grabbed my hand and twirled me around. I laughed, and he twirled me again, looking very pleased with himself.

Char was a great dancer, but Harry wasn't. He seemed at a loss for moves, and after standing still for a moment, he just twirled me around once more. This time, I caught Char's eye as I spun. He made a *come here* motion with his fingers.

Harry opened his mouth, as if to say something to me, but before he had the chance I said, "One second, okay?" I dropped Harry's hand and made my way to the DJ booth.

"Is everything okay?" I asked Char when I reached him. "Do you want me to take over for a while?"

"Everything's fine. I just thought you could use some rescuing."

I looked back across the room. Harry had returned to dancing with Dave and Vicky. "I was doing okay," I said to Char. "But thanks."

"Do you want to stay up here?" Char asked. "We can go one-to-one until the night's over. It's quieting down."

I slid in next to him. "Sounds great."

Char and I alternated songs for the next half hour or so. I played some oldies; the Contours, James Brown, stuff like that. That was my dad's favorite sort of music to play, and I wondered how he had spent a Thursday night at home without me. Char was playing more eighties: Prince, Edwyn Collins, Transvision Vamp. He put on New Order's "Temptation," and we both took off our headphones and relaxed for a moment, leaning against the booth's railings. "Temptation" is a long song.

"This one could be about you," Char said, looking at me.

I tilted my head. "Why?"

"Because it's about a girl whose eyes are green and blue and gray all at the same time. Just like yours."

"They're usually blue," I said. "Bluish gray."

He stared into my eyes deeply, unblinking.

"They only look green when I wear a green shirt," I said. "So it's not really like this song."

"This song is about never having seen anyone like you before. And I haven't ever seen anyone like you," Char said.

"I haven't seen anyone like you either," I said.

We both fell silent and looked at each other for a moment.

And then he kissed me.

I pulled away almost instantly, as if I'd received an electric shock. "What did you do that for?" I demanded, my hand flying to my mouth.

Char reached out and gently removed my hand from my face. "Because I wanted to," he answered quietly, and, still holding my hand in his, he kissed me again. This kiss lasted longer than the first, and I didn't know what to do with my lips. But Char knew exactly what to do.

When he leaned away from me, I stared at him for a moment, my heart thundering so fast in my chest that I thought I might throw up, or just collapse to the floor, if he weren't still holding on to me.

"You know, *I'm* not going to have sex with you." The words flew out of my mouth. I immediately felt myself turn bright red. *You never know when to* shut up.

But Char laughed and laughed. "Don't worry," he said, kissing the top of my head. "I never thought you would."

I narrowed my eyes at him, unable to tell if he meant that as compliment or criticism.

"What about Pippa?" I asked.

His face was unreadable, and his eyes kept straying to my lips. "This isn't about Pippa," he said. "This is about you."

"But—"

"Come here," Char said. "It's okay." He opened his arms to me. I slowly sank into his embrace, and he rocked me back and forth. Dimly I was aware of the song fading out, the silence that followed, the lights coming on overhead. I slid my arms around him and pressed my face to his chest, trying to hear through his thin T-shirt if his heart was pounding as hard as my own. But his heart seemed fine.

"Come on, Elise," he said after a time, softly into my hair. "Let me drive you home."

11

WHEN MY ALARM WENT OFF ON FRIDAY MORNING, I woke up in my mom's house, not my dad's, which still felt a little crooked. I could hear Alex downstairs, banging around with her poetry castle construction project. I could hear Chew-Toy scratching at my door. But I stayed still for a moment, just thinking about last night—five hours ago, really. Me playing songs. Strangers dancing. Char kissing me. Me kissing Char. Char and me kissing each other.

In the dark and in the night, it made some kind of sense. There we were, two DJs, standing close together, sharing an evening where every song we touched felt golden. But in the harsh light of morning, I couldn't wrap my mind around it. He was nearly twenty, I was in high school. He was cool, I was not.

So why had he kissed me?

I got out of bed, threw on a pair of jeans and a plain T-shirt, and braided my hair so it would be out of the way. Before I went downstairs for breakfast, I opened up my laptop. I clicked away from the DJ program I'd been using the night before and opened up my Internet browser. Then I googled "Flash Tommy" and clicked over to his Web site.

It was filled with party photos. I saw boys smoking in bathrooms, girls pretending to take off their clothes, boys and girls making out in every combination. I saw lots of shots of Pippa: Pippa dancing with Vicky, Pippa downing a glass of wine, Pippa with her arms around Char. I quickly scrolled away from that last one.

And then I came across what I'd been looking for: a photo of me. It wasn't one of those that Flash Tommy had taken when I first arrived last night. I hadn't noticed him shooting this one. In the photo, I am standing alone in the DJ booth. I have my headphones half on, and I'm looking out just past the camera, smiling like I have a secret. The dress that Vicky helped me buy makes me look like a punk-rock ballerina, and my eyes look wider and bluer than I remembered them ever looking before.

I glanced toward my mirror, but I bore only a passing resemblance to the Elise in that photo on that Web site. My eyes were puffy, and the most punk-rock thing about me was that the cuffs of my jeans were frayed. But I was still smiling like I had a secret. Because I did.

I decided right then that Flash Tommy's big fancy camera, no matter how much it had cost him, was worth every single penny.

I hummed my way through breakfast and the bus ride to

school, all the way to my locker. I was working on my combination when my friends showed up. You know, Chava and Sally. Those friends.

"Just the people I wanted to see!" I said to them, and I wasn't even being sarcastic for once. I have watched enough popular television to know that when a boy does something inexplicable, like kiss you out of nowhere, you are supposed to discuss it with your girls. Especially if your girls are people like Chava and Sally. There is nothing they love more than trying to explain the behavior of boys they don't know.

Yet neither of them responded by saying, "Girlfriend! Spill the gossip!" which is how your girls are supposed to talk to you, according to popular television. Instead, Chava said to me, looking very serious, "Elise, Sally and I just want you to know that we are here for you. We are your friends and we are here for you," she went on grimly. "Like, in your times of need."

"Okay, that's great." I raised my eyebrows at her. I assumed she wasn't talking about Char kissing me, since that wasn't exactly a "time of need."

"And you can tell us anything," Sally added. "In fact, you *should* tell us anything. That's what friends do."

"You should tell us anything so that we can be supportive," Chava said. "You know, of whatever it is that you tell us."

"Plus, we tell you everything," Sally added. "So it seems only fair."

"I do tell you everything," I said, which was not true. But I told them more than I told anyone else at school, so it seemed like a lot.

Sally said, "You didn't tell us that you want to kill yourself."

I heard a loud *whoosh* in my ears, and I felt dizzy, like the earth was suddenly rotating around me very, very fast. I pulled my sleeves down over my wrists in an instant, like a reflex.

"I don't want to kill myself," I said in a shaky voice.

"You see, she doesn't tell us anything," Sally complained to Chava.

"Who said I wanted to kill myself?"

"You did," Sally said.

"You just claimed that I never tell you anything!" I slammed my fist against my locker, and Sally and Chava exchanged a look of concern.

"We read it in your blog," Chava said.

"I don't keep a blog."

"Okay, your 'online journal,' then," Sally said with a sigh.

"I don't keep one of those either."

"Elise, you can trust us," Chava said gently.

"Then can I trust you to tell me who claims that I have a goddamn blog about my suicidal tendencies?"

Sally wrinkled up her nose. Predictably, Sally's parents do not allow her to swear. She was probably supposed to put a quarter in a jar just for listening to me.

"Everyone," Chava said, blinking hard, like she was trying to hold back tears. "Everyone has read it."

I shoved past them and ran down the hall to the computer lab. I sat down and typed in "Elise Dembowski" to Google. The first option that popped up was "Elise Dembowski, MD." The second was "Elise Dembowski Tampa Florida school superintendent." But the third line read, "Elise Dembowski suicide."

I clicked on the link, then stuck my fist into my mouth and

bit down while I waited for the page to load. When it came up, it was a design scheme of orange stars, with the heading "Elise Dembowski's Super-Secret Diary," and the sheer juxtaposition of my name and my least-favorite color was shocking to me.

I started reading.

May 6: *i hate my life and i just want to die. nobody likes me, and i deserve it. why WOULD anyone ever want to be friends with me? i'm ugly and boring and stuck up. i wish i could kill myself, but ever since the last time i tried, my parents keep our medicine cabinet locked up and they hide our knives. i hate my parents—why won't they just let me die? i'd be doing them a favor. xoxo elise dembowski*

May 1: *just think of all the attention i would get if i killed myself. i bet they would have a school assembly about me and people would have to say nice things about me, even if they didn't mean them. maybe the paper would even run a feature on me! xoxo elise dembowski*

April 27: *confession time: no boy has EVER kissed me. actually i guess that's not a surprising confession since i am so awkward and gross. i know that i will be alone for the rest of my life, so i just hope that the rest of my life is short. xoxo elise dembowski*

April 21: *today i made a list of everyone who i hate. my name is at the top of the list, obviously. amelia kindl is second. if only she hadn't turned me in that first time i tried to commit suicide. then i could just be dead right now and wouldn't have to keep living my pathetic, worthless life. but no. i told her, and she betrayed me. she puts on this 'nice little girl' act, but it's just an act. i won't ever forgive her. xoxo elise dembowski*

I stopped reading not because I wanted to but because I couldn't see the computer screen anymore. Black spots crowded across my vision, and I realized I hadn't taken a breath since I started reading. I took my fist out of my mouth and exhaled, and my eyes got better, but nothing else did.

Somebody had taken my life, my identity, every negative thought I had ever had, and they had perverted them, twisted them into something grotesque. A version of me, but not me.

There was no question in my mind that this was what Amelia Kindl had been talking about during scoliosis testing when she spoke to me, for the first time all school year, to say, "And now there's *this*."

Who had done this, and why? Who would possibly expend the time and energy just to hurt me this much?

But the answer to that came to me instantly: lots of people. Jordan DiCecca and Chuck Boening had easily managed that iPod theft last year, so there was no reason why creating a fake Web site about me would be beyond their abilities, except for the fact that they may or may not know how to type in full sentences.

Lizzie Reardon, it seemed, had endless time to devote to bullying me. Writing a dozen blog posts over the past two weeks wouldn't be nearly as hard for her to pull off as the time in seventh grade when she orchestrated a supposed date between me and Mike Rosen that wound up with me getting pelted with water balloons while waiting alone in front of the Baskin-Robbins, wearing my favorite lace dress.

Then there was that "Elise Dembowski: Let us give you a makeover!" ad that Emily Wallace and her friends had run in the eighth-grade yearbook. If they were each willing to chip in $25 to have a laugh at my expense, I felt sure they could get it together to create a free Web site that would give them an even bigger laugh.

It didn't matter who had created this fake diary. In a way, that was the worst part about this: there were *so many people* who didn't like me, I couldn't even narrow down a list of suspects. It could have been anyone.

I logged out of the computer and went to class then, because I didn't know where else to go. Amelia glared at me from her desk, and Mr. Hernandez gave me a demerit for being late. I sat at my desk, taking notes on autopilot, and writing affirmations in the notebook margins, like the psychiatrist had told me to. *I am a good person. I like myself the way I am. Many people love and care about me. I have a purpose in life. I don't want to kill myself.*

I wrote over and over the words, pressing my pen down as hard as I could, until I broke through that sheet of paper and ink bled onto the page behind it.

As Mr. Hernandez lectured, I looked around the room and tried to figure out who had read my fake diary. Chava had said *everyone*. But what did that mean? Amelia had read it, that much was clear from the way her face scrunched up when she looked at me. Which meant that Amelia's friend, the mummy documentary girl, must have read it, too, since she crossed her arms and glared at me when she noticed me looking at Amelia. A few rows ahead of me, two boys were whispering, and then I clearly heard one of them say "suicide girl." Mr. Hernandez clapped his hands and said, "All right, folks, can I get some attention up here?" but I still felt the eyes on me.

Chava was not an exaggerator. Everyone had read it.

The moment class ended, I grabbed Amelia's arm. My voice shook as I said, "Look, Amelia. About that thing you read—I didn't write that. That wasn't me."

For some reason, I felt this intense need for her to know. I wanted to clear my name, of course. But also—and this is pathetic—there was some part of me that couldn't give up on this dream, the dream of friendship between me and this normal, nice, happy girl. The dream had already died, it had died on the first day of the school year, yet I still felt like if I just told her the truth . . . if she could just understand . . .

But Amelia pulled her arm away and said, "Of course it's you. Who else would have known enough to write all that?" And when I didn't say anything, she went on, her voice trembling, "Please, Elise. I can't handle any more of this. I never did anything to you. Please just leave me alone." Then she hurried after her friend.

The rest of the day, I couldn't stop thinking about what Amelia had said. *"Who else would have known enough to write all that?"* Because she was right: it wasn't enough just to enjoy torturing me, like Lizzie or Jordan or Emily or anyone I had already thought of. Whoever did this also had to know, somehow, that I had once thought I wanted to kill myself, and that Amelia Kindl had ratted me out. Someone had to know what really happened on the first day of school.

After I cut myself, after I called Amelia, after she called 911, an ambulance drove up to my house, filling my dad's quiet block with sirens and flashing lights. I opened the door to let in the EMTs because I didn't know what else to do. "What's the situation here?" one of them asked. So I held out my left arm. I hadn't meant to, but I also hadn't planned for anything like a 911 response team, and it seemed somehow like it would be rude to send them away with nothing.

Plus, I was scared. What if I had really screwed up my arm? What if I had cut through a tendon? Everything from my elbow down felt numb. I wanted to be saved.

The next thing I knew, the EMTs had loaded me into an ambulance and we were speeding toward the hospital. Some time after that, my parents showed up. Both of them, in the same room, which may have been the scariest and most disjointed part of the whole situation. Mom got there first, and she was completely calm and reassuring—until Dad arrived, at which point she freaked out at him, like this was all his fault. And Dad started out by crying and hugging me nonstop, until Mom's hysterical ranting got to be too much for him, at which point he stopped crying and hugging and started defending his parenting skills.

Some time after that, and after my arm had been examined and disinfected and rebandaged, a woman came to talk to me. She was wearing a skirt and heels, not hospital scrubs, and she explained that she was a psychiatrist, and she needed to ask me a few questions.

"Have you ever tried to kill yourself?" she asked me.

And I answered, honestly, "No."

"Do you ever feel so bad that you think about suicide?" she asked me.

And I answered, honestly, "Sometimes."

So they kept me in the hospital for a couple days on suicide watch. Eventually I was allowed to go home, but my parents didn't want me to go back to school right away. They wanted to keep an eye on me. I didn't argue, because I didn't want to go back to school either. I just went to therapy and downloaded new music. It was a fine life, but after a week or two of that, my parents decided that I was ready to go back into the world. I don't know what made them think that. As far as I'm concerned, I have never been ready to go into the world.

I returned to school having been through so much, but somehow school was exactly the same. It still smelled like cleaning supplies and meat loaf. My locker still jammed when I tried to open it. Lizzie still criticized me when I walked past her. No one asked where I had been, because no one had noticed that I was gone. All I really wanted was attention, but I didn't even get that.

Amelia was right. Who knew enough of that story to write it? I knew, Amelia knew, my parents knew. Some doctors and the school guidance counselor. But that was it. Even my little brother and sister only knew that I had been sick for a while, and then I got better.

By the time school ended for the day and, thank God, the week, I had become overwhelmed with the feeling that maybe I really *had* written that journal. Yes, those were someone else's words, someone else's story of me. But it was so close to true that it almost didn't feel like a fiction. If everyone else believed that this was me, did it matter if it was true or not?

At night my dad and I ordered in Chinese food and watched an action movie on the living room couch together. If I seemed quieter than usual, he didn't comment. He was quiet, too, which was fine by me. I didn't want to talk to him. I didn't want to talk to anyone.

After my father went to bed, I went to my room. I brushed my teeth and washed my face and tried to fall asleep. This should have been easy, since I had gotten so little sleep the night before. But it wasn't. I lay in bed and watched the changing pattern of lights on my ceiling as cars drove by. *Why is it always like this?* my brain kept repeating. *Why are you always like this?*

I got up, opened my laptop, and went back to Elise Dembowski's online journal. I didn't want to. I did it anyway.

> May 7: *i know that some people don't like the things that i write in this diary, but to them i say SHUT UP! this is MY diary, so i can say how i really feel. if you don't like it, don't read it. xoxo elise dembowski*

As I sat alone at my desk in the dark, I thought about suicide. Sometimes I did that, thought about suicide, though not in an active way—it was more like pulling a lucky stone out of your back pocket. It was a comforting thing to have with you, so you could rub your fingers over it, reassure yourself that it was there if you needed it. I didn't want to try to kill myself, didn't want the blood and the hysterical parents and the guilt, any of it. But sometimes I liked the idea of simply not having to be here any-more, not having to deal with my life. As if death could be just an extended vacation.

But now what I thought about suicide was this: *If I died to-night, everyone would believe this journal was true.*

Like Amelia, Chava, and Sally, everyone would forever be-lieve that I had written that diary. Everyone would believe they knew how I "really felt." And how dare they?

When I thought about suicide, I thought about Start. I thought about Char and Vicky and Pippa and Mel, and I thought about all the songs I had left to discover and all the songs I had left to play.

I closed out of the Elise Dembowski diary, revealing Flash Tommy's photo of me on the window below it. Tonight the In-ternet seemed filled with versions of me, like a fun house filled with mirrors. Some of them made me look prettier, and some of them made me look uglier, and some of them chopped me right in half, but none of them were right.

I changed out of my pajamas, put on my sneakers, grabbed my iPod, and slipped out of the house. I planned to walk as I did any night: I would walk until I was tired.

But songs and songs went by, and two miles, then three, and I never grew tired. Whenever I blinked, what I saw behind closed eyes was that diary Web page, a searing orange. I couldn't go to sleep. I would walk until morning.

After a while, I looked around me at the darkened apartment complexes and I realized: I knew where I was. I had been here before.

I was just a few blocks from where Char lived.

And it hit me that this was where I had been walking all night long.

I found Char's apartment in a courtyard surrounded by buildings that all looked the same. I leaned my head back to look up at the windows. They were all dark. I pressed my finger to Char's buzzer, and I held it there for a long moment.

Silence.

A couple minutes went by, and I was just about to walk away when the door opened.

"Elise?" Char said, rubbing his eyes. His hair was sticking up in all directions, and he was wearing nothing but an old New Order T-shirt and a pair of boxer shorts. Even his feet were bare. It was all I could do to keep from throwing my arms around him and burying my face in his chest.

"What are you doing here?" Char asked, his voice confused. "It's four in the morning."

I didn't say anything.

"Is everything okay?"

I shrugged.

"Do you want to come in?" He opened the door wider, and I stepped inside.

I followed him upstairs and down the hall to his apartment, which clearly hadn't been cleaned since the last time I was here. His DJ setup still rested on boxes in the middle of the room, and the window beside his bed was open, letting in the fresh spring air.

"So what's going on?" he asked as he locked the door behind us.

I found my voice enough to say, "I don't want to talk about it."

"Okay." Char rubbed the back of his head. "That's okay. We won't talk."

He leaned forward and kissed me. I kissed him back this time, and his mouth was warm and soft. It felt like he was breathing life into every part of my body. I pressed my lips harder against his, and I felt his hands on my lower back, pulling me toward him.

I didn't even notice that he was walking me backward until my legs hit his bed, and I collapsed onto it, pulling him on top of me, our mouths never separating. I didn't know what to do with any part of myself, so I tried to mimic his movements as he ran his hands from my shoulders, down my sides, all the way to my thighs, before coming back up again.

"One sec," he whispered to me. He stood up, and I readjusted myself on his bed while he went over to his laptop. I stared at the giant GIRLFRIEND IN A COMA poster on the wall opposite me. It seemed almost like a threat, which was creepy, but then I reminded myself that I wasn't Char's girlfriend, and that made me feel better.

After a few clicks on the keyboard, a song began to play from Char's speakers. It was my Cure song, "A Letter to Elise."

"You like this one, right?" Char asked.

"Yes," I whispered back.

Before getting back into bed, Char pulled off his T-shirt, and when he lay down beside me again, I could feel the heat radiating from his body. He had a small tattoo of a record player a few inches below his collarbone. I brushed my fingers across it, scared to touch his naked torso anywhere else. I'd never touched anyone's tattoo before. It just felt like skin.

Char kept his word: we didn't talk. The only sounds were the music, and his breathing, and my breathing. He took off my shirt and my bra, and when I began to shiver, he pulled me closer to him, covering my body with his own. Time passed, but I lost track of it. Neither of us spoke at all until Char was pulling my jeans down my legs, and then it was me who broke the silence.

"I don't even know your real name," I said.

He paused, his hand resting on my stomach. "Does it matter?" he asked.

"Yes, it matters. I don't even know who you are."

"I don't know your full name either," he pointed out. "Just Elise." He murmured into my ear, "I'll tell you mine if you'll tell me yours."

I thought about this. What is a name for anyway? It's for looking up people online. I thought about what Char would find if he searched for me. *Elise Dembowski, MD. Elise Dembowski Tampa Florida school superintendent. Elise Dembowski suicide.*

"Never mind," I said. "Forget names. Just Elise is perfect."

"Personally, I prefer DJ Elise," he said, touching his nose to mine.

I kissed him. "DJ Elise works for me, too."

We went back to rolling around on his bed. I grew braver, my hands exploring more and more of him: his head, his shoulders, his back.

After some time, our hands became less restless. Char rolled me over so that my back was to him, pressed against his chest, with my legs curled against his legs. I could see out his window now, to the dawn that was just beginning to break. "Elise?" he said sleepily. "What did you come here for?"

I thought about that. I hadn't consciously planned to come here at all, but it wasn't an accident either. Yet what had I expected to happen? Had I thought Char would erase my fake online diary, and erase the memories of everyone who had read it, too? Had I thought I would pour out all my secrets to him and he would grant me absolution? He wasn't a priest or a psychiatrist or a magician. He was just a boy.

"I came here because I didn't want to be alone anymore," I answered him.

"That's a good reason," he murmured.

After a few minutes I felt his arms slacken around my waist, and I heard his breathing grow deep and regular. Char fell asleep. And then finally, mercifully, so did I.

12

THE NEXT THREE WEEKS FELL INTO A PATTERN. I went to class. I did my homework. At home, Alex's poetry castle continued to grow larger and more elaborate until eventually Steve had to move it into the sunroom so we weren't constantly tripping over it. At school, I ate lunch with Chava and Sally, who spent most of their time, when they weren't trying to decide who might invite Sally to the Freshman/Sophomore Summer Formal, trying to convince me that life was worth living because a beautiful future awaited me.

"Someday you'll get your driver's license," Chava told me.

"Someday you'll go to prom," Sally told me.

"Prom is even *better* than the Freshman/Sophomore Summer Formal," Chava added.

It was unclear why these predictions would make me want to stay alive, but I didn't argue. And I learned quickly that joking about suicide with these girls got me nowhere. The day I brought in a sharp knife to cut an orange for lunch, Chava started to tremble as though I had already slashed my throat and blood was now pouring out of my mouth. One day I said something along the lines of "I have so much homework, I want to die," and it took me the rest of lunch period to talk my friends off the running-to-the-guidance-counselor ledge.

"I don't want to kill myself," I kept telling them.

But everyone else at school was saying that I did. And who do you think Chava and Sally believed, me or everyone else at school?

Actually, though they would never admit to this, I think they were secretly thrilled to be friends with someone who other people were talking about. Granted, what other people were saying about me was "If I were Elise Dembowski, I would want to off myself, too." Nonetheless, my classmates knew who I was, which meant they practically knew who Chava and Sally were, too, which meant it was only a matter of time before my friends could ascend to their rightful places as Brooke Feldstein's ladies-in-waiting.

It was funny: When I called Amelia, it was because I wanted attention. And now I was getting it. But this wasn't the attention I had wanted.

Throughout it all, as May went on, Fake Elise kept updating the online journal. Some days I was talking about various ways to die. Some days I was talking about all the reasons why I hated myself. Some days I was talking about how I wished I had Ashley Mersky's body, or Gina McKibben's boyfriend, or Alexandra Pleet's parents—whatever it was that could turn me into someone other than me, someone better.

The blog wasn't updated every single day, and I know this because I looked at it every single day.

I don't know why.

More than once I thought about showing it to someone in power. The vice principal, maybe, though I had never interacted with Mr. Witt outside of the iPod incident last spring. And honestly, that hadn't gone so well for me, and I didn't have reason to believe that he would handle this problem any better.

I could have shown it to Vicky or Char, because isn't that what friends are for? And weren't we friends? But just thinking about doing that made me feel ashamed. It would be like saying to them, "Here. This is what everyone thinks of me. What about you? What do you think of me now?"

I thought about telling my parents, or Ms. Wu, who was so eager for me to have a personal problem so that she could solve it. But ultimately I didn't tell anyone. I just didn't see what good it would do. Anyway, if I showed this blog to a parent or a teacher, wouldn't they believe that it was true, too, just like Chava and Sally did? Wouldn't they, like Amelia, believe that this was just another one of my cries for help?

On Wednesday evening, as my father and I sat in the living room, him reading the newspaper and me working on math problems, both of us munching on our takeout Thai, the room silent except for the Doors album on the stereo, I considered just saying it. If I opened my mouth, I felt like the words would fall out: *Dad, some kids at school are being mean to me.*

But here's a question for you: *And then what?*

I remembered sixth grade. The first year of middle school, which seemed like a very big deal. We got an *arts elective*. We were eleven years old now, so we were finally trusted to make decisions about our own lives.

I took my arts elective choice very, very seriously. The options were painting, theater, chorus, or reading. Reading is not actually an art; it was a remedial class. I felt bad for the kids who had to take reading. It didn't seem fair that they weren't allowed to learn how to paint until they were able to read at grade level.

Anyway, after much deliberation, I chose theater. I liked to play pretend, and theater class seemed like an opportunity to play pretend, only with everyone paying attention to me.

What *actually* happened in theater class was that we played a lot of "theater games," like the one where you make a sound and a motion at the same time, or the one where you walk around the room at different speeds, or the one where you mirror a partner's motions. After three weeks of this it occurred to me that maybe our teacher, Madame Chevalier, did not actually know anything about theater.

One day she had us play a game where you alliterate your first name with an adjective about you. Like Lizzie Reardon was "Likable Lizzie"—even though I would describe a dead skunk as likable before assigning that adjective to Lizzie.

Maybe I will someday discover that all Broadway actors audition for roles by playing a game where they alliterate their first names with adjectives. Maybe I will discover that Madame Chevalier was some kind of method acting genius. *But I do not think that is going to happen.*

Anyway, when it came to my turn, I said, "Eloquent Elise." Which is following the rules of the game, right? But then everybody laughed at me. And called me "Eloquent Elise" for the next three days. Which you wouldn't think would be a bad thing; I mean, *eloquent* is a compliment. But I could tell that no one was saying it as a compliment, and that was what confused me.

Eventually I went to my dad and I told him what was going on. I remember crying and just repeating "Why?" over and over.

"They're teasing you because they're jealous of you," Dad said, taking my hands in his and looking into my eyes.

"Why?" I sniffled. Were they jealous that I was eloquent? Were they jealous that I knew what the word *eloquent* meant?

"They're jealous of you because you're smart and you're talented and you know who you are."

I stopped crying then. The words buzzed around my brain like hummingbirds, filling me with air. *I'm smart and I'm talented and I know who I am.*

But now my father looked upset. "Come on," he said, and he took me to the basement. There are four units in my dad's building, so there's a lot of stuff in his basement: baby strollers and washing machines and broken furniture.

Dad found a softball bat and used it to gesture at an old futon. "When I feel bad," he said, "I like to come down here."

The basement was cold, and I hugged my arms to my chest. "Why?"

"Because," he said, "it gets all the bad feelings out of me."

And then he raised the softball bat and started whacking the futon like a lunatic, screaming and swearing the whole time, his arms wild, the futon sagging underneath the impact of the bat again and again. *Don't you dare talk to my daughter that way!* he hollered, his voice guttural, like a bear's roar.

After a minute he stopped and turned to me, breathing hard. "Here." He held the softball bat out to me. "Your turn."

I hugged my arms in tighter and backed away. I didn't want to hit that futon. *I wasn't mad.* I didn't need to scream and attack a piece of furniture. I just needed someone to like me.

After a long moment, my dad laid the softball bat down. We went back upstairs. And we never spoke about that incident again, even though I couldn't shake the feeling that my dad was disappointed in me. Like he had wanted me to be as angry as he was, when I wasn't angry at all.

The next day at school, we were forming our circle at the beginning of theater class when Lizzie slipped in next to me and cooed, "Eloquent Elise, how many words do you know?"

I blinked at her.

"A million?" she pressed. "A thousand? A hundred? You must know more than a *hundred* words, Elise. After all, you are *so* eloquent."

"I . . . don't know," I said.

"You don't *know*?" The kids nearby giggled. "But how can that be? Eloquent Elise, I thought you knew *everything*."

So I took a deep breath, and I drew myself up to my full height—which, at the time, was roughly four feet—and I recited, "You are just jealous of me. You're jealous because I'm smart and I'm talented and I know who I am."

There was a moment of silence in which I thought that maybe, finally, I had bested them. Maybe Lizzie was about to be like, "Oh my God, *you're right*."

Instead, Lizzie and her friends began to shriek with laughter. I felt like I was surrounded by a thousand cawing birds. *"I'm smart and I'm talented and I know who I am,"* they sang at me, over and over, for the rest of the period, and throughout every theater class thereafter, until the words that had once sounded so uplifting became an insult, a joke.

Eventually I couldn't take it anymore, so I quit theater for another arts elective. But painting and chorus were full. So I had to switch into remedial reading. I spent the rest of the semester learning to read picture books of *Goldilocks and the Three Bears.* Because that is where the eloquent go.

So now, four years later, as I thought about confiding in my dad, I tried to figure out what it was that I thought he might be able to change. And the answer was: nothing.

So I said: nothing.

But it was okay. The blog and the silence and the secrets and the Chava and Sally lunchtime suicide help line. It was okay because that wasn't everything. I had my night life, too, and that was what was real.

I hung out with Vicky more and more. I could tell from their raised eyebrows and suppressed smiles that my parents were thrilled about this, clearly thinking, *A friend! Elise has a real, live friend!* But aloud they played it cool, acting like, "Oh, yeah, Elise has friends all the time." And for my part I volunteered no information about Vicky. She belonged to a different world from my parents', and I was going to keep it that way.

Vicky brought me to her favorite clothing boutiques and I brought her to my favorite record stores. On Friday night I skipped dinner with my dad to meet Vicky downtown for pizza and a movie at the indie cinema. We spent most of dinner playing a game called When We're Famous.

"When we're famous," Vicky said, "I'll perform at Radio City Music Hall and my rider will include a bucket filled with cinnamon jelly beans. Just cinnamon, no other flavors. A stage-hand will have to go through and pick them out. And if he accidentally leaves in any cherry jelly beans, because he mistakes them for cinnamon, I will have him fired on the spot."

"When we're famous," I said, "people will buy action figures that look like us. No little girls will play with Barbies anymore. They will only want rock music action figures."

"When we're famous," Vicky said, "we can open a camp for girls who are artists, and it will be free, so even if their parents say 'No one makes a *career* as a musician' and refuse to spend a penny on their arts education, they can still afford to come."

"When we're famous," I said, "everyone will know our names."

The next week I met up with Vicky and Harry at Teatotaler, which is like a coffee shop except for (surprise!) tea. Harry and I individually took notes on *Macbeth*, which we had both been assigned at our respective schools. My English class was a full act ahead of his, so I kept spoiling it for him.

"Oh, no," I murmured, turning a page.

"What?" Harry asked. He glanced up from his book.

"Nothing."

A moment passed.

"Oh, *no*," I said again, sounding even more horrified.

"What?" both Vicky and Harry asked this time.

"You don't want to know."

"Okay," said Vicky, and she went back to pretending to read a thick book of literary criticism for one of her classes while texting with Pippa.

"I want to know," Harry said.

"Well, if you're sure . . ." I leaned in and whispered, "All of Macduff's family just got murdered."

Harry groaned and tossed his copy of the play aside. "I hate you."

I shrugged. "I told you that you didn't want to know."

"Excuse me, babe." Vicky looked up from her phone for long enough to flag down the male barista who was clearing the table next to ours. "Any chance you'd treat a girl to another tea bag?" She batted her long lashes. "Something *steamy*."

The barista looked confused. "You can order up at the counter, ma'am." He walked away.

Vicky sighed and her eyelashes went back to normal. "No one appreciates my feminine wiles."

Harry snorted.

"Hey." Vicky turned to me. "Do you want to hear the new Dirty Curtains song? We just recorded it last weekend."

"I'd love to!" I answered at the same time that Harry whined, "Aw, Vicky, *no*."

"Why not?" Vicky demanded.

"Because." Harry's face was red. "It's *embarrassing*. We're just going to watch Elise while she has to sit there and pretend to like our music? I mean . . . she's a DJ!"

I giggled into my teacup.

"Harry," Vicky said, "I don't know how to break this to you, but you are in a band. And that means that sometimes people are going to hear our music. Deal with it."

She pressed a few buttons on her cell phone, and then the opening drumbeats of a song kicked in. Vicky turned up the volume as loud as it would go. The guitar came in next—rich, raw, powerful. And then Vicky's voice.

"Screw you, too.

No, I don't want you back.

With your sneers and your jeers

And your worthless attacks."

The barista came over to us again. "Hey," he said, "could you guys turn that off? This is a public place, and it's annoying the other customers."

"Sorry," we said in unison.

"Did you like it, though?" Harry asked me after the barista walked away.

"I can't wait to listen to the whole thing."

Harry flushed. "You're, like, obligated to say that, though."

"I still mean it," I said. "You guys are *really* good."

"Way too good for this place," Vicky agreed, slamming shut her book. "Let's get out of here and go annoy strangers somewhere else."

It was good to have Vicky.

And then, of course, there was Char.

Char and I fell into a pattern, too. Every Thursday night, I would walk over to Start as soon as my family was asleep. Char would say hi to me like we were just friends, nothing more, and I would plug my laptop into his mixer like we were just friends, nothing more. We never greeted each other with a hug or a kiss; nothing. I would start each Thursday night convinced that whatever Char and I had between us was over now, and I would be walking home at a relatively reasonable hour.

And by the end of each Thursday night, Char and I were

making out in the DJ booth like our lives depended on it, my hands in his back pockets, his hands in my hair, our tongues exploring each other's mouths, coming up for air only when it was time to transition into a new song.

It wasn't because we got drunk as the night went on. I didn't drink at all, and Char didn't drink much because, as he pointed out, "This is my *job*. You can't get wasted at your job."

It wasn't an effect of alcohol. It was more like we got drunk on the night.

Invariably, even if I was done with my half-hour set by one a.m., I would hang around until Start ended, at two. Then Char and I would load the equipment into his car, and he would drive us to his apartment, where we would fall into bed and continue what we had started in the bar, only with far, far fewer clothes. We would keep that up until one or both of us fell asleep.

At five thirty, my phone alarm would go off.

"Jesus *Christ*," Char groaned into his pillow. "It's the middle of the goddamn *night*."

Then I would make Char drive me home immediately, before my mom woke up and noticed that I wasn't there.

This was easier the first night, when I walked over to Char's from my dad's. My dad was late to bed and late to rise, especially on weekends. So when I jolted awake at eight a.m. on that first Saturday to the feeling of Char kissing my neck, it was easy to scramble out of bed, into Char's car, and home before Dad had even gotten out of bed to collect the morning paper.

Getting back to my mom's house before she woke up, however,

presented a different sort of challenge. This was a woman who operated on about six hours of sleep every night. "There's just too much to do in a day," she often said, as if this were a bad thing, though you didn't have to know her well to know that she *loved* doing too much in a day.

Thus, Char and I woke up at five thirty a.m.

"Remind me why I'm doing this?" Char asked on the second Friday morning that we did this, as we sat in his cold car, the streetlights still on overhead.

"Duh, because you love me," I joked. But Char was practically asleep in the driver's seat, and he didn't laugh.

And that was the last I would hear from Char until the next Thursday night. No text messages. No Saturday night dates. Nothing. Just a friendly greeting when I showed up at Start six days later, followed by a thousand kisses.

I knew Char wasn't my boyfriend. But was he anything to me? And was I anything to him? I wanted to ask him to explain this to me, but I couldn't, because I suspected that I was supposed to understand already. I suspected that our relationship, if I could even call it that, was just one more thing covered in the Handbook for Being a Real Person, which somehow I had never received.

"How do you know so much music?" Char asked me late on the following Thursday night as we lay in his bed together, my head resting on his chest. At Start earlier, I had played a set of late sixties soul. Char hadn't recognized any of it, and I could tell he didn't like this, because he told me it was his turn again well before my half hour was up, while the crowd was still enthusiastically dancing. I wanted to keep playing, but I didn't. After all, it was *his* night.

I had discovered that Char knew a lot of *facts* about music. He knew the names of drummers from famous bands, and then what other bands they had later gone out to start. He knew the names of dozens or possibly hundreds of music labels, and who had produced Fleetwood Mac's *Rumours*, and which members of the Beach Boys were brothers and which were cousins.

I didn't know any of that stuff. Music wasn't history class; I didn't need to memorize a thousand dates and names. I just *cared* a lot about music.

You'd think this might make me cool, since music is supposedly cool, but it doesn't work like that. It turns out that caring a lot about anything is, by definition, *uncool*, and it doesn't matter if that thing is music or *Star Wars* or oil refineries.

"My dad introduced me to a lot of music when I was very little," I told Char, then added, because we were in bed together and this seemed like an intimate thing to reveal, "He's in a band."

Char propped himself up on his elbow. "You have a cool dad. What band?"

"The Dukes."

"I don't know them," Char said.

"Yes, you do." I sang the chorus of the Dukes' big hit: "Take my hand, baby, and run away with me. Take my hand, and I'll be your man."

"That's your *dad*?" Even in the darkness, I could see how wide Char's eyes had grown.

"Well, he's the bassist," I said.

"But didn't the Dukes break up ages ago?"

"No way. The Dukes have been together for *decades*. They play cruises, casinos, seventies revues. You know. The big time. The four of them all grew up together in Philadelphia. They started the Dukes for a middle-school talent show. And then they just stayed together. Forever. My dad says that the band has been the most long-lasting relationship of his entire life."

"Is that, like, his full-time job?" Char ran his hand through my hair, twisting it around his fingers.

"Being a Duke would not be much of a living. The drummer is a lawyer now, the guitarist and the singer started an accounting firm, and my dad works at a music store. They just do Duke shows occasionally. Like when Frankie Valli and the Four Seasons are unavailable."

That last bit was intended to make Char laugh, but he didn't. "I can't believe you never told me this before," he said, as if he and I were constantly having long, meaningful conversations about our personal lives and I had for some reason kept this particular piece of information a secret.

I shrugged. "I don't know what *your* parents do."

"Yeah, but they're not in a *famous band*."

He didn't, I noticed, tell me what his parents did.

"My dad's band isn't famous," I said. "They had one song that was a huge radio hit, and then two LPs of songs that no one has ever heard. Honestly, it's kind of sad."

"Sad?" Char echoed.

"Yeah, like, every couple months these middle-aged guys put on fringed leather jackets as if they're thirty-five years younger and sing about 'dancing to the radio,' or whatever. Like the best part of their lives happened when they were our age. They play an afternoon show for a sparse crowd of equally middle-aged people who only know one of their songs, and they do it all so they can make a couple thousand bucks that they can use to fix the plumbing in their houses and send their kids to summer enrichment programs."

Char laughed a little, his breath tickling my ear. "When you put it like that, it does sound pretty sad." He paused. "But I guess that's not how it feels to me. I mean, I don't know your dad. Maybe he is just forcing himself through the motions so he can bring home some extra money. Maybe he really hates it, and maybe every day he wishes he was eighteen again. But *maybe* he found something he loved to do and people he loved to do it with when he was a kid, and he's lucky enough that he still gets to do it years later."

"If you were fifty-three years old and still DJing the exact same songs, except at the Illinois State Fair Big Tent at two in the afternoon, would you feel like your life was *sad* or *lucky*?" I asked Char.

Char shrugged. "I guess you'd have to ask me again in thirty-three years. I think I would feel lucky. I think what would make me feel sad would be if I were fifty-three years old and I *wasn't* playing music anymore."

"I would be sad if you weren't playing music anymore, too," I told him.

He rolled on top of me then, and kissed me long and hard. And there was nothing sad at all.

* * *

The following Thursday night, I was in the middle of my set, and everything was going smoothly. People jumping around to the Rolling Stones. Vicky was there with Dave, and they had claimed dance space right in the middle of the floor. Char was at the bar, talking to some college-aged girl with highlighted, flat-ironed hair, but I didn't mind, because he had already pressed his fingers into my lower back earlier, which meant I was basically guaranteed yet another night of getting home at dawn. I was wearing the rhinestone pumps that Vicky insisted I buy, one of my dad's old band shirts that I had resewn to fit me, and a multicolored scarf that Vicky had lent me. Even Mel hadn't found anything to criticize with tonight's outfit.

Everything was going smoothly. Until the door opened a bit before midnight and Emily Wallace, Petra Davies, and Ashley Mersky walked in.

I was thrown into shock, like a queen whose castle's ironclad fortress has somehow been breached. *What were they doing here?* This wasn't high school. This wasn't driver's ed. This was Start. This was *mine*.

Emily and her friends hadn't noticed me yet. They clustered in a tight circle, looking around the room, pointing and giggling. I could tell they had gotten all dressed up for their big night out, like this was a school dance. Emily wore a tight black strapless dress and fake eyelashes. Her makeup was perfect.

They looked ridiculous here, obviously high school girls costumed as make-believe adults. Ridiculous, but beautiful. There's a reason why Emily is a model. There's a reason why Ashley's chest was voted "best rack" by the guys' lacrosse team when she was only a freshman. Because they are the beautiful ones.

This song was winding down, so I put on my headphones to find a new one, but everything I tried sounded suddenly out of place. I tried to focus on my computer, but my eyes kept flickering up, and I was terrified that I would find Emily smirking at me. I wanted to drop my headphones and let the song play out while I ran straight out the door and all the way home.

But *you are a professional.*

I transitioned into the Smiths' "How Soon Is Now?" I messed up the beat matching, so it sounded disorienting and wrong, but I didn't even care. I scanned the room again for Emily and her friends. They were waiting in line at the bar. Still not looking at me. But they could look at me at any time. At *any time,* I could be discovered.

And then what?

Char left the girl with the highlighted hair, and for one second I was convinced that he was going to walk over to Emily, as he had walked over to me weeks earlier. That he was going to introduce himself to her, and ask her to dance, and invite her into the DJ booth. Just like me, only prettier and cooler and normal. I remembered how Char explained to me why he had sex with Pippa: *"Because she's hot."* What if he saw that Emily was hot, too?

But Char walked past Emily, seeming not to notice her. He walked through the dance floor and into the DJ booth, to me. "What is going on in here?" he asked me.

I blinked fast. "What do you mean?"

"I *mean* that it's prime time on the dance floor, you had this crowd in the palm of your hand, and now all of a sudden you've decided to play the world's most downer of a song."

"It's the Smiths," I defended myself. "Everyone loves the Smiths."

Char raised his eyebrows and quoted the lyrics to me: "'There's a club if you'd like to go. You could meet somebody who really loves you. So you go and you stand on your own, and you leave on your own, and you go home and you cry and you want to die.'"

I shrugged.

"Do you want me to take over for a while?" Char asked, his hands already moving toward the mixer.

"No," I said.

He paused.

"What I *want*," I said, my voice rising, "is for you to get those girls *out* of here."

Char's eyebrows knit together. "What girls?"

"Those girls!" I screeched, pointing at Emily, Petra, and Ashley.

"Um, why?" Char asked, and I saw them, just for a brief flash, as he probably saw them: three harmless-looking teenage girls, delicate features, pretty smiles. Like they couldn't cut you until you were so disfigured that you hardly recognized yourself.

"Because they're *underage*!" I screamed.

"Yeah . . ." Char said dubiously.

"Don't they have *parents*?" I raged. "What the hell kind of parents let their teenage daughters go to a bar on a school night? This isn't the goddamn Freshman/Sophomore Summer Formal. This is the real world."

Char cleared his throat pointedly. "Seriously?"

I grabbed his skinny tie and pulled him in close to me, and I spoke right into his face. "Char, listen to me. *I am the DJ*. And I don't want them here."

As soon as I let go of him, Char left the booth. He headed straight for the exit and stepped outside. A moment later, he returned with Mel. Char pointed to where Emily and her friends stood, now with pink drinks in their hands.

Mel strode directly over to them. He towered over all the people on the floor; everyone moved aside to let him pass. I watched him speak to the girls briefly. I saw them smile and bat their eyelashes, trying to flirt their way out of it. Then I saw their mouths harden and their eyebrows narrow. Mel just stood there with his arms crossed. Emily pulled a card out of her pocket and handed it to him. A fake ID, I bet. Mel glanced at it briefly before snapping it in half with one hand. Then he escorted them to the door.

Emily took one look back at the club, her mouth hanging open in the astonished expression of a girl who has never before been denied anything. And now she saw me. Her eyes caught mine right before the heavy metal door slammed shut behind her.

I had once thought that I wanted to get revenge by dying. But getting revenge by living, and living well, was much, much sweeter.

Char came back to the booth. "Do you want to explain what that was all about?" he asked me.

"Nope."

He rubbed the back of his hand across his eyes. "Well, are you happy now?" he asked.

"Yes." And I transitioned into "Walking on Sunshine." The

crowd perked up immediately. Vicky shot me a thumbs-up sign from the floor.

"Elise," Char asked, leaning in close, "are you, you know, okay?"

I closed my eyes. "Kiss me," I said. And he did.

I remembered how Pippa had described the thrill of being friends with the DJ. *You always have somewhere to stash your coat, and sometimes he'll play songs for you.* But that was kids' stuff. That was nothing compared with the power of *being* the DJ.

But I also felt like an eggshell that had gotten a tiny crack. You can't repair something like that. All you can do is hope that it sticks together, hope that the crack doesn't grow until all your insides come spilling right out.

13

WHEN I GOT TO OUR LUNCH TABLE ON TUESDAY, Sally and Chava were already seated. With some guy. Seriously. Sally and Chava knew a guy, apparently. His hair was dyed slime green, he had a fake septum piercing, and his face was riddled with acne scars.

Don't get me wrong; I'm not blaming anyone for having pimples. At this particular lunchtime, I myself had one massive pimple on my chin and one that looked kind of like a mini uni-corn horn right in the center of my forehead. These things can't be helped. But here's what *can* be helped: removing your fake nose ring and using it to more effectively pick at your pimples while sitting at a lunch table with Sally and Chava. Which is what this guy was doing.

Nonetheless, he was a guy.

I sat down. "Hello, friends."

"Elise!" Sally cried in delighted surprise. "You're just the person I wanted to see."

"Sure," I said.

"This is Russell," Sally went on. She reached out her arm as if to put it around him, but then she seemed to think better of it and just pointed instead.

"Hi," Russell wheezed out around a mouthful of his burger.

Chava started to laugh cheerily. I stared at her. "Sorry," she said. "It's just that Russell is so clever!"

I unwrapped my peanut butter sandwich.

"Why don't you tell Elise that funny story you were telling us earlier?" Sally prompted him.

As Russell launched into a description of this one time when his online role-playing game turned particularly violent and he had to resort to inhumane tactics to save the day, I let my attention wander. As I gazed into the distance, who did I see walking toward my table but Emily Wallace. She led a group of five beautiful people. Her hair swished with every step she took, and she carried her books in a gleaming leather shoulder bag.

This was one of the other rules that started at some point, maybe around eighth grade. It turned out that it wasn't cool to carry your school supplies in a backpack. I didn't know that it wasn't cool to have a backpack. It *used* to be cool, I think. Even after Lizzie Reardon told me not to, I still kept using my backpack. Because textbooks are heavy. Do girls like Emily Wallace never ache from the weight of all those books?

I could hear Emily's high-pitched voice float above the din of the cafeteria. "Yeah, we had *so* much fun," she was telling her minions. "It was way overpriced, though. Like, six dollars for a hard lemonade? But these college guys fully offered to buy us drinks. We left kinda early, though. Petra's mom would have lost it if we'd stayed out any later. I mean, it was a *Thursday.*"

"Hey!" I heard Petra object.

"The bouncer was kinda weird, though. I mean, he . . ."

And at that moment, Emily's eyes met mine. I resisted the urge to look away, to play ostrich. Instead I stared right back at her, and I tried to send her this message through my eyes: *Don't you* dare *talk about Mel like you know him.*

Emily's voice faltered. She blinked and looked away. Then she made an abrupt turn and led her posse down an aisle toward their table in the center of the room, away from me.

I had never seen anything like it.

"So do you want to?" Russell was asking, and it took me a moment to come back to earth and realize he was speaking to me.

"Do I want to what?" I asked.

He coughed a number of times, his hacking getting louder and louder until I half expected him to expel an owl pellet. Sally flinched away, like he might be contagious. At last, Russell coughed out, "Do you want to go to the summer formal with me?"

Chava clapped her hands delightedly. She is a sucker for romance.

"Me?" I asked.

Russell nodded a bunch and slurped down his Coke, which seemed to help with the coughing.

"Do you even know my name?"

He nodded again, less vigorously.

The Freshman/Sophomore Summer Formal is a relatively new addition to the Glendale High social calendar. It used to be that there was only one formal dance at the end of the year, and that was prom. Obviously. Only juniors, seniors, and their dates are allowed to go to prom, so this led to some seriously immoral and occasionally illicit maneuvering on the part of lower classmen trying to score tickets. Two years before I started at Glendale High, some sophomore girl apparently offered to tell everyone that she had given a senior guy a blow job in exchange for him agreeing to take her to prom as his date.

At this point, the school administration must have realized that they desperately needed an occasion for freshmen and sophomores to spend their money on; thus, the Freshman/Sophomore Summer Formal was born. It's now a very big deal among the community of people who care about school dances, and almost no one bothers to bribe or blackmail her way into actual prom anymore.

I breathed out, slowly. "Thank you for asking me, Russell," I said, "but I'm afraid I already have plans that night, so I won't be able to make it."

"You don't even know what night the formal is," Sally pointed out.

This was true.

"It's in two weeks," Chava piped up.

"Two weeks from *Saturday*," Sally said.

I nodded. "I have plans."

Russell didn't seem terribly devastated. He didn't say anything like, "Don't leave me, my love!" He said, to Sally, "Can I go now?"

She shrugged. He took off, leaving his burger wrapper and soda cup behind.

"Wow, Elise." Sally turned on me. "You really *are* a snob, aren't you?"

"Excuse me?" I blinked.

"All your journal entries about how nobody at this school is good enough for you. I was always like, 'Oh, she can't really mean that.' But you *do* mean that."

"Sally, what are you talking about? Who do I think I am better than?"

"Russell!"

"I don't *know* Russell. Where did you even find him?"

"He's a freshman," Chava said.

"So what was he doing here?" I asked.

"He wanted to ask you to the formal," Chava explained.

Suddenly it all became clear to me. "*You* wanted him to ask me to the formal."

Silence from my friends.

"You made this poor freshman come over here and ask me out. Why? Just so you'll have company at the dance, Sally, so you won't have to stand there alone like always?"

"No!" Chava sounded shocked.

"For your information," Sally snapped, "I *won't* be alone. Larry Kapur asked me to be his date."

"Oh." I didn't know how to respond to this. "Um, that's great, Sally."

"I just thought it might be fun for us to double-date," she said. "Share a limo or something. You know, like *friends* do."

"Plus," Chava said, "you're always talking about how no boys ever like you and how lonely you are."

"I'm not," I said, flashing back to last Thursday night, Char's mouth on mine, our bodies pressed together—

"You know, in your journal," Chava said. "We didn't want you to be sad anymore. That's all. So that's why we encouraged Russell to ask you to the dance."

"Encouraged," Sally repeated.

"We didn't say he *had* to. We just wanted you to know that boys do like you. Like Russell."

I thought of Char's breath in my ear, his tongue on my neck, his hands on my stomach.

"Thank you," I said. I shook my head, like I was trying to shake Char right out of my mind. "That's really sweet of you guys."

And it was, actually. That was the surprising thing of it. I'd assumed Sally and Chava had some malicious or at least self-serving reason for "encouraging" Russell to ask me out, because in my experience, when my classmates acted like they were trying to help me, they were usually just trying to help themselves. But all my DJing had taught me something about reading a crowd. And when I read Sally and Chava right now, all I saw in them was exactly what they claimed: they wanted me to be happy.

It was weird. But being friends with Vicky had made me realize that some people were just like that. Some people were nice to you, simply because they liked you.

"So will you go to the dance, then?" Sally asked.

I smiled and took a bite of my sandwich. No matter how pure my friends' motives were, they were not getting me into any non-mandatory school event. "I really do appreciate it, guys," I said. "But no way."

During my DJ set on Thursday, Pete came over to the booth. He scribbled a note on a Post-it, stuck it to the hem of my dress, and walked away.

I picked it up. *When you're done playing, come talk to me,* it said.

Pete didn't have to wait long. I was done about twenty seconds later, when Char ran over. "What did Pete want?" he asked me.

I shrugged and showed Char the note.

Char's forehead wrinkled. "I'll take over. You should go talk to him, I guess. I'm right over here if you need backup."

That didn't sound good. I smiled weakly and climbed down from the booth.

I found Pete sitting alone on a stool at the bar. "Elise!" he exclaimed, adjusting the brim on his fedora. "DJ Elise. Wait, you don't have a DJ name, do you?"

"DJ Elise is fine," I said.

"Do you have a last name?" he asked.

No one at Start knew my full name: not Char, not Vicky, not Harry. But Pete was a real grownup. He clearly expected me to have a real name. "It's Dembowski."

"It's great to talk to you again, Elise Dembowski," Pete told me. I hadn't seen him since the first time I met him, when Vicky was trying to get his attention. He booked Start, but he didn't come every week. Tonight he was wearing loose jeans, a plaid button-down shirt, and a dad-like haircut. The only giveaway that he wasn't an elementary school teacher was his hat.

"Do you know what I want to talk to you about, Elise?" Pete asked.

I could think of a lot of options, none of them good. He wanted to talk to me because he'd found out I was only sixteen, for example. Or he wanted to talk to me because Char *was* supposed to have gotten permission to let me DJ Start with him, after all. Or maybe Pete wanted to talk to me because it was against the rules for two DJs to hook up with each other.

Some people will tell you that honesty is the best policy, but I disagree. In instances like this, I fully believe that feigned ignorance is the best policy.

"No," I said. "What do you want to talk to me about, Pete?"

He smiled. "May I buy you a drink?"

I narrowed my eyes. If this was some trick to catch an underage drinker, I wasn't falling for it. "That's okay, thanks."

Pete nodded. "I hear you. I don't drink, myself."

My gaze flickered to the glass on the bar in front of him.

"Ginger ale," he explained. "I've been on the wagon for five years. I used to party way too hard. I gave up all the substances back then, but I've never been able to give up the scene."

"What made you stop drinking?" I asked, interested despite my concern that this was all some elaborate setup to get me banned from Start forever.

"Well, I was at the Mansion one night—do you know the Mansion? Downtown? No, never mind, you're too young. Anyway, I was at the Mansion and accidentally sober. We'd all taken ecstasy, but I'd gotten mine from some shady dealer—shadier than normal drug dealers, if you can picture that—and I guess he gave me a placebo pill, hoping I wouldn't notice. But I definitely noticed. We were all on the floor, dancing and talking and hitting on girls, and I had this moment where I looked at my friends and realized *they were all acting like idiots*."

I laughed a little. I couldn't help it.

"I know," Pete said. "*Obviously* people on drugs act like idiots. Didn't we all learn that in junior high? But I didn't get it until I saw it. It was chilling, I tell you. Anyway, that was my moment.

"Three months earlier my girlfriend at the time had overdosed on painkillers and spent a week in the ICU, all hooked up to IVs and shit. But that was not my wake-up call. My wake-up call was at the Mansion. The next day I enrolled in Alcoholics Anonymous and Narcotics Anonymous and every other Anonymous club I could find. I even remember the song that was on the speakers the moment it happened, when I decided I wanted to quit, start a better life."

"What song?" I asked.

"LCD Soundsystem. 'All My Friends.' I still go back to it sometimes, even now. When I'm tempted by something I shouldn't do, I'll listen to that song, and it reminds me of the life I don't want anymore."

I pursed my lips. "That's a pretty powerful song."

Pete stared into my eyes, like he was searching for something inside me. "A great DJ can do pretty powerful things."

I stared back at him, willing myself not to look away.

"Elise," he said, "do you want your own night here?"

I blinked. "Excuse me?"

"Your own night. Here, in this space. Char DJs Start on Thursdays, and he does a great job, but I want to expand. I want a Friday night party. The big time. It'd be all you. Whatever kind of music you want, however you want to set it up. Costumes, bands, decorations, your call. And you'd get paid, obviously. Ten percent of the bar ring, if that's okay with you. We can negotiate it later. You can charge a cover at the door, if you'd rather make the money that way."

"Wait." I held up a hand. "*That's* what you wanted to talk to me about?"

Pete nodded. "It's a weekend night, so it'll be more crowded than this. People will stay out later, too. I need to know if you can handle it."

"But I'm just—" I began, then stopped myself before I finished with "a kid." "I haven't been doing this for very long," I said instead. "I'm sure you could find someone with more experience . . ."

Pete took a swig of ginger ale. "If you're saying that you're sure I could find some thirty-six-year-old guy who's spun 'Love Will Tear Us Apart' so many times that he's able to play Tetris on his phone while he's DJing, *while* chugging Red Bull so he can stay awake until four a.m., then yeah. I'm sure I could find that guy, too. But I don't want that guy. I want someone with something to prove.

"Char probably told you that I first booked him to play Start when he was barely eighteen years old. This was back when Start was at the Harts Lofts, you know, before the police busted that place and we moved down here. Char was just a kid with a big mouth who really wanted to be cool. I remember thinking, *I should kick this guy out*, but I could tell that he genuinely loved the music. And he had talent. But, Elise, believe me when I tell you this: your talent, your natural talent, puts Char's to shame."

I shifted on my bar stool. "Char's an amazing DJ."

"I'm not denying that," Pete said. "He wouldn't be here if he weren't. And it's not a competition. But you have got the goods to be big. Really, really big. If you want this, then I know you can do it. So just tell me: do you want this?"

My body felt as if it were filled with electricity, and I started to smile. "Yes," I said quietly, like I was signing a legal contract. "Yes! I want this. When can I start? Tomorrow?"

Pete chuckled. "Why don't you give me a little time to promote it, get your name out there, so we can make sure people actually show up. We're going to make a star of you. Let's say two weeks from tomorrow. Ten p.m. Yes?"

"Yes," I said to him. "Thank you so much. I can't even tell you how much this means to me."

Pete tipped his fedora to me. "Just make sure you do something powerful," he said, "and that will be thanks enough."

I almost floated away from the bar. I needed to share this with someone. I needed to tell Vicky right now. I needed to tell Char. Fortunately, I saw that Vicky was standing right next to the DJ booth. I ran across the dance floor toward them, kicking up my legs behind me . . . then slowed to a walk when I saw who was with them.

Pippa.

"You're back!" I exclaimed. "How was Manchester?"

"What the bloody hell is your problem?" Pippa spat at me.

I took a step backward. I tried to catch Vicky's or Char's eyes, but they were both staring at the floor.

"I don't . . ." I began, the electricity seeping straight out of my body.

"My mum makes me leave the country for all of a month and a half, and you think this is an opportunity to just jump right in there and start banging Char?"

Shit.

"Pippa, it wasn't like that," I tried.

"Oh, really? What was it like? Did you wait a whole week after I was gone? Come on, do you think I'm an idiot? If you were trying to keep your little romance a secret, maybe you shouldn't have let Flash Tommy photograph it. We do have the Internet in England, you know."

I saw Char wince.

"Pippa, honey," Vicky said gently, "it wasn't Elise's fault."

"Oh, so she just *accidentally* pulled Char one night? And what about you?" Pippa turned to Vicky. "You never mentioned this to me because you thought I wouldn't care, or because you weren't brave enough to tell me?" Her voice rose and her tiny hands clenched into fists as she stared down Vicky and Char. "I was gone for six weeks. You can't both just *replace* me!"

"That's not fair," Vicky said in a low voice. "You're my best friend, Pippa. I missed you every day."

"Just tell me why you did it," Pippa demanded of me, and I could see her long lashes fluttering as she blinked back tears. "Why did you have to steal him?"

Why did I do it? I didn't know. I didn't have a reason, really. Char kissed me, so I kissed him back. I hadn't thought of it as stealing him from Pippa. He had told me he wasn't interested in her. He didn't want to be her boyfriend. How could I have stolen him if he was never hers?

"Do you love him?" Pippa asked, her voice pained.

I glanced over at Char. He was still studying the floor.

It was a ridiculous question. Did I *love* Char? Did I feel about Char the same way I felt about the Beatles, string instruments in pop songs, the way Little Anthony sang high notes, the way Jerry Lee Lewis played piano?

"No," I said.

Pippa frowned. "So *why*, then?"

Because you were swept away by someone liking you.

I took a deep breath and tried to explain. "I didn't know. I feel sometimes like . . . there are all these rules. Just to be a person. You know? You're supposed to carry a shoulder bag, not a backpack. You're supposed to wear headbands, or you're not supposed to wear headbands. It's okay to describe yourself as *likable*, but it's not okay to describe yourself as *eloquent*. You can sit in the front of the school bus, but you can't sit in the middle. You're not supposed to be with a boy, even when he *wants* you to. I didn't know that. There are so many rules, and they don't make any sense, and I just can't learn them all."

"Well, here's a simple rule for you, Elise," Pippa snapped. "Don't steal your friend's man."

And she turned on her heel and marched toward the bar.

Vicky ran to catch her. Char started after them.

"Char," I said, catching his sleeve. "I have something to tell you."

He pulled himself free and said, his voice clipped, "It's not really a good time, Elise."

"Oh." Of course, he was right. Pete's giving me a Friday night party seemed silly and irrelevant now. No one was interested.

I had a sudden flash of wondering just how Char was going to take that news. He would be proud of me. Wouldn't he? Proud that he had taught me so well that Pete would trust me with this?

Yes, of course, Char would be proud.

But maybe I wasn't so sure of that, because I let the subject drop.

"Can you take over the decks so I can deal with Pippa?" Char asked me.

I nodded mutely. He turned away again. "Char," I blurted out. "Am I going over to your place later tonight?"

I sensed instantly, staring at Char's half-turned shoulder, that I had broken yet another unspoken rule. To ask for what I wanted.

My question seemed to hover in the air between us, while I wondered what it would be like to have a real boyfriend. Someone who you could make plans with. Someone who called you when he thought of you. Someone who would say that he wanted you to come over. I wondered what it would be like to be Sally, and to have Larry Kapur tell you that he wanted to take you to a formal dance. Someone where you didn't have to guess.

"I don't think it's a good idea," Char said. "Not tonight. It would just upset Pippa even more if we went home together."

"You're right."

Char reached out and squeezed my shoulder briefly. "Thanks for covering for me, Elise. I owe you."

Then he went to the bar to handle Pippa, and I went to the booth to handle the music, and that was the last we spoke all night.

I liked being up there in the booth, separate from everybody. Pete was right: I was good at it, and it was safe. But on a night like tonight, it was lonely, too.

When I was done, I walked home for the first time in weeks. When I reached my mother's house, I eased open the front door into darkness and then closed it behind me as quietly as I could. I leaned back for a moment, resting my head against the door. Home safe.

Then someone screamed.

I bolted upright.

"Alex?" I whispered.

A pause. Then my little sister emerged from the shadows, brandishing an empty paper towel roll like a sword.

"Are you okay?" I asked softly.

"What are you doing here?" she hissed. "You scared me!" She didn't quite lower the paper towel roll, like she still wasn't sure whether she would have to physically fight me or not.

"I'm sorry, honey," I said. "I just went for a walk."

Alex stepped forward so I could see her better. "Now?" she asked. "It's the middle of the night."

It was much later than the middle of the night. "I couldn't sleep," I explained.

Alex blinked a few times, then asked, "You're not sick again, are you?"

And I knew we were both thinking about September, when I was rushed to the hospital and then had to miss weeks of school, because I was "sick." I felt a sudden surge of love for my baby sister. Even if no one told her what was going on, she was no fool.

"No," I said. "I'm not sick."

"So why—" Alex began, at which point I decided that the best defense was a good offense.

"What are *you* doing up?" I asked.

Alex twirled the paper towel roll around in her hands. "Working on my poetry castle," she said. "Come see."

She led me into the sunroom. The cardboard castle sat proudly in the middle of the room, flags flying from its two turrets. Paper and markers were spread out all over the rest of the floor.

"It looks great," I told her.

Alex looked at it critically. "I still need to paint the front," she said. "And I need to finish writing the poems. I'm going to sell poetry, and I don't know how many people will want to buy them. I need to be sure I have enough. Everyone in the whole school is coming, even the fifth graders. And all the parents. You're coming, right?"

"Of course," I said. "I wouldn't miss it."

"How many poems do you think people will want to buy?" Alex asked.

"Well, I'll want to buy at least ten," I told her.

Alex nodded like she had expected as much. "I need to write more poems," she concluded.

"But, Alex," I said, "you don't have to write them *now*. You have two whole weeks. It doesn't have to get done at three o'clock in the morning."

"I know that," Alex said, picking up a piece of paper and carefully setting it on top of the stack inside her castle. "I wanted to do it now."

I looked into her gray-blue eyes and saw myself in them, as clearly as looking in a mirror. Building a miniature record player for my dollhouse long past bedtime. Teaching myself to code a Web site under the covers, so my dad wouldn't come in and tell me to go to sleep. DJing alone in my bedroom in the dark. These things could always wait until daylight, but I wanted to do them in the night.

"I'm going to bed, Poet Girl," I said. "Want me to tuck you in?"

Alex tapped the end of a marker to her teeth, considering. "Okay," she said at last. She put down the marker and followed me upstairs.

"Alex?" I whispered in the darkness of her bedroom. "Can you not tell Mom and Steve that I went for a walk tonight?"

"Okay," Alex said, snuggling into her covers. "Don't tell them that I was working on my castle either."

I wrapped my arms around her and she kissed my cheek. It wasn't the person who I'd thought would be kissing me at the end of tonight. But it was better than ending the night alone.

14

BY SUNDOWN THE NEXT DAY, I COULD BARELY KEEP my eyes open. I was curled up on the couch in Dad's living room, holding a book but not really reading it. Mostly I was just staring at my cell phone, willing Char to call or text. I wanted to know what had happened between him and Pippa. I wanted to tell him that I was going to have my own Friday night party. I wanted to talk to him. But so far, nothing.

Of course, this was normal, I reassured myself. Char and I didn't have a talking relationship. We had the other kind, the kind where you don't talk. So his silence meant nothing.

My dad sat in his armchair, fiddling with his guitar. He strummed a few chords and mumbled to himself. It mostly sounded like, "Hmm, mmm, mmm. Yeah yeah yeah. Mmm la la. Yeah yeah."

"New song?" I asked.

"Yeah. I was thinking the Dukes could play it at Solstice Fest, if I could figure out some lyrics. What do you think?"

What I thought, silently, was that no one at Solstice Fest, or anywhere for that matter, was interested in hearing a new Dukes song. They just wanted to hear "Take My Hand," and they would put up with other songs if they had to.

I had traveled with my dad to a lot of his shows. The best destination concert was when I was twelve. I got to go on an oldies cruise to Jamaica with him. I got my hair done in dozens of tiny braids with beads on the ends, and I swam in the Caribbean.

But what I remembered most clearly about this trip was the Dukes' set. They played a bunch of new songs and B-sides while the audience sat there politely. Then they played "Take My Hand," and the audience went nuts for it, obviously.

Once the song was over, the lead singer said to the crowd, like it had just occurred to him, "Hey, do you want us to play it again? It's only two minutes and twelve seconds long, after all." The crowd roared its approval, and the Dukes started "Take My Hand" right back from the beginning.

Even as a twelve-year-old primarily focused on eating a pineapple popsicle, I felt that there was something heartbreaking about this. Because the Dukes knew the truth: that nobody at all gave a shit about what they'd been up to over the past thirty-five years.

The Dukes seemed just as happy to be playing their hit single the second time around, and the audience seemed just as happy to hear it. Somehow I was the only one who wasn't happy.

After that, Dukes concerts just weren't as fun for me. Mostly, I tried not to go at all anymore. It felt like watching a magic show after you've already learned how the magician does all his tricks.

"The song?" Dad prompted me now, as he strummed out the chorus again. "Do you like it?"

I checked my cell phone again. Still nothing. "It was nice," I said.

"Oh." Dad cleared his throat. "I'm still working on it."

I had missed my cue somehow. I could tell. "I think it's going to be really good, Dad. I think the hippies at Solstice Fest will eat it up."

He half smiled and ran his thumb over one of the guitar strings. "Hey, do you want to go with me? To Solstice Fest."

"Um, when is it?"

He gave me a weird look. "During the solstice."

I guessed that made sense.

"We could drive up on Friday night and camp out. I think the Dukes' slot is around noon on Saturday."

"I can't," I said.

"Oh," Dad said. "Of course, you probably already have plans. Are you and Sally and Chava going to that school dance?"

I had told my parents about Sally and Chava because I wanted them to know that I was a normal person with friends. I had never told my parents about the Freshman/Sophomore Summer Formal because I wasn't insane. Apparently my father had been reading the PTA newsletter.

"The dance is that night," I said noncommittally.

"Do you have a date?" Dad asked.

"*God*, Dad. No." I thought about what that could possibly look like: Char showing up on my doorstep in a tuxedo, slipping a corsage around my wrist, posing for photographs in front of the fireplace? He wouldn't even call me.

Dad nodded sagely. "We guys, Elise, are easily intimidated. When I was sixteen, I would not have had the guts to ask a girl like you to my school dance."

This was a lie on multiple levels, since 1) the reason why boys weren't asking me out was absolutely not because they were intimidated by me, and 2) by the time my dad was sixteen, he was already playing sold-out shows at his local concert hall, and any girl in Philadelphia would have given her left arm to go to a dance with a Duke.

"Dad," I said, "would it be okay with you if I spend Friday night at Mom and Steve's house?"

He paused in his strumming. "You mean the weekend that I'm at Solstice Fest? Of course that's okay. I was going to suggest that myself."

"No, I meant, like . . ." I hugged my knees into my chest. "Every weekend."

He set his guitar down. "So I would only get you on Wednesdays? And you would stay with your mother six nights a week? Every week?"

"Well . . . We could rearrange things so I could spend some other weeknight with you . . . like Tuesdays?"

"Why?" Dad asked, his voice raw.

I couldn't answer that. I opened and closed my mouth, but I had nothing to say.

"Okay," Dad said, "forget 'why.' How's this? No."

"What?" I stared at him.

"I said, *No*. No, you can't stay with your mother six out of every seven nights. No, I am not going to rearrange my work schedule just because you feel like it. I don't care if you don't want to be here, or if when you are here you don't want to talk to me, or if your mother's house has all sorts of marvelous puppies and children and swing sets and fresh-baked goods. I am your father, and that means I am every bit as much your parent as she is. No, you can't spend Fridays there, too."

I stood up. "Look, this has nothing to do with Mom or swing sets or anything like that. It's just that her house is a lot more conveniently located to . . . well, to . . . stuff."

Dad stood up, as well. "I don't really care," he said. "What I'm hearing you say is that you don't want to spend time with me. And what I am saying to *you* is, you don't have a choice."

I felt panic bubbling up in my chest, and my breath started coming out in short gasps. What was I supposed to do, go to Start next Thursday, hope that Pete was there, and tell him, "Hey, look, my dad won't let me go out on Friday nights. Good luck finding another DJ!" I might as well just wear a sandwich board proclaiming, *I AM ONLY 16*. I couldn't do that. I didn't *want* to do that.

"You can't stop me," I said, my voice shaking. "Don't you love me at all?"

"Don't I *love you*?" Dad's words got louder and louder. "Jesus Christ, Elise, are you kidding me?"

I felt my face puckering like a prune. "Mom wouldn't keep me from doing something I care about." And even as I said it, I knew it was a cheap shot. One of the unspoken rules that I *did* understand was that my parents were not supposed to criticize each other in front of me, and I was not supposed to play them off each other.

Plus, Mom would absolutely keep me from doing something I cared about, if it came down to that. The only reason why she hadn't stopped me from going to Start was because she didn't know that was happening. Not because she was the superior parent.

"So that's why you want to spend Friday nights with her, too?" Dad asked. "Because she doesn't get in your way as much as I do?"

"No!" I protested. "It's just that . . . this is important to me. You don't understand."

"I don't," he said. "Explain it to me."

He looked at me closely, and I thought for a moment about telling him everything. What Start was, why I needed it. After all, he was on national tour with his band when he was just two years older than me. Maybe he would be cool with it.

But what if he wasn't?

I shook my head. "I can't explain it to you."

Dad kicked his guitar, and I flinched at the sudden atonal squawk as it hit the ground. "You know what, Elise?" he said. "Do what you want."

I stood still, hardly breathing.

"You want to spend every single night at your mother's house? Fine. I'll be here if you ever decide that you need me."

He lunged to pick up his guitar and lifted it over his shoulder like he was about to smash it into something. I clapped my hand to my mouth. Then slowly, painfully, he laid the guitar down on the armchair and walked out of the room. I heard his footsteps hard on the stairs to the basement. And a minute later I heard the sound, unmistakable to anyone who has heard it before, of a softball bat whacking a futon.

"Look, if you want to go to Start tonight, you should go," Vicky said over the phone the following Thursday evening.

I lay down on my bed, my cell phone pressed to my ear, and glanced at the clock on my bedside table. Nine o'clock.

"I think I want to stay home," I said.

"If you want to, sure." I heard the sound of spritzing through the phone, like Vicky was putting on hair spray or perfume. "But you shouldn't not come tonight just because of Pippa. You're the DJ. You do what you want."

"Does she want me there?" I asked, already knowing the answer.

"Well, whenever she's mentioned you over the past week, it's been as 'that slag,' so I'm thinking probably not."

"What's a slag?"

"I asked her that," Vicky said. "It's British for *slut*."

"How am I a slag? Char is the first and only guy who I have ever . . ." Kissed. Seen naked. Slept in a bed with. "Anything," I finished.

"I don't think she means it literally," Vicky reassured me. "And for whatever it's worth, I'm on your side. They weren't together. Pippa can't call dibs on every guy who she thinks is hot, because that would be *every* guy. Except for the Dirty Curtains. She thinks Dave looks like a caveman, and not in an 'I will protect your young' way. And Harry isn't 'man enough' for her. You know, because he's not actually a legal adult."

"Oh, so speaking of the Dirty Curtains," I said, "I have a proposal."

"Shoot."

"You know how I get to DJ Friday nights now?"

"I'm so excited," Vicky replied. "Goddammit, I am so excited. *Glendale's hottest DJ.* Do I or do I not keep saying that?"

"Well, Glendale's hottest DJ wants the Dirty Curtains to play a set at her first-ever gig next Friday."

There was silence for a moment.

"What do you say?" I asked.

Vicky let out an earsplitting shriek. "I say *yes!*" she squealed. "Harry and Dave also say yes, or they will once I tell them, since they do basically everything I say. Elise, this is awesome. I can't believe you would share your big night with us."

"There's no one I would rather share it with," I told her.

"You *have* to come tonight, then," Vicky said. "So we can celebrate together our impending fame. Honestly, Elise, don't worry about Pippa. You need to understand, the past few weeks have been hard on her." Vicky's voice grew quieter. "Pippa likes being in the action. Like the sun, with everyone revolving around her. When she was in Manchester, I think she felt like she was completely in the dark, closed off from her own solar system. So to come back here and discover that all of us kept orbiting without her . . . well, she's not happy. It isn't about *you.*"

"Isn't she in the room with you?" I asked. "Aren't you two getting ready together?"

"I locked myself in the bathroom." I heard the sound of a toilet flushing. "See?"

I sighed. "I don't want her to hate me. Enough people already hate me."

"I don't know if this matters, but *I* want you to come tonight."

I pulled my quilt over my head.

"This will all resolve itself on the dance floor," Vicky told me.

"Oh, really?" I said. "How's that going to work?"

"How could anyone hate anyone when we're all out there together, moving to the same song? How can we not be united? Come out tonight and join in—it'll be good for you. Oh, and wear that top you got from Calendar Girls. The lacy one."

"It makes me look like a snowflake," I mumbled.

"Just trust me!" Vicky chirped. Then she hung up the phone.

I sat for a moment under the fortress of my quilt. Tiny flecks of light peeked through the stitches. I could just live the rest of my life under here. I could pay Neil to bring me food three times a day.

I groaned and threw the blanket off my head. Unfortunately I hadn't thought to make feeding time arrangements before hiding in my bed, and now I was hungry.

Before I went to forage for a snack, I glanced at my computer to see what Fake Elise was up to right now. I hadn't checked in on her since right after coming home from school this afternoon.

June 10: *nobody likes me. sometimes i think people like me, i pretend that i have real friends, but i know i'm just kidding myself. why would they really like me? why*

195

would anyone ever *really like me??? whenever someone is nice to me i know it's just because they're taking pity on me. xoxo elise dembowski*

I looked in the mirror on the back of my door. I stuck my fingers in the corners of my mouth and pulled my face into a hideous grimace. Then I practiced some affirmations.

Lots of people really like you!

For example . . . your mom!

Alex!

Neil!

People who gave birth to you or who still have most of their baby teeth totally like you!

Sure, the only thing your dad said to you during the entire time you were at his house last night and this morning was, "Well, I'll see you again one week from now, since that's what you want." But that doesn't mean he doesn't *like* you. He's just mad at you. And he will get over it, if only because he is your legal guardian!

Vicky likes you! She is not just taking pity on you. Really. Her kindness to you is genuine.

How do you know this?

Because you're awesome at reading a crowd!

Char likes you! Okay, he kind of ignored you at Start last week, and okay, you haven't heard from him since then. But this situation with Pippa is delicate. He doesn't want to hurt her. Who does? You don't want to hurt Pippa either. Why would he have taught you to DJ if he didn't like you? Why would he kiss you? Because he likes you!

You are a likable girl, Elise Dembowski!

Affirmations complete, I headed toward the kitchen to make myself a hot chocolate. On my way back, I noticed my mother sitting on the couch in the sunroom. Alex was with her, which surprised me. Neil's weeknight bedtime is 8:15 and Alex's is 8:35, so the fact that it was past nine and Alex was still awake was definitely *not fair*.

"What's up?" I asked them.

"We're just admiring the poetry castle," Mom answered. She took a sip of her tea and gestured at Alex's creation.

I sat down on Alex's other side, and the three of us stared contemplatively at the castle.

It was massive. I had no idea how Mom and Steve planned to transport this thing to Alex's school next Friday. It stretched well over my head, cardboard boxes and duct tape everywhere. She had painted the boxes all the colors of the rainbow, and streamers hung from every corner. I could see the poems stacked neatly inside, ready for sale.

"It's amazing, Alex," I said.

"It's not done yet," Alex warned me. "It's not perfect yet."

"It's going to be the best one at the fair," Mom said proudly, and I remembered all the times she had said those same words to me. When I designed and sewed a dress for the Girl Scouts' fashion show; when I practiced reciting a monologue for the Shakespeare competition in eighth grade; when I baked pecan-raisin-banana-chocolate bars, my own invention, for the Election Day bake sale three years ago. My mother always said this: *It's going to be the best one.*

"Does Mr. Berger give a prize for the best booth?" I asked Alex.

Alex snorted and said, "Of *course* not," like I was an idiot for not understanding the exact rules of the second-grade spring fair.

"Well, if he did, you'd win," I told her.

"But for now, Alex sweetie, it's *way* past your bedtime." Mom stood and lifted my sister from the couch.

"But I'm not tiiired," Alex whined, and I wondered if this was the curse of all women in my family, to never get tired.

"It's bedtime anyway," Mom said. "You can work on it more tomorrow. Right, Elise?"

"Right," I said. "Even I am going to bed, Alex. See?" I picked up my hot chocolate, yawned dramatically, and headed to my room.

Two hours later, I crept out of the house and walked to Start. I meant what I had said to Vicky. I meant to stay home tonight. But I wanted to see Char too much, and I couldn't resist.

Like Char himself once told me, we all want things that aren't good for us.

15

WHEN I GOT TO START, I DIDN'T IMMEDIATELY SEE
Vicky or Pippa. Char was in the booth with his headphones on,
playing a Marvin Gaye song, and this seemed a good omen;
Char knew how much I liked old soul singers.

I slipped into the booth next to him. "Hey, stranger," I said.
"Long time no talk. You miss me?" I was aiming for jokey, but it
came out wrong, too honest. I saw Char flinch a little.

nobody likes me, Fake Elise chanted inside my head. *why would*
anyone ever *really like me???*

"How was your week?" I tried.

"Fantastic," Char muttered.

"Really."

"Oh, yeah. Probably my best week ever. Have you ever been
to Disney World?"

"Yeah."

"My week was like that, only about eighty times better."

He stared down at his computer. The song playing was "Panic" by the Smiths, which is the one where Morrissey repeats the line "hang the DJ" for about a minute straight.

"Sure, it totally seems like you're having an eighty-times-Disney-World week," I agreed. When he didn't respond, I said, "So what exactly happened with Pippa last week?"

"We frolicked through rainbows together," Char answered in a monotone.

"Char."

He sighed and ran his hand through his hair, making it stick up in tufts. "I don't know, Elise. She was pissed."

I fought the urge to smooth down his hair with my hand. I never touched Char first. I always waited for him to touch me.

"What did you think was going to happen when she came back from Manchester?" I asked him. "Did you think she wasn't going to find out about us? Or she wasn't going to care?"

"I didn't," Char said, "think about it. Anyway, I told her I didn't want to be her boyfriend before she left. You know that. So why did she expect me to celibately wait for her return for a month and a half?"

"Because," I replied, wondering if Char was secretly an idiot not to already know this, "you had sex with her *after* you told her you didn't want to date her."

"So?" he asked.

"So, what was she supposed to think that meant?" I asked. "What do you *think* people think it means when you hook up with them?"

He shook his head. "I have no idea. What do people think it means?"

I gave a long exhale, then said, "For someone who's supposed to be so great at reading a crowd, you have some serious blind spots."

Char flicked a number of dials on his mixer. "If you're such an expert, Elise, why don't you just tell me?"

I tried to look him in the eye, but he just kept looking at his equipment. "People think it means that you want to actually be with them. In a serious way. People think it means you care about them. That's the point of the whole thing, isn't it?"

Char shrugged. "Guys don't think that way."

I didn't know if he was right about that or not. I didn't know how guys thought about anything.

"Is Pippa coming tonight?" I asked, even though I already knew the answer from Vicky.

"No idea." Char put on his headphones.

I waited until he had transitioned into the next song, but when he still didn't take off his headphones, I tugged at his arm.

"What's up?" he asked, taking off one earphone. "I'm working."

"I can *see* that," I said. "I wanted to tell you my big news from last week."

Things were weird between me and Char right now. Things were weird because Pippa was back. But when I told him my news, he would be proud of me. He would remember how much we had in common. Things would be good again.

Right?

I felt like a cat bringing home a dead bird to her master. *"You'll like it, won't you? I killed it all by myself. You* must *like it."*

Did bird-murdering house cats get this fluttery feeling in their stomachs, too?

"I'm going to be DJing Friday nights!" I told Char, a smile erupting across my face. I couldn't not smile whenever I thought about it. "Starting next week. I can do whatever I want with it, Pete said. It's going to be the best."

Char took off his other earphone. He stared at me. "You're DJing Friday nights," he repeated, and I thought that maybe the loud music had garbled my words. "Here?"

"Right!" I shouted, to make sure he could hear me this time.

But his expression was still confused. "Pete gave you a Friday night party? Just you, no one else?"

"Just me," I confirmed.

Now Char's expression was more than just confused. It was mad. He responded with only one word. "Why?"

"Because he thought I'd be good at it."

"Why?" Char asked again, and I felt the ground slant ever so slightly underneath me.

"He said . . . I have a lot of natural talent, and—"

"Do you have any idea what a big deal it is to get a weekend party at one of Pete's venues?" Char interrupted. "Do you have any idea how many times I've asked him to move me to Friday, so no one has school or work the next day and can really *go out*? And then he just gives it to you? You, a sixteen-year-old girl who started DJing all of two months ago?"

I didn't speak for a moment. Then, quietly, I said, "It's not my fault that I'm only sixteen. And it's not my fault that I only started DJing now."

Char lowered his voice, too. He sounded gentle, helpful. "Why don't you just tell Pete that you don't feel ready? Tell him you need more practice. Tell him you're worried about what will happen if you have technical problems and you don't know how to fix them. I'm sure he'll understand."

"Because," I said, "I *do* feel ready." I cleared my throat. "This is so silly, but I guess I expected that you would be happy for me."

Char tapped on his computer keyboard and was silent for a minute. If I were someone else, I might have been impressed. But I knew enough about DJing to know that he wasn't actually doing anything.

"Listen, Elise," Char said at last. "I hadn't wanted to get into this tonight. But I think we should . . . stop."

"Stop?" I repeated.

"Yeah. Like, break up."

And the world tilted again, harder. "How can we break up?" I asked. "Were we even together?"

"I think the age gap is too much for us," Char said. "We're at different stages in our lives, and we're looking for different things."

"Now?" I said. *"Now* this bothers you?" I felt my breathing coming funny, like I had to gasp to get enough air. "What did I do, Char? What is it? Are you breaking up with me because Pippa's mad at you? Are you breaking up with me because"—my breath caught in my throat and I almost couldn't go on—"because I got offered a stupid Friday night party and you didn't?"

"You said you didn't love me," Char said quietly, looking at his computer screen, not me.

"When?"

"Last week. When Pippa asked you. You said no. You almost *laughed*, and you said no."

"I'm sorry," I said. And then I said, "No—I'm *not* sorry. You don't love me either. You never said you did. You never once called me, or hung out with me in daylight. How could you love me? Do you?"

My body tensed. Part of me hoped that he might say yes. That he would say, "Yes, I love you, and that's why I'm breaking up with you—because it kills me that you don't feel the same."

Because that would be it, then. The ultimate proof that I was lovable.

But what Char actually said was, "That's not the point."

"How the hell is it not the point?" I was almost screaming by now.

"You don't need me," Char said. "*That* is the point."

He put his headphones back on.

When do you want me to take over? I wrote on a Post-it and stuck it to his computer screen.

The corner of Char's mouth twitched, and he pulled my note off his monitor. "Don't worry about it," he said, crumpling the paper in his fist. "You have a full night of DJing ahead of you next Friday. You deserve to take tonight off."

It took me a minute more of standing there before I realized that I'd been dismissed. Before I realized that a relationship can end just like that.

Dazed, I left the booth and walked outside. I would have kept walking, too, I would have walked forever, except that Vicky, Harry, and Mel were standing right there.

"Hi, Elise!" Harry said. "Look, I'm here!" He went on to explain, "My parents are on a business trip, so Vicky's quote-unquote 'in charge.'"

I pasted a smile on my face and joined their circle. I don't know why I bothered to act like everything was okay. Start is small, and news travels fast. Soon enough they were all going to find out that Char had dumped me. But I wanted, for as long as I could, to pretend like he hadn't. I wanted not to be there when they heard the news and said, *Well, of course he did.* Boyfriends are for pretty girls, normal girls, girls who know what they're doing. Everybody knows that.

nobody likes me, and i deserve it.

Shut up, Elise.

"The Beatles," Vicky was saying to Mel.

"All quit," Mel replied.

"Not John," Vicky countered.

"Right, because he was murdered before he had the chance."

"George never quit either," Vicky said.

"And then he died from *lung cancer*," Mel said.

"But when he was, like, *sixty*. I'll quit before I'm *sixty*."

"Sixty comes sooner than you think, honey," Mel countered.

"We're taking a poll," Harry explained to me, "on whether or not Vicky should quit smoking. So far it's two for quitting, one against. You want to even out the score?"

"No," I said.

"Oh, come on," Vicky whined. "This isn't a majority-rule situation. It's my body."

Mel cleared his throat. "Well, maybe—"

"Hey," I interrupted. "Were you guys popular in high school?"

They all stopped talking and stared at me.

"You know," I said. "Friends. Did you have them? If so, how many?"

"Well, now," Mel rubbed his bald head. "You're asking me to remember back pretty far."

"Oh my God, Mel," Vicky said. "You are, like, one-eighth as old as you pretend to be."

Mel scowled at her. Then he said to me, "Honey, I was a gay black teenager in Arkansas. How popular do you *think* I was?"

I tried to picture a younger Mel getting bullied by his own versions of Chuck Boening and Jordan DiCecca. But it didn't work. If they had tried to steal his iPod, he would have stood up to them. He was Mel. Standing up to people was his job.

"I'm definitely very popular among the Dungeons & Dragons players at my school," confided Harry. "Also, I rule at Settlers of Catan, and that has won me a devoted fan base of at least two or three classmates. Oh, and I *shred* on the drums. The girls go wild for that."

"You can't shred on drums, dipshit," Vicky told him. "Only guitarists shred."

Harry winked at me, then screwed up his face and mimed a very intense drum set. He stopped after a few seconds, when he noticed that I still wasn't smiling.

"I don't believe that anyone who is a legitimately interesting person can be popular as a teenager," Mel went on. "Or ever, maybe. Popularity rewards the uninteresting."

"I take offense," Vicky cried, throwing her cigarette butt to the ground. "I am at least a somewhat interesting person, and *I* was popular in high school."

Mel and I both gaped at her. I felt betrayed. "*You* were?" Mel asked.

"You don't have to sound so shocked about it." Vicky shook out her thick, wavy hair.

Mel said, "I just can't picture you as a blond cheerleading girlfriend of the class president, that's all."

Vicky snorted. "Exactly how many teen movies have you watched? You know that's a huge stereotype, right?"

Mel shrugged. "I'm a John Hughes fan."

"Well, I was never blond, but I was a cheerleader sophomore year, and I never dated the class president, but I *did* once make out with the quarterback at a party."

"And the wide receiver," Harry added.

"And him," Vicky conceded.

"And the tight end," said Harry.

"I did not."

Harry nodded at me and mouthed, *She did.*

"Anyway," Vicky said, "I was popular. Well, for the first half of high school. I was a very popular fifteen-year-old."

"Then what happened?" I asked.

"Well . . ." Vicky's eyebrows knit together. "Don't laugh or anything, but I used to be skinny."

She paused, her face red.

"Why would we laugh at that?" I asked.

"I don't know," Vicky said. "Like, maybe you'd think it's ridiculous that someone like me could have ever possibly been skinny."

"You're not *fat* now," I said.

"I'm fat enough," Vicky said. "But when I started high school, I was skinny. I really, really was. I also threw up pretty much everything I ate. Everyone loves a skinny girl. I do, too, frankly.

"At the end of tenth grade, my parents made me start seeing a therapist, and she literally changed my life. After a few months of therapy, I stopped making myself throw up so often, and then I did it less and less, until I never did it at all. So *naturally* I gained weight. There were actual calories in my body for the first time since I was twelve. And so my friends, who were, by the way, huge bitches, just ditched me."

"That's crazy." I tried to imagine, as I looked at Vicky, not wanting to be friends with her. I couldn't do it.

"That's actually why I started smoking," Vicky said. "Because it's supposed to be an appetite suppressant. As you can see, it doesn't work as well as all that." She lit another cigarette and arched her eyebrows at Mel, as if daring him to tell her not to. He didn't say a word.

"To be fair to my high school friends," Vicky went on, "it wasn't just that I didn't *look* like I used to. It was like this spell had been broken, and all sorts of things that used to seem important to me now just seemed stupid. So I quit cheerleading. And student council. My so-called friends could *not* figure out what was going on."

Vicky giggled and added, "My parents weren't that thrilled either. Their plan had been for me to give up vomiting, not for me to give up *everything*. They even fired my therapist, as if it was all her fault that I had decided that I wanted to be myself."

"And it meant that I never got a therapist either," Harry added. He sighed. "Yet more proof that Vicky is their favorite. So unfair."

"But then," Vicky said, "I made friends with these other kids at my school—you know, the 'uncool' ones. And one of them turned out to be really into music. She and I started writing songs together. Eventually we formed my first-ever band. She played guitar, I played keyboards and sang. We never performed anywhere, but we recorded a bunch on our computers. And that"—Vicky flung her arms out to the sides—"is how I discovered who I am. And *that* is why I'm here tonight, hanging out with you."

I tried to picture one of the girls at my school secretly being Vicky, hiding in the skin of a popular clone. What if Lizzie Reardon in three years would look back on the time she spent making my life hell and think to herself, *Well, that was really petty, wasn't it?* Would Lizzie Reardon someday be nice to a stranger on the street the way Vicky was to me the first night I met her?

But it was too hard to imagine. I couldn't see it.

"Enough sad tales of my youth," Vicky said. "Your turn, Elise. Who are you in the teen movie of our lives?"

I opened my mouth, then closed it. *I'm a super-cool underground DJ sensation,* I wanted to say. But that wasn't right. Char had just made it clear that I was nothing of the sort. *I'm the super-cool underground DJ's girlfriend.* But I wasn't that either. Who was I?

I extended my left arm toward them, palm up, my pale white skin illuminated by the stars and a lone streetlight.

"Jesus Christ," Harry said. "What happened to your arm?"

Vicky smacked him on the side of the head.

"Ow!" Harry exclaimed. "What was that for?"

Vicky shook her head at him, then took my arm in her hands and looked at it. Really looked. "Why didn't you tell us?" she asked in a low voice.

"Tell you what?" I asked, trying to shake her off. "Tell you I'm unpopular? Okay, I'm telling you now: I'm not Glendale's hottest DJ. My name is Elise Dembowski, I'm sixteen years old, and nobody likes me. One time I pretended to try to commit suicide, but I didn't really do it, and for a while I pretended to date Char, but I didn't really do that either. I'll pretend to be anyone or anything other than myself, but the problem is that *no one is ever fooled.*"

I wrenched my arm away from Vicky and shoved past a startled Mel, back into Start. I wanted to lock myself in one of the filthy, graffitied bathroom stalls and not come out until daylight.

But once inside, I couldn't help but find Char with my eyes. So I couldn't help but find Pippa, too, next to him.

Her body was angled toward him, her button nose and rosebud lips turned up toward his face. From across the room, I could see his mouth moving as he spoke to her, his headphones resting on the table. She threw back her head and laughed, and Char laughed, too, as he placed his hand on her lower back.

I felt the warmth and weight of his hand as strongly as if I were the one in the booth right now, not Pippa. How many times had Char touched me in exactly that same way? And it always made me relax, because it was the most certain reassurance *you will be coming home with me tonight.*

Pippa would be going home with Char tonight. I could see it as clearly as either of them up there could. Maybe even more so, because I knew how to read a crowd. And I could read them both perfectly.

I felt my stomach flip, but it wasn't because of Char. Not

really. It was because I could pinpoint exactly how I had lost him. I knew because it was the same way I lost everyone.

Pete had offered me my own Friday night party, and I had accepted. I had been too precocious. Again. Again and again and again.

I had always thought that if I just did something extraordinary enough, then people would like me. But that wasn't true. You will drive away everyone by being extraordinary. You will drive away your classmates and your friends, and tonight you will drive away Char. But you, you never learn your lesson. The world embraces ordinary. The world will never embrace you.

Of course Char wanted Pippa. It was so clear to me now: why he ended things with me, why he would keep Pippa around and around, no matter how much he didn't care about her. He wanted a girl he could mold just the way he wanted. And me? No one can mold me. I know because I've tried.

So I turned and ran. I left them all behind, and I ran the whole way home.

When I got through the front door of my mom's house, I saw the poetry castle looming in the sunroom in front of me. I was panting, my heart racing. I bent over, resting my hands on my knees, trying to steady myself. But nothing felt steady.

It was too late for me to turn into the sort of girl who people would like. It was too late for me to be normal and unremarkable. Fake Elise had seen this long before I had. Every word in that journal was true, truer than me fooling myself into thinking that maybe this new world of Start gave me a new lease on life, a new chance to alienate no one.

Silly. Silly Elise. It is too late for you.

But there was one person it wasn't too late for.

Alex.

And, crying so hard that I didn't know if I would ever stop, I tore her entire castle to shreds.

When I was done, silence set in. The only sounds were my ragged breathing and the buzzing of my cell phone. I sat down on the floor and opened it.

I had three missed calls from Vicky and a text message.

I THINK YOU'RE WRONG. I LIKE YOU. HARRY AND MEL DO TOO. SO THAT'S THREE TO START.

16

I WOKE UP TO SCREAMING.

"I'm going to kill you! I'm going to cut you open with a sword and feed your insides to the dogs!" That was Alex. That's how she thinks. She reads a lot of books.

"It's not my fault! I didn't do it! Help!" That was Neil.

My eyes were stuck together with dried tears. I rubbed them away and glanced at my bedside clock. 5:53 a.m.

"Alexandra Myers, stop that *right now*!" That was Steve.

"Violence is not the answer!" And Mom. Of course.

I slipped out of bed and padded out of my room. When I got to the sunroom, I stopped.

The ruins of Alex's poetry castle looked even worse in the daylight than they had a few hours before. It wasn't just broken. It was utterly destroyed.

Alex was weeping in the middle of the foyer, hugging a collection of torn papers to her chest. Neil was in Steve's arms, wailing into his shoulder. Mom sat on the floor next to Alex, and I could see that she was crying, too.

"If Neil didn't do it," Alex said, "then *who did*?"

"Maybe Chew-Toy?" Steve suggested hopefully.

Hearing his name, Chew-Toy came trotting into the front hall, his tongue hanging happily out of his mouth.

"I hate you, Chew-Toy!" Alex screamed. She smacked him once and raised her hand to do it again, but he fled before she had the chance.

"Alex, *violence is not the answer!*" Mom shouted again. She grabbed Alex in a tight bear hug, pinning her little arms to her sides.

"Maybe it was a robber," Steve suggested, again in that hopeful tone. Like he really, really wanted to believe that a burglar had broken into our house in the middle of the night just to wreck Alex's poetry castle.

I took another step into the foyer. Mom, Steve, and Alex turned to look at me. Neil just kept crying into Steve's shoulder.

"Good morning, Elise," Mom said. And I could tell from the tone of her voice that she didn't blame this on Chew-Toy, and she wasn't hoping a robber was going to show up to take the blame. My mother knew exactly whose fault this was.

She stood up slowly and spoke to me, her words coming out low and shaky. "What do you have to say for yourself?"

I steadied myself against the wall. "I was just trying to . . ."

"To what?" Mom said sarcastically. "To hurt Alex? To hurt me? What?"

"To protect her," I said. "Like a big sister should."

Mom laughed, a bitter, clipped laugh. "Protect her," she repeated. "I can't believe you. This really takes the cake."

"How do you not see it?" I snapped. Neil stopped crying. He looked back and forth between me and Mom, sucking on his thumb, even though he stopped sucking on his thumb a full year ago. "How do you not see what Alex is going to become if you let her go on like this? What kind of a person do you think she's going to be?"

"She can be whoever she wants to be," Steve answered.

"No," I said. "She can't. Nobody can. And you're not doing her any favors by telling her that she can because she's special. Look at me. *Look* at me. I'm ugly and boring and stuck-up. I'm awkward and gross; I'm pathetic and worthless. Do you think that's who *I* wanted to be?"

I blinked and behind my closed eyelids could see only Char, again, dismissing me.

"Alex doesn't need to have the best booth at the second grade fair," I went on. "She needs a reality check, diminished ambition, and some non-imaginary friends. And that's what I am trying to give her."

"Elise did it?" Alex's gray-blue eyes grew wide as she finally figured out what we were talking about. Her face contorted into an ugly, silent howl, and Mom held her even more tightly.

"Do you honestly believe that?" Mom asked me. "That you're boring and worthless and all of that? Because you're not, Elise. You're nothing like that."

"Open your eyes!" I screamed. "That's exactly who I am. And I am trying to be a good big sister, so instead of two screwed-up daughters you'll have only one. I'm sorry if you don't like it, but I am doing the best I can. And in ten years, when Alex is happy, maybe you'll see that I was right."

I didn't want Alex to ever have to lose someone the way that I lost Char. She deserved better than that.

"Elise, this is unacceptable," Steve said. He cleared his throat. "I'm not comfortable having you near my children right now."

His words were like a slap in the face. I *was* Steve's child. He had been my stepfather for nine years. And since my own dad was so angry with me these days, Steve was the next best thing.

"What are you saying?" I whispered. My legs felt suddenly weak under me, and I sat down, right there on the floor.

"I want you to stay at your father's until this whole situation has cooled down," Steve said, rubbing the bald spot on the back of his head. "Maybe for a few weeks. I'm sorry, but I can't have you putting my children in danger."

My children.

"You are so grounded, young lady," Mom added. "You are going to go to school, and then you are going straight to your father's house, and you are not leaving there. End of story." To my sister, she said, "Come on, sweetheart. Let's go wash off those tears."

I pulled myself to my feet and dragged myself back to my room.

I had done Alex a favor. In the long run, this would make Alex happier. It would make everyone happier.

But right now, I didn't feel happier at all. If anything, I just felt worse.

* * *

By next Thursday, the day before my first party, I had made up my mind: I wasn't going to do it. I was going to tell Pete that I couldn't, I wasn't experienced enough, I didn't have the technical skills. And I was going to offer the party to Char. Pete had said I could do whatever I wanted with Friday nights, and this was what I wanted to do.

Because I was grounded, I hadn't seen Vicky for a full week. My parents had taken away my cell, so I didn't even have her phone number to call her. In a way I was glad for this, since I knew that if I told Vicky my plan, she would try to talk me out of it.

I was going to go to Start tonight and tell Char that he was right: I wasn't as good as all that, and I needed him. And he would take over Friday nights. Maybe he would even be generous and let me do a guest slot. And everything would go back to the way it had been, back when things were good enough, before I ruined it all by trying to make it better.

I knew this plan was a last-ditch effort, coming too late and unlikely to work. But I also knew I had to try. Because what else did I have?

My first obstacle was figuring out how to get from my dad's house to Start on Thursday night. My dad had taken the week off from work so that he could constantly monitor me. I hadn't been allowed back at my mom's house since Friday. I hadn't even been allowed to talk to Alex on the phone.

The problem was that my dad's house was about nine miles from the club. I was grounded. And it was pouring rain, one of those June storms that sounds like the God of Weather roaring at you, "You shall never have your summer!" Even if I wanted to sneak out of the house and walk nine miles, I wouldn't have made it.

What I needed was a ride.

After dinner on Thursday, I sat on my bed and ran through my options. Vicky didn't have a car. Neither did Pippa, and even if she did, she wouldn't have helped me with any plan to win back Char. Asking Char for any help was obviously out of the question. I didn't have Mel's phone number, and anyway, I was pretty sure that he was enough of an adult that he wouldn't help me break out of my dad's house. In fact, without my cell phone, I would have had a hard time figuring out how to get in touch with *any* of them.

No matter how I thought about it, I kept coming up with one idea. She wouldn't like it, but desperate times called for desperate measures.

I grabbed my father's landline. I grabbed my school directory. And I dialed.

"Hello?"

"I need your help," I said.

"Oh, thank goodness," said Sally. "I thought you would never ask. Okay, the first thing is: *You are not alone.* The second thing is: *Suicide is not the answer.* The third thing is . . . Wait, I forget." Her voice became muffled and I heard her say, "Chava, what's the third thing?"

"Sally," I said. "That's not what I need your help with."

"Oh. Wait, what else do you need?"

"Do you have any plans tonight?"

"It's a *school night,*" Sally answered.

I paused. "So is that a no?"

"Chava's over," Sally said. "We're doing homework."

"Great. Can you pick me up at my dad's and then drive me somewhere?"

"Um . . . why?" I could almost hear Sally raising her eyebrows.

"I just have this thing I need to do."

Sally lowered her voice. "Is it a drug deal?"

I sighed, very quietly. "It's not a drug deal," I said.

"Let me ask."

I overheard some footsteps and shuffling and muffled conversation. A couple minutes later, Sally got back on the line. "Yes," she said.

"Yes!" I squealed.

"But I can't take the highway."

"You don't have to."

"And I can't drive faster than twenty-five miles an hour."

I paused. "Sally, your parents won't *know* if you drive, like, thirty miles an hour."

"They told me about this story they once read about a boy who went drag racing in the rain, and then he crashed his car."

"Wow," I said.

"And died," Sally added.

"Fine," I said. "We can drive at twenty-five miles an hour. Can you come get me at ten?" I gave her my dad's address, then added, "But can you just wait down the block, not right outside the house?"

She was silent for a moment. "Are you *sure* this isn't a drug deal?"

"Positive."

I told her my dad's address, we hung up the phone, and I

swung into action. I told my dad that I was going to be in my room the rest of the night. I said it in a way that seemed both sulky and exhausted, so he would be clear on the fact that I really, really did not want to hang out with him tonight. Then I stomped around the house in my pajamas and brushed my teeth in the hallway to make sure that he saw me all ready for bed.

"Good night, Daddy," I said. Then I shut my bedroom door. I turned on my music, and I got ready.

I put on the same outfit I'd been wearing the first night Char kissed me. It felt like good luck. Like maybe if he saw me looking just like I had then, he would remember just how he felt about me then.

The last thing I did, as part of my preparations, was check Fake Elise's journal.

June 17: *tonight is the night. i don't want to do this anymore. i give up. goodbye. xoxo elise dembowski*

In a way, Fake Elise knew what she was talking about. In a way, she always did. I *was* giving up. But sometimes you have to give up something you are to get to who you want to be.

I gave myself one last check in the mirror and whispered the line from my fake journal: *"Tonight is the night."* Then I grabbed my ladybug umbrella and snuck out of the house.

It was easy. I had done it before, just to go for walks. Being officially grounded didn't make it any harder to slip out my first-floor window and jump to the ground.

Keeping my head down, I ran through the pounding rain to the street corner. Sally and Chava were already there, headlights cutting through the downpour. I crawled into the backseat of Sally's parents' SUV.

"Thank you so much, guys," I said.

"You look crazy," Sally responded, looking at my outfit.

"But pretty!" Chava added as Sally started to drive. Chava gave a little sigh of pleasure. "I love to drive at night. It feels like we own the streets, you know?"

"Seriously?" I asked. Not that driving was such a weird thing to enjoy doing. Just that it had never occurred to me to wonder what Chava and Sally might like to do when they weren't at school.

"One time," Sally whispered, looking around as if for hidden cameras, "I let Chava drive this car. And she only has her permit."

"Did you get in trouble?" I asked.

"No!" Chava exclaimed, and they both burst into giggles.

"Hey, guys?" I said. "Thank you."

"For what?" Chava asked.

"For giving me a ride tonight. I really needed your help."

Chava's face cracked into a huge grin, like she had been waiting for me to say this to her for her entire life.

"That's what *friends* do," Sally said slowly, like she was explaining something to a hearing-impaired child. "They're there for each other."

I didn't know much about friends. But the more friendships I saw up close—with Vicky, Pippa, Harry, Char—the more I suspected that Sally knew what she was talking about.

"Look, Elise," Sally said matter-of-factly. "We know you think you're too good for us."

Chava nodded in unemotional agreement.

"What, did you read that on my quote-unquote blog, too?" I asked.

"No," Sally said. "But we're not *stupid*. Okay, we're not popular, but we're not blind either."

"I don't think that I'm too good for you," I said, but they both acted like I hadn't spoken.

"And you're clearly using us right at this instant," Sally went on.

"For Sally's license," Chava added.

"For my license," Sally said.

And I couldn't argue with that, because that was true. I treated Sally and Chava in the same disposable way that Amelia and her friends treated me. The only difference was, I'd never made them clean up my trash. "I'm sorry," I said.

They shrugged in unison. "Honestly?" Chava said. "It's okay. We don't really mind."

"What?"

"We like you," Chava said simply. "You're interesting." She added quickly, "Good-interesting, obviously."

"I wouldn't ask my parents for permission to take the car out at ten p.m. on a *school night* if I didn't like you," Sally said.

"I like you, too," I said, and realized that, in a way, I meant it. I didn't feel about Sally and Chava the way I felt about Vicky. I never would. They didn't *get me* like Vicky did—and, honestly, I didn't get them either. But that didn't stop me from liking them.

"We know," Chava said with an understanding nod. "You're just bad at showing it, that's all."

As we drove down the street of warehouses toward Start, Sally muttered, "There's, like, *nobody* out here."

But she was wrong.

A small cluster of people stood at the end of the alleyway, waiting for Mel to let them into Start. On the otherwise desolate gray street, the cluster of brightly colored umbrellas stood out like a poetry castle in a field of cardboard boxes. Sally slowed the car, and together we took them in: the giggling girls in high heels or colorful sneakers. The boys in galoshes, jumping in puddles in the street. The couple sharing one umbrella, kissing, pressed up against the concrete wall.

I saw Sally glance down at her own mom-fitted jeans and too-big sweatshirt, then back out the window. "Who are they?" she asked.

I thought of all the answers to that question. Students. Artists. Dancers. DJs. Guitarists. Photographers. Bartenders. Designers. Club kids. "People," I said.

"What is this place?" Chava asked.

I had thought I'd never be able to explain what Start was to anyone, but my response actually came out simply. "It's called Start," I said. "It's the greatest underground dance party in the world."

Sally's forehead creased. "Why are we here?"

"Um." I tugged down my skirt. I didn't want to explain about Char, not now, so I went with the easier explanation. "Because I DJ here."

"You DJ an underground dance party?" Chava shrieked.

"Only on Thursdays," I said lamely.

"You never mentioned that on your blog," Sally accused.

"Sally, I've been telling you this for weeks: *I don't write a blog.*"

Sally still looked shell-shocked. "But you never mentioned it to *us*, either."

"I know." I stroked the inside of my left wrist. "Don't you ever want to have just one thing that no one else knows about, so no one can ruin it for you?"

Sally just stared out the window at the line of people and didn't respond. I was about one second away from saying, "Never mind," when she opened her mouth. "I have a boyfriend," she said.

I stopped stroking my wrist. "What?"

"Do you mean Larry Kapur?" Chava asked, looking as surprised as I felt.

"No." Even in the dark I could see Sally blushing. "He's an online boyfriend. I've never actually met him in person. He lives in California. But we message each other all the time. Our first anniversary is coming up in August."

"How did you never mention this to me?" Chava demanded.

"I don't want to talk about it," Sally said. "I'm just saying . . . yeah. I get it. About having a part of your life that's secret, so no one can take it away from you." She looked down at her short, plain nails. Sally had told me before that the only nail polish she was allowed to wear was the clear kind, and, as she herself pointed out, "What's the point of that?"

"Do you want to come in to Start?" I asked suddenly. I wanted to give them something in exchange for the things they'd given to me—not just the ride tonight, but things I'd taken for granted: letting me sit with them when I had no one, welcoming me into their little group of two when we all knew they didn't need me. "I'm the DJ," I went on. "The bouncer won't care if I bring in underage friends, I bet."

Chava looked hopeful, but Sally shook her head. "I have to get home by curfew."

I nodded and opened the door. "Thanks again for driving me."

"Sure," Sally replied. Then I got out of the car and watched her drive away, at twenty-five miles per hour. My friend Sally was two-timing Larry Kapur. The world is a weird place.

"You're here pretty early," Mel commented when I reached the door to Start. "For you, I mean."

I shrugged.

"Can't wait for your party tomorrow night," Mel went on. "It's gotten fantastic press online. All about Start's vibrant young DJ sensation, Elise Dembowski, rising from nowhere to night-life fame. I'm sure you've seen it. They got some great shots of you from Flash Tommy."

"No," I said, my heart sinking. "I haven't seen it."

"Look yourself up, honey!"

"Mel . . ." I took a deep breath. "I don't think I'm going to do the party tomorrow."

"Why?" he asked.

"I don't think I'm . . . technically proficient enough. I mean, I'm just not good enough, probably . . ." I trailed off, waiting for Mel to fill in the blanks.

I wasn't selling this at all. When I told Char, and Pete, I was going to need to sound a lot more convinced of my inability.

Mel frowned. "Honey, when you came here to me and I asked you whether you had talent or issues, do you remember what you said?"

I nodded and swallowed. "Both."

"So why are you letting your issues get in the way of your talent?"

"Mel," I said, "I want to."

I went inside. Char was alone at the DJ booth. I supposed it was too early in the night for Vicky or Pippa to be here, and I was glad for that. This would be easier if it was just between me and Char.

I stood alone in the back of the room for a moment, watching him. It was early, so almost no one was dancing yet. Char's eyes were focused on his computer, and he brushed a lock of hair off his forehead. I could see his fingers tapping out a beat on the table next to him.

One last time, I thought about what it could be like, twenty-four hours from now, at my party. If I were the one standing up there, tapping out a beat. If Char were the one in the audience, watching me, swaying to my music.

One last time, I said goodbye to that, and I started toward the booth.

One foot in front of the other, until you reach him. Open your mouth and tell him. Just tell him you give up. It's easy. Fake Elise did it. You can, too.

I was almost at the DJ booth, reaching out for Char, when I felt a hand clamp down on my shoulder. I turned around, and the disco ball overhead illuminated the man behind me.

It was my father.

17

"WHAT ARE YOU DOING HERE?" I ASKED MY DAD.

"What are *you* doing here?" he asked. Then, "We're going home."

He propelled me out of Start, past Mel, and into his car. Whether Char noticed that I was there or noticed that I left, I don't know. I never spoke to him.

"How did you find me?" I asked.

Dad ignored me and pulled out his cell phone. "Danielle," he said into it. That's my mom. "I found her." He paused. "No, she's fine." Another pause. "Okay, yes. See you there."

He hung up and started to drive, his windshield wipers flicking furiously back and forth.

"Daddy, I'm sorry," I said. "I'm sorry I snuck out. I'm sorry I lied to you. I'm sorry I'm so . . ." I started to cry then. "I'm sorry," I repeated over and over. "I'm so sorry."

When we pulled up to Dad's house, Mom was already

waiting in her car outside. She jumped out and ran through the rain to meet us at the front door.

Inside, we dumped our umbrellas and wet shoes by the front door and went into the living room. Mom sat in one arm chair, Dad in the other. I sat alone on the couch. I noticed Mom glancing around the room. I didn't know if she had ever been to Dad's house before. They almost never saw each other at all, because they didn't have any reason to. They had both been at my middle school graduation ceremony two years ago. And at the hospital on the first day of the school year. Big events only.

But here we were, the three of us alone, together. Just like a family.

I was still crying, but I shut up when Dad opened up his laptop and showed me the screen. "Does this look familiar to you?"

It was Elise Dembowski's Super-Secret Diary.

My stomach clenched. "Yes."

"Around ten o'clock tonight," Dad said, "I received a panicked phone call from a nice-sounding girl named Amelia Kindl. She said that she didn't know you very well, but that she had read something online that concerned her. She directed me to a blog, saying she didn't know if it was serious or not, but she was worried. I thanked her and went to the Web site address she'd given me. This is what I found." He read aloud. " 'June seventeen. Tonight is the night. I don't want to do this anymore. I give up. Goodbye. xoxo Elise Dembowski.' "

"Oh my God," I whispered.

"What do you think I did?" Dad asked me.

"You got worried?" I asked.

228

"Elise, 'worried' does not begin to cover what I got. If anything had happened to you, I literally would not be able to go on. I ran upstairs and opened your bedroom door, no idea what I was going to find. I was terrified. And what I found was . . . nothing. The room was empty. That was when I called your mother. She wasn't happy about hearing from me so late at night."

"Only because I didn't know why you were calling," Mom objected.

"We didn't know where you were," Dad said. "All we knew was that you had left a suicide note online, and then disappeared."

"I still don't understand how you didn't notice her leaving," Mom said to him.

"She said she was going to bed," Dad defended himself.

"Didn't you *hear* anything? Do you expect me to believe she snuck out of the house absolutely silently?"

"I wasn't sitting outside of her bedroom all night, preparing to bust in if I heard a single sound other than a snore. I believe kids need a little privacy."

"She was grounded. How much privacy did she need?"

"So how did you find me?" I interrupted. There's nothing interesting in my parents' bickering. I've heard it all before.

"This other Web site," Dad answered. He said the name like it was in quotation marks: " 'Flash Tommy'? You had it open on your computer, and I saw photos of you at a big party. So I headed to the street address given on the site. I didn't know if you would be there. I was just hoping."

Thanks a lot, Flash Tommy.

"So you probably want to know what I was doing at that party," I said dully.

"What we *need* to know," Mom said, "is, what is this diary of yours?"

"I didn't write it," I told them.

"That's what I thought," Dad murmured.

Mom shot him a look.

"What?" he asked. "The girl on this Flash Tommy Web site is not the same girl writing these diary entries. They directly contradict each other. And she's been at this party a number of times. I saw photos on that site. Sorry to tell you this, Danielle, but your daughter has snuck out of *your* house before, too. More than once."

Mom blinked rapidly, but otherwise acted like Dad hadn't spoken. "So you didn't set out to kill yourself tonight," Mom asked me.

"No!"

"And you don't . . . hate us?" Mom asked.

I bit my tongue to keep from swearing. "Does that blog say I hate you?" I asked, already knowing the answer.

They both nodded.

"No," I said. "You're my parents. I don't hate you."

"Then you shouldn't have been sneaking out of our houses, Elise," Mom said. "It's dangerous. Not to mention incredibly disrespectful. Your father and I set rules, and we expect you to follow them. When I tell you that you're grounded, I need you to take me seriously."

"I'm sorry," I whispered.

"How many times have you left the house in the middle of the night?" Mom demanded.

"I . . . don't know. A lot, I guess."

"And were you always going to this . . ." Mom gestured at Dad's laptop, at a loss for a word to describe Start. "This event space?" she finally said.

"No." I'd never put this into words before, to explain it to someone else. I didn't quite know how to begin. "Sometimes I just wanted to walk. I wasn't trying to hurt you or disrespect you or anything . . . It had nothing to do with you. I just really love Start. That's all."

"Here's what I want to know," Dad said, tapping his finger against his computer. "If you don't write this blog, then who does? And why?"

"I have no idea," I answered.

"Then that," said Dad, "is what we really need to figure out."

When I walked into the kitchen the next morning, my father was not only awake and reading the newspaper, he was dressed in a suit. The last time I saw my dad in a suit was at his own mother's funeral.

"Let me guess," I said, grabbing a banana. "You're pursuing a new career as a real estate broker."

He raised his eyes over the paper. "I want your school to take me seriously when I go in there and give them hell. Here." He slid a carefully cut-out newspaper article across the table to me.

It was a brief piece, more of an event listing than an actual story. It just said there was a new indie, new wave, and soul dance party tonight, from the promoters who brought you Start, and it featured up-and-coming DJ wunderkind Elise Dembowski. Above it was a color photograph, small but unmistakably showing me behind the turntables.

This wasn't the first time I'd appeared in our town paper. Getting into the *Glendale Gazette* is actually not that competitive. You can accomplish it for far less than DJing a warehouse party. I got mentioned in the paper when I won the eighth grade spelling bee, and before that in fifth grade when I was a youth volunteer on Steve's friend's mayoral campaign. I still had those clippings in my desk drawer, cut out for me by my father. This wasn't the first time.

But it felt the best.

"So that's why you wanted me to get you DJing equipment, huh?" Dad asked, not looking up from his paper. "Very clever. Now, were you planning to tell me that you're going out tonight, or were you just going to try your hand at sneaking out again?"

"I . . ." I rubbed my eyes. "Neither. I was planning not to go."

"Because your mother would blow a fuse if she knew her underage daughter was at a nightclub?"

"Because . . . It's complicated, Dad."

"Try me," he said. "I'm a relatively smart guy."

Yeah, my dad was smart. Smart enough to kill me if I told him I'd been hooking up with a guy who was three and a half years older than me. I said, "Because some people there don't want me to play. And they have a good point."

"The thing about being an artist," Dad said, folding his newspaper and setting it down on the table, "is that there are always going to be people who want to stop you from doing your art. But this usually says more about them and their issues than it does about you and your art. Trust me. I've been a musician since I was younger than you. And if I had a penny for every person who has told me the Dukes are dead, we should stop trying to write music, I should do something productive with my life, I'll never be as good as this other bassist or that other bassist—well, I would be rich enough to buy you something fancy. But those people don't *know* me. So I just keep playing my music. That's what I've been doing for forty years, and that's what's always worked for me."

"So you're saying I *should* sneak out of the house tonight to DJ a warehouse party?"

Dad gave a little laugh. "You wish. No, Elise, all I'm saying is: don't let anyone else decide your life for you." He stood up and straightened his tie. "Let's go."

Dad drove me to school. We met Mom in the parking lot, and then we headed to the principal's office, united.

Of course, the principal wouldn't see us. The principal never sees anybody; he is way too important for that. We met instead with the vice principal, Mr. Witt, most famous for his masterful handling of the Jordan DiCecca–Chuck Boening iPod Crisis. My parents showed Mr. Witt Elise Dembowski's Super-Secret Diary and explained what was going on.

"What are you going to do about this?" my dad asked.

Mr. Witt suggested the following things:

1. Most likely, I *had* actually written this diary, but now that my parents had discovered it, I was just acting like I hadn't so I wouldn't get in trouble.

2. Even if somehow I didn't write this blog, there was no reason to believe that the blogger was a student of Glendale High. It could have been anyone in the world! In fact, the blog might even be referring to a *different* Elise Dembowski!

3. Glendale High had zero tolerance for bullying, and therefore it was impossible that any one of the school's 850 angel-faced students was the culprit.

"I hear what you're saying, Mr. Witt," Mom said, "but I have to disagree. I would appreciate your conducting a real investigation into this question. This *is* harassment. This *is* bullying. We need to know that the school is taking this as seriously as we are."

"If any of our students is somehow running this blog, we will find out about it," Mr. Witt promised, in the tone of someone who has only one week left in the school year and after that doesn't have to give a shit about any adolescent problems until September.

After our meeting, my parents left matters in Mr. Witt's capable hands and headed to work. "I'll pick you up at three to bring you to Alex's school fair," Mom said before she left.

I blinked. "I'm ungrounded?"

"No way, José. You are definitely still grounded. But you're going to that fair."

"Why?" I asked.

"Because," she said, "you told me you wanted to be a good big sister. And *that's* what a good big sister does." She gave me a quick hug. "I'm sure Mr. Witt will sort this out."

I was sure of nothing of the sort, but I put on a smile and waved goodbye.

* * *

As I headed to lunch a couple hours later, I braced myself for more questions about Start from Chava and Sally. But what I didn't brace myself for was the dozen other kids who showed up at our table as soon as I sat down.

Emily Wallace slid in right next to me. A few of her friends joined her. And of course wherever Emily goes, boys follow. The guy who had once offhandedly called me a "lesbo" sat down next to Chava, who looked like she was maybe going to faint. A bunch of other guys in T-shirts, sweatshirts, track pants, and other gear that proclaimed GLENDALE LACROSSE gathered around, too.

"What's going on?" I asked, looking around the table. Looking for escape routes. Looking for a lunch monitor.

"Nothing," replied one of the girls. "Just eating lunch with you."

And you might think I would be happy to have the popular kids sitting with me, like: This could be it! The moment when my fortune changes! Next stop is homecoming queen, student council president, and juggling three boyfriends at once!

But that wasn't what I wanted. It never had been. Leave those dreams to Sally and Chava. I hadn't wanted popularity; I had only wanted friends.

"Tuna fish," said another girl, pointing at my sandwich. "Good choice."

"For real," agreed another. "I wish I'd brought tuna fish today."

I looked at Sally and Chava and raised my eyebrows as high as they would go, to say, *This is weird, right?* But Sally and Chava were too busy beaming at all our lunch guests, like desperate hostesses who hadn't been quite sure that their party would ever begin.

"I wish I had tuna today, too!" was Chava's contribution.

Conversation continued in this vein for a few more minutes before one of the less tactful guys, who clearly couldn't handle the suspense any longer, burst out: "I saw you in the paper!"

"Me, too," I said, eating a bite of my sandwich, which, if the girls were to be believed, was the most miraculous sandwich ever to grace the Glendale High cafeteria. I tried to ready myself for what these people, these people who did not understand, would have to say about Start.

"Did you really go to that warehouse party?" asked another guy.

"Of course she did," said the first one. "There was a *photo* of her there."

"Chava and I drove her there last night," Sally answered proudly. "She was grounded, so she snuck out of the house. I was the getaway car."

"That's cool," a girl said to Sally, in a tone like she legitimately meant it. Sally beamed. Then the girl turned to me. "So you actually DJ there?"

I tried to smile as the walls I'd built between Start and school, my real life and my dream life, came crashing down piece by piece, battered away by lacrosse sticks and mascara wands.

"I went to see her once," Emily butted in. All eyes snapped to her. "Guys, it was *so* much better than a school dance."

Everyone murmured their approval and envy of Emily's lifestyle.

"How did you get to do that, though?" one of the guys asked me. "I mean, why *you*?"

"I don't know," I answered. "Luck of the draw?" But that was a lie, and I couldn't do it; I just couldn't leave it at that. "And I'm good at it," I added.

Oh, you think you're so great. You think you're so special. You think you're so much better than everyone else.

But no one said that. Just my own mind.

"Here's the bit I don't understand," Emily began, and again everyone turned to listen to her. "Why do you write that super-depressing blog about how nobody likes you and you hate your life, wah wah, when you get to be a *DJ*? I wouldn't complain that much if I were you."

"Oh, that's easy," I responded. "Because I don't actually write that blog."

Emily paused for just a second, and then she said, "Okay, that makes more sense."

Mr. Witt couldn't believe that someone would write a blog pretending to be me, because he is an adult, and adults don't do things like that. And Amelia Kindl couldn't believe it, because she is a nice girl, and nice girls don't do things like that either. But Emily Wallace believed it immediately. Because she's a mean girl. So she knew exactly the things that mean girls do.

"Who writes it, then?" asked one of Emily's friends.

"I have no idea," I said. "Mr. Witt is supposedly trying to figure that out."

Everyone at the table snorted as one. "Oh, yeah," said a girl. "I bet he'll get real far with that."

"Remember that time he thought I'd stolen Colin's phone?" said a guy. "Mr. Witt doesn't know shit about how this school works."

"Anyway, Elise," said one of the girls, "tell us more about the club. It was hidden in a warehouse, right? How did you even find out about it?"

So I told them, sort of. I talked about Start for the rest of the lunch period, but the safe parts: what kind of music we played, how people there dressed. I didn't mention Char, or Vicky, or anyone specific. Sally and Chava delightedly shared their celery sticks with all our guests, and contributed to the story wherever they could, like by saying, "Yeah, Elise has always liked music a lot!" and so on.

It felt good, this sense of power. I had something, or I knew something, that these kids wanted. And for that reason, they were treating me with respect. They had seen I wasn't the person who they'd thought I was, so now they were treating me differently, like the new person who they thought I was. Perhaps this was how it felt to be popular all the time.

But power was not friendship. And these people were not my friends.

When the bell rang, everyone got up to throw away his or her trash. But before I could leave the table, Sally and Chava each grabbed one of my arms.

"Thank you," whispered Sally.

"That was the best lunch I've ever had," whispered Chava.

I guess I had managed to give them something, after all. "Thanks, guys," I said. "Me, too."

Sometime during last period, the PA crackled to life. "Please send Elise Dembowski to Mr. Witt's office," the staticky voice said. "Elise Dembowski, to Mr. Witt's office."

Everyone in my history class went "Oooh," which is pretty much the only appropriate response when one of your classmates gets called into the vice principal's office.

I don't know what I expected to find in Mr. Witt's office. But what I know I did *not* expect to see was Amelia Kindl's friend there. The one who had won the prize for making that documentary film about people at mummy conventions.

"Oh, hey," I said to her, and, "Hello again," to Mr. Witt.

He replied, "Elise, we have something important to discuss with you. Marissa, would you like to start?" He gestured toward the *Wrappers* documentary girl.

Her face was almost as red as her crocheted scarf when she said to me, in a mechanical tone, "I wanted to apologize. For the blog. Elise Dembowski's Super-Secret Diary."

"What?" I said.

She looked at Mr. Witt and he nodded. "I wrote it," she muttered.

"You . . ." I stared at her. She was short, with a bob cut and cat-eye glasses. Her fingernails were stubby, with chipped nail polish, and the toes of her Converse sneakers were scuffed.

"*You* wrote it?" I said. "Why? You don't even know me. I didn't even know your *name* until two seconds ago." I took a breath. "How could you not even know me and still hate me enough to do something like this?"

She drew herself up to her full height, which still left her a couple inches shorter than me. "It's postmodern," she explained, drawing out the word as if she were speaking to someone who had only recently learned English. "It's a piece of experimental art."

"It's not art," I told her. "It's my *life*."

"Watch that tone, Elise!" Mr. Witt murmured.

"Oh, you want to hear a tone?" I asked. "Here's one for you. 'Nobody likes me. Why would *anyone ever* really like me?' Does that *tone* sound familiar to you?"

A feeling was welling up inside of me, so strong that I felt it spilling out of my eyes and mouth and nose. It was strong, but it was nothing I was accustomed to, so it took me a moment to identify it.

I was angry. Not at myself. I was angry at someone else.

"It's an exercise in storytelling," Marissa appealed to Mr. Witt. "Trying to get in the mind-set of someone else, trying to see the world through their eyes."

"Don't you *dare* tell me what my mind-set is," I said.

"I'm using the blog as part of my application for the Gutenstein arts fellowship," Marissa said to Mr. Witt. "They really like this sort of thing. Giving voice to the voiceless. I'm sorry you didn't like the writing, Elise, but you have to remember it's not really about *you*. It's about a character who just happens to share your name."

"Marissa," Mr. Witt said, "this is bullying, and here at Glendale High, we take bullying very, very seriously."

This was news to me.

He went on, "I'm going to call your parents so we can discuss how to proceed. But for now, I can tell you that you're suspended, and this will go on your permanent record. You will take down the blog and replace it with an explanation and apology post, to be approved first by me. You will not be allowed to attend the graduation ceremony or the Freshman/Sophomore

Summer Formal. And the school will no longer support your application for the arts fellowship."

"What?" she shrieked. "Are you serious?"

"Very," he said. "Now I'm going to let Elise get on with her day, while you stay here and we sort this out. But before she goes, is there anything else you want to say to her?"

Marissa stood still for a moment, her mouth moving, like she was trying to figure out what words to form. At last, she settled on, "Nobody at this school appreciates artists."

"Give me a break," I said, and I walked out.

And what I realized in that moment, as I turned my back on the voice of Fake Elise, is this:

Sometimes people think they know you. They know a few facts about you, and they piece you together in a way that makes sense to them. And if you don't know yourself very well, you might even believe that they are right. But the truth is, that isn't you. That isn't you at all.

The final bell was minutes away from ringing, so I didn't see any point in going back to class. Instead I walked outside to wait for my mother to pick me up. I stood for a moment on the wide stone front steps of the school, turning my face up to the almost-summer sunshine. And I smiled. Because I had met Fake Elise. I had seen her face-to-face. And she was *nobody*.

I heard a voice behind me. "Did Mr. Witt talk to you?"

I turned around to see Emily, alone. Two words that do not go together. "Yes," I said.

"Cool." She stepped out of the shade of the building and immediately pulled her Gucci sunglasses down over her eyes. "I told him," she added.

"Mr. Witt?"

"Yeah. I told him who wrote that blog."

"You knew?" I asked, surprised that someone like Marissa would discuss her insane creative pursuits with someone like Emily.

"Of course not." Emily made a face like she'd taken a bite of raw meat. "I've never talked to that girl before. She's weird. I just found out."

"How?" I asked.

"What do you mean, 'how'? The same way anyone knows anything. I ask. People tell me stuff."

"Well." I cleared my throat. "Thank you, Emily. That was really . . . like, surprisingly kind of you. I appreciate it."

"You're probably wondering what I want in exchange," Emily said, immediately undermining any credit I had given her for surprising kindness.

"Now I am." I shut my eyes for a moment. If there's one thing I never asked for, it was to sell my soul to Emily Wallace.

Emily turned her head to glance around, as if to make sure no one was there to hear her. Then she leaned in and said in a low voice, "I want to go to your party tonight. You know, the one that was listed in the paper. Also, Petra's coming. And Ashley. *Do not* get us kicked out again. That is not acceptable."

Emily flashed me her pearly white teen-model smile. If she'd been trying to sell me toothpaste, I might have even bought it.

I considered telling her that I didn't even know if I was *going* to my party tonight—didn't know if I wanted to, didn't know if I was allowed—but that was, frankly, none of Emily's business. "That's it?" I asked.

She pursed her lips, like it hadn't occurred to ~~her~~ that ~~she~~ might wrangle yet another payment out of me f~~or her~~ good deed and she wanted to make sure she use~~d it well. At~~ last she asked, "So did you actually try to kill yourself? Or did that weird bitch just make up the whole thing?"

Silently, I held up my left arm, wrist facing Emily. She crossed her arms and kept her lips squished together as she examined me for a moment, sizing up those three perfect scars. Finally, she said, "You know that you're supposed to cut *down* to kill yourself, right? You did it wrong."

I looked at Emily and thought about what would have happened if I'd cut the other way. Or what wouldn't have happened. Char wouldn't have broken up with me. Alex wouldn't be mad at me. Pippa wouldn't hate me.

And I would never have met Vicky. I would never have had my first kiss. I would never have worn rhinestone pumps. I would never have heard Big Audio Dynamite. I would never have discovered Start. I would never have known I could be a DJ.

Emily Wallace didn't know what she was talking about. She never had.

You did it wrong, she said.

"No," I said to her. "I didn't." Then my mother's car pulled up in front of the school, and I turned my back on Emily, and I walked away.

18

"YOU COULD HAVE TOLD US," MOM SAID AS SHE drove me to Alex's fair. Before my mother picked me up, Mr. Witt had called her to reveal the identity of the blogger and reassure her that Glendale High was once again, as promised, a Very Nice School. "You could have shown that diary to your father, or me, or Steve, and we would have put an end to this long ago."

You couldn't have put an end to it, I wanted to tell her. *You don't have the power of Emily Wallace.*

"Don't you think having a conversation about what was going on would have been more productive than ruining Alex's school project?"

"I thought I was helping her," I said. "At the time."

"And now?" Mom asked.

"Now . . . no. I don't think that anymore."

Mom nodded. "You're a smart cookie, Elise."

I had always loved when she said that to me, because she was one of the only people in the world who didn't make it sound like a put-down.

"So can I stop being grounded?" I asked.

Mom laughed lightly as she paused at a stop sign. "No matter how much you've seen the error of your ways, you really hurt your sister. And you really hurt this family. I can't let you off the hook so easily. It wouldn't be fair. You can't be ungrounded, but here's what you *can* do: you can come home."

The idea of walking back into my mom's house after a week away, lying in my big bed there, wrestling with Bone and Chew-Toy, sitting with Alex and Neil and Steve around the breakfast table, having Dinnertime Conversation . . . it made me smile.

"I'd like to come home," I said. "I'd like that a lot."

Mom parked the car at Alex's school's parking lot, and together we walked into the fair.

At Glendale East Elementary School, everyone was in high spirits. The soccer field was filled with the second graders' booths. Older kids ran around selling popcorn and cotton candy. There was even a bouncy castle. Steve, Neil, and Alex had already arrived, and they were standing at Alex's replacement booth, which consisted of a few cardboard boxes duct taped together with a handful of quickly scrawled poems sitting on top of them. It was nothing like the real poetry castle. It was more like a condemned poetry shack. Looking at it made my stomach turn.

"Hey," I said, bending down to address my little sister. "Can I talk to you for a second?"

Alex shook her head and hid behind Mom's legs. I briefly

wished that my genetic code did not include quite so much stubbornness.

"Just hear your sister out, Alex," Mom said, stepping aside. "Let her say her piece."

Alex scowled and followed me a few paces away from her booth. She was tightly clutching one of her favorite Barbies, glaring at me like I might lunge out and start tearing her doll limb from limb.

"Alex," I said, "I'm sorry. I shouldn't have ruined your poetry castle. I'll never do anything like that again."

She pretended to ignore me, mumbling to her Barbie as she made it crawl across a nearby tree branch, clearly playing some imaginary game.

This gave me an idea.

"You know that game you play, Underwater Capture?" I asked her.

"I can't play it anymore." Those were the first words my sister had spoken to me since last Friday. "Because of the new couch."

"But you know the evil sea witch in Underwater Capture?" I pressed on. "The one who gets inside the dolls' heads and turns them all evil?"

Alex nodded once, not looking at me.

"That's like what happened to me, Alex."

She looked at me then, her forehead wrinkled.

"It wasn't a real sea witch," I explained. "It was people I know. But that's how it felt—like all these bad thoughts were in my head, and I didn't know they weren't really mine. And that's why I wrecked your castle. It wasn't the sea witch's *fault*, since

I'm the one who did it. But I did it because I was listening to her too much. Does that make sense?"

I couldn't tell if I had taken this analogy too far, or if seven-year-olds even understand analogies, but after a moment, Alex nodded. "I'm sorry you had a sea witch," she said.

"Me, too."

"But—" She shook her head, as if shaking herself free from feeling any sort of sympathy for me. "You *ruined* my *poetry castle*. That's mean, Elise. That's the meanest thing anyone has ever done to me. And I know sea witches are evil, but *I don't care* why you did it. You *shouldn't have done it*."

"I know," I said. "I'm so sorry, Alex. I know."

But it was too late; Alex had already stalked off.

And after that, I didn't know what to do. What do you do when you say sorry, but that still isn't enough?

I walked slowly around the fair. I saw a post office and a cookie store and a booth that sold worms and caterpillars, although the second grader in charge told me they were all out of caterpillars.

I smiled at all the kids and told them what good jobs they had done. But inside, I felt like my heart was breaking. Because Mom was right: Alex's booth would have been the best one.

The thing was, Alex's replacement booth was no worse than half the other ones out on this field. In a week, she had thrown together something that was just about as good as what her classmates had done. Just about as good as theirs, but a fraction of how impressive she was capable of being.

Because of me, and what I had done to her.

In that moment, paused between a booth that sold papier-mâché flowers and a booth advertising mud sculptures, I knew this, suddenly but finally: I wanted to DJ my party tonight. Not to prove Char wrong, not to put Emily and her friends on the guest list, not for anything like that. Simply because Alex deserved to be the best that she could be. And I did, too.

After the fair was over and all the booths had been broken down, Mom and Steve took me, Alex, and Neil out for pizza.

Pizza is a rare treat in the Myers household, reserved for special occasions like winning art contests, performing the lead role in the school play, definitively triumphing over the oil industry, or making it through the most traumatic second-grade school fair in all of history.

"Let's get it with pepperoni," Alex said as we headed to the parking lot.

"Let's get it with maple syrup," Neil said.

"Let's get it with pepperoni *and maple syrup*," Alex said.

We would get it plain, and with soy cheese. We always did.

Alex and Neil rode in Steve's car, while I traveled to Antonio's Pizzeria with my mother.

"Mom," I said as we left the school, "I know I'm still grounded. But—can I be a *little* ungrounded?"

"Tell me what that means, and I'll tell you yes or no."

I took a deep breath. "Can I get, like, a furlough, just for one night? Tomorrow I swear I'll go back to being grounded. But tonight I'm . . . supposed to DJ a dance party. At that warehouse where Dad picked me up last night."

Mom sighed. "I know."

"You do?"

"Your father told me he saw it listed in the paper." She glanced at me sideways, and my face must have conveyed my surprise, because she said dryly, "Just because we're divorced doesn't mean we don't know how to exchange a civil e-mail, you know."

"So can I?"

Her fingernails drummed against the steering wheel, and her voice was tense as she answered, "You shouldn't be out of the house that late at night. You're way too young to drink—"

"But I *don't* drink," I protested.

"—and I can't have you hanging out with drunk people either. Especially not *ever* drunk people who are driving you somewhere."

"I don't," I said. "I wouldn't."

"It terrifies me to think of you wandering the streets alone at night, because you're a sixteen-year-old girl and you're an easy target. And I don't want you spending your time with so many people who are so much older than you, because I worry they are going to take advantage of you, just because you're young. I don't think you appreciate how recklessly you've been acting, and how lucky you've been so far. I can't let this kind of behavior go on."

So this was it, then. The moment when my mother forbade me to go back to Start. I wanted to feel shocked, but instead I felt only sadness.

And now, what would I have?

Well, I would have Sally and Chava. And that was something worth having; at least, more worth having than I had known.

I would have the respect of Emily Wallace and company. I didn't expect that they would ever honestly like me, but that was okay; I didn't expect to like them either. But I also didn't believe that they would offer to give me a makeover any time soon.

I would have Vicky and Harry, and maybe someday, if she could ever forgive me, Pippa, too. They weren't nightlife friends. They were real-life friends.

I would have memories of when I was golden.

I would have less than I had two weeks ago. But more than I had in September.

"But," Mom was saying, as she turned onto the street that Antonio's was on.

"But," I repeated, coming back to the present.

"I'm not going to tell you that you can't go."

I blinked. "You're not?"

She scanned the street for a parking space. "More than anything else that I don't want, I don't want to keep you from doing something that you love so much. I can't do it. It wouldn't be fair."

I felt tears pricking my eyes, but not the same sort of tears that I had cried last Thursday night, coming home from Start. "Thank you," I whispered.

"One condition," Mom said, finding a spot and backing into it. "Your father will need to drive you there and home."

I rubbed my eyes to clear them. "You're kidding, right? You think Dad actually wants to hang out in a warehouse nightclub until, like, three a.m.?"

"No," she said. "In fact, I know for sure that he doesn't. But he wants to know you're safe. We *both* want to know that you're safe, always. And if that means your father stays up until sunrise sometimes, then that's what we'll do." I opened my mouth, but she said, "Don't even try to argue, or you're not going anywhere."

"Okay," I said in a small voice. "It's a deal."

She turned off the car and faced me. "I'm really disappointed in you, Elise."

"I know."

"Not just because of how you treated Alex. I really believe you're in the process of making that right, even if it takes time. But because of how you treated *me*. If you want to do something like go for a walk in the middle of the night, or party at a nightclub, tell me. I know I'm your mother, but I'm a reasonable person. I think we can work these things out."

I brushed my hair out of my face. "You can't always make me safe," I said. "Just by having a parent home with me every evening, or grounding me, or giving me a chaperone every time I want to go out past nightfall. That's not how it works."

There are dangers everywhere, I wanted to explain to her. On the school bus, in the cafeteria, at Start, inside of me. No parent—no one at all—can step in and vanquish every one of them.

"I know that," Mom said. "But I *want* to always make you safe."

We got out of the car and joined the rest of the family in line at Antonio's. Neil can handle standing in line for roughly three seconds before he gets bored and starts roaming and twirling around poles. Alex quickly convinced him to play a game where they pretended to be lions who were being harpooned by hunters, so they started crawling on all fours, stepping on other

251

customers' feet. Steve said reasonable things like, "Champ, the floor's pretty dirty. Do you really want to get dirt all over your hands?" while I pulled out my iPod and pretended like I had never seen these people before in my life.

At last we got to the front of the line. "What can I get for you?" asked the guy behind the counter.

I looked up. I knew that voice.

It was Char.

The guy taking our pizza order, the guy in a tucked-in white button-down shirt and an apron, the guy speaking to my mother right now, *was Char.*

When he saw me, his eyes widened. He opened then closed his mouth.

"Roooawr!" Alex shouted from underfoot.

"One plain pizza, please," Mom said to Char, fumbling in her purse for her wallet. "With soy cheese."

It had been just over a week since Char and I had last spoken, since he had told me he didn't want to see me anymore. A week isn't very much time. Weeks often go by where nothing much happens at all.

But so much had changed in this past week. Even Char, here in the fluorescent lights, with his tomato sauce–stained apron, did not look quite the same. And while a week ago losing him cut me to the bone, today I saw him and just felt sad. I was sad that Char was never going to be the person I hoped he would be.

But I was never going to be the person he hoped I would be either. And I was just fine with that.

"Do you take credit cards?" Mom asked.

"Sorry, we're cash only," he replied.

This wasn't how I imagined things going. But imagination is so often no match for the absurdity, the randomness, the tragedy of reality.

"So what brings you all to Antonio's today?" Char asked as he made change for my mother.

"Just celebrating our kids," Mom answered. "That lion on the floor just had the best booth at the second-grade fair."

Alex made mewing noises and crumpled to the side, like the safari hunters had successfully stabbed her. She fell onto my feet, which seemed maybe like progress, since earlier she wouldn't even let me touch her. I thought about how funny it was that Alex's cobbled-together poetry hut still counted as "the best" for my mother.

"And this one"—Mom put her arm around me and squeezed—"is about to be the disc jockey at the best party this town has ever seen."

"Mom!" I hissed. I wriggled out of her embrace.

On the floor, Alex also hissed. The murdered lion had somehow turned into a snake.

"She gets easily embarrassed," Mom told Char. "Teenagers."

If I had one of Alex's imaginary hunting sticks in hand, I would not have hesitated to ram it into my mother's mouth at that moment.

"Sounds like a big night," Char replied. He looked me straight in the eye, as he had so many times before, and I wanted to throw my arms around him just about as much as I wanted to punch him in the stomach. "Good luck."

I unstuck my tongue from the roof of my mouth. "Thank you," I said.

A bell dinged. "Pizza's up," Char said. He reached behind him and handed the box to my mother. "Have a nice night, folks."

"Oh, don't worry," I said as we turned to go. "I will."

Together, the Myers household walked out of there: the founders of BOO OIL, a teenage DJ, and two mountain snakes, slithering all the way out the door.

19

WHEN MY PHONE RANG A COUPLE HOURS LATER, I knew who it was. I knew because this was one of the only phone numbers programmed into my cell phone, which my parents had kindly given back to me at school this morning. After what had happened last night, they said they wanted to know that they could reach me.

"Hello, Amelia," I answered.

"Elise?" she said, her voice tentative, gentle, hopeful.

And just the way she said my name sent me back, back almost ten months. I looked over to the corner of my room, like I expected to see a ghost of myself still there, back pressed up against the wall, left arm cradled up to her chest, right hand holding the phone that connected her to Amelia Kindl.

"Elise?"

"Hi, Amelia."

"What's going on?"

"I cut myself."

"Oh, no! Are you okay?"

"I don't know."

"Are your parents there? What happened?"

"I cut myself. Three times."

"You poor thing. How?"

"With an X-Acto knife."

"Wait. What? Elise, what did you say?"

"My dad really likes to cut out articles from the newspaper. You know, to give to people when he thinks they'd be interested. Well, mostly just me. I don't think he cuts out stories for anyone else."

"Elise, is your dad there with you? Is anyone there?"

"No, it's just that's why he has an X-Acto knife. For the newspaper."

"Are you bleeding?"

"Yes, but it doesn't actually hurt that much. It's weird; it doesn't hurt as much as I thought it would. When I was six years old I got mad at my mom and slammed the door, only somehow I slammed the door on my fingers. There was blood everywhere that time. It hurt a lot more than this. It was an accident, though."

"Elise, I'm going to call 911, okay?"

"You don't have to do that. I think it'll be fine."

"No, I want to do it, okay? I want to help. Can I put you on hold so I can call 911?"

"You want to help me?"

"Yeah, I do. Of course I do. Can I put you on hold for just one second?"

"Great. Since you want to help me so much: do you see me, Amelia?"

"I don't know what you mean."

"Do you see me! *I've gone to school with you every day since sixth grade. Do you understand me? Do you understand why I did this to myself? Do you see?"*

"Sure, Elise, of course. Let me—"

"Then can you please explain it to me?"

"I'm calling 911 now. Help will be there soon. It will be okay."

"But can't you just talk to me?"

Nothing. Just silence. And then, sirens.

"Elise, are you there?" Amelia asked, her voice in my ear jolting me back to present day.

"I'm here," I said.

"Great! Look, I'm calling to apologize about Marissa. I only found out this afternoon that she's the one who was writing that whole blog about you, and I feel awful about it. Just *awful*. I shouldn't have accused you of saying mean things about me online, because of course it wasn't you at all, but I thought it was.

"And I shouldn't have ever told Marissa that you called me that time in September when . . . well, you know. It wasn't any of my business, I know that. I promise I only told a few people: my parents, Marissa, one or two of my other best friends. I want you to know I wasn't spreading it all over school that you . . . you know, hurt yourself. I was just so panicked after you called me, and I didn't know what to do, so I talked it through with a few close friends. I wasn't trying to spread rumors about you or anything."

"Amelia," I said, "it's fine."

"I really am sorry about the way Marissa treated you, though," she said. "I had no idea she was like that."

Amelia, it occurred to me then, was not very good at reading a crowd.

"I just feel like this whole thing is my fault," she went on. "Is there anything I can do to make it up to you?"

I thought of all the responses I would have rattled off had she asked me this same question just a couple months ago. *Let me sit with you at lunch. Invite me to hang out with you on weekends. Text me sometimes. Listen to this mix I made for you. Have dinner with my family, and when that's over, pretend to do homework in the living room with me while my sister and brother distract us, and we pretend to care, but we don't.*

But Amelia is nice. That's all. That doesn't make her my friend, that doesn't make her special, and that doesn't make her anything I want her to be. It has nothing to do with me. She's just nice.

So I said, "Amelia, don't worry about it. It isn't your fault."

"I just . . . when I called 911 that time . . . I was trying to help. And I feel like it totally backfired, you know?"

"You did the right thing, calling an ambulance," I told her. "You didn't know how serious it was; you weren't there with me." I thought about how I would have responded if someone had called me in the way that I called Amelia. How scared would I have felt? How responsible? "I would have done the same thing if I were in your position."

"Honestly?" she asked.

"Yes," I said. "I would have. It's okay, Amelia. I'm not mad at you."

After Amelia and I hung up, I sat on my bed for a moment, my phone cupped in my hand. There was still one other person that I needed to talk to. So I lifted the phone again, and I dialed Vicky's number.

She answered after one ring. "Where the hell have you been?"

"Grounded," I said.

"Grounded," Vicky repeated.

"Yeah, I . . . It's a long story. I did something mean to my sister, so my mom took away my phone."

"You could have e-mailed or something," Vicky pointed out. "You could have found some way to let me know you were all right."

"I know," I said. "I'm sorry."

"The last time I saw you, you basically told me that you're suicidal because nobody likes you. The next thing I knew, you'd disappeared, Pippa and Char were making out, and you weren't talking to me for a week. I've been freaking out, Elise. *Harry* has been freaking out. And he *never* freaks out."

"I'm not suicidal," I said. I held my arm out in front of me and twisted it back and forth. Palm up. Palm down. Now you look fractured. Now you look whole.

"That's not the story your arm told."

"I did that a long time ago. Before I knew you or Harry or Mel, or Pippa or Char or Pete, or Start. I didn't know then how good life could be. But now I know. And I would never do it again."

"I think I can speak with some expertise on the issue of personally inflicted bodily harm," Vicky said. "May I?"

"Go for it."

"*It's not worth it.* Sure, high school sucks sometimes. Some people will mess with you, whenever they want, and for no reason

259

except that they can. But hurting yourself is giving those people all the power, and they *don't deserve it.* Why would they deserve to have control over your life? Because they're cool? Because they're pretty? That's completely illogical."

"Where did you learn all this?" I asked her.

"Like I said. Lots and lots of therapy." She paused. "Also, almost dying from malnutrition. It gave me a lot of clarity."

"Thanks, Vicky."

"Anyway," Vicky said, "now that you're alive, the second most important thing: Is the party still on for tonight? You're ungrounded?"

"For about the next nine hours," I replied.

"Okay, then I need to go find something to wear that isn't a nightgown." She paused. "One last question on the self-mutilation thing."

"I don't really feel like having this conversation, Vicky."

"We won't. Just one last question. What did Char have to say about it?"

I frowned, confused. "Nothing. I mean, he doesn't know. Why would he?"

"Because you were hooking up," Vicky said softly. "For weeks."

I thought about that—the number of times he had pulled my shirt off of me, or grabbed my hands in his, kissed my shoulder. "I guess he never noticed?"

"No," Vicky said. "I guess he wouldn't." She didn't say anything more.

"Speaking of Char," I said, "I ran into him at a *pizza parlor* this afternoon."

"What did he say?" she asked. "Did he apologize?"

"No."

"Did he beg you to give him another chance?"

"No."

She sighed noisily. "He's such a waste of a good haircut."

"Hey," I said. "Do you know Char's real name?"

Vicky didn't even pause. "Sure. It's Michael. Michael Kirby. Why?"

"No reason," I said. "I'll see you tonight."

We hung up after that. Then I opened my computer, and I googled "Michael Kirby."

I wanted to know who Char really was. No more personas, no more images, no more pretending.

It was easy—so easy that I had to wonder why I had never asked Vicky for his real name before. Within ten minutes, I had a whole picture painted of Michael Kirby.

He was nineteen years old, turning twenty next week. He'd grown up in Westerly, about forty miles from here, the middle of three kids. On the high school track team, he would occasionally, but not all that often, finish in the top five in the 400-meter. He was one of eight trombone players in his high school's marching band. I watched a video of them playing at a county fair, but I had to watch it twice before I could tell which one of the blue-uniformed trombonists was him. Michael's dad worked in construction and his mom worked part-time as a secretary for Russell Gold, DDS, "Where Your Smile Makes Us Smile."

In Michael's freshman year at state college, he'd joined the college radio station and lived in Hutton Dorm. There was a photo of him wearing pajama pants at a study break, with a caption reading, *Michael's special snack: Chex Mix!* Now in his second year, he was only a part-time student; he spent the rest of the time as a server at Antonio's Pizzeria. He maintained Antonio's Web site, and when I clicked the "contact us" button at the bottom of the page, it opened an e-mail addressed to michael @antoniospizza.com.

That was Char. It was all laid out for me across the Internet. It was a simple portrait of a person, like a million other people, and I felt the magic of Char float off into the air, as if I'd blown on a pile of dust.

But you know better than anyone how the Internet sees everything and nothing, all at the same time.

After I had learned all I cared to learn about Michael Kirby, I looked up my own name.

Why do you do this? Why do you want to see what other people say you are?

I suppose it's because old habits die hard.

The first two search results were the same as always. *Elise Dembowski, MD. Elise Dembowski Tampa Florida school superintendent.*

But the third result was different. *Elise Dembowski suicide* had fallen down on the list. The third thing that came up when I typed in my own name was *Elise Dembowski DJ.*

I stared at my computer screen for a long moment, and I smiled. Then I closed my laptop and got ready for Start.

20

"SO YOU DECIDED TO SHOW UP AFTER ALL, HMM?" Mel said when I arrived at Start later that night. "Just couldn't stay away?"

"What can I say? The scene needs me," I told him.

Mel laughed. "Atta girl." Then he noticed who was behind me. "Hello," he said, sticking out his hand for a shake. "I'm Mel."

"I'm Joe Dembowski. Elise's dad," said my dad.

I closed my eyes briefly. *Please don't do anything to embarrass me, Dad.* Actually, my dearest hope had been that he wouldn't identify himself as related to me, period. Let everyone think he was just some lecherous old guy who enjoyed hanging out at warehouse parties on his own.

"You've come to see your daughter's big premiere?" Mel nodded his approval. "You've got a good dad," he said to me. "And don't worry about it, Joe; I don't need to see your ID."

"You've been taking care of Elise?" Dad asked, looking Mel up and down.

Mel shrugged modestly. "When she lets me."

Dad laughed and clapped him on the shoulder. "I know what you mean," he said. Then we entered Start.

"So this is where you've been spending all your time?" Dad asked, looking around the room. The party hadn't started yet, so it was almost entirely empty. The bartender's iPod was playing faintly on the speakers.

"Some of my time," I said cautiously.

Dad shrugged, like he wasn't impressed. Then he laughed. "You know what? You've come to enough of my gigs over the years. I'm glad to finally have the chance to return the favor."

"I'm glad, too," I said, and I was. Glad that we were back on speaking terms, glad that my dad understood what it meant to fall in love with music, glad that I had my own father and not Sally's. I hugged him suddenly.

"I'm proud of you, baby," Dad murmured. "Go out there and knock 'em dead."

"Thanks, Dad," I said. "Now would you please sit over by the bar and act like you don't know me all night?"

He nodded. "You got it."

I headed over to the DJ booth and started setting up. Char had always taken care of this part before, so I went slowly, checking and double-checking to make sure that everything was plugged in correctly.

Just as I was plugging in my last cords, the Dirty Curtains arrived.

"Helloooo, Glendale!" Harry shouted, raising his drumsticks in the air. "How y'all doing tonight? Glendale in the hooooouse!"

"Harry," Vicky said, a step behind him. "We've been over this. The drummer doesn't get to banter with the audience."

"What about the guitarist?" Dave asked, setting his guitar on the stage. "Does the guitarist get to banter?"

"No," Vicky said.

Dave shrugged. "That's cool. I didn't want to banter anyway."

"*I* did," Harry said. He raised his voice again. "Glendale, get your hands in the air if you're sexy! All sexy hands, in the air! Unsexy hands, you can just hang out."

"I swear to God," Vicky said, "I have the bantering under control. *I will handle the banter.* Just play your goddamn instruments."

I stepped down from the booth and gave Vicky a hug.

"Okay, I am *freaking out*." Vicky let go of me and took a step back. "Now tell me the truth: do these false eyelashes make me look like a My Little Pony?"

"Vicky!" I laughed. "Since when do you get stage fright?"

"Uh, since my whole life?"

"But you've performed in a zillion things. You were a cheerleader," I reminded her.

"Yeah, and shouting, 'Roosevelt Roosters, go go go!' in a yellow-and-green unitard really prepared me for singing in front of Start. Anyway, this is the first time I've performed *my* songs. Songs that *I* wrote. Not to mention the first time the Dirty Curtains have performed anywhere, ever. Like, all of a sudden the Dirty Curtains are a real band, instead of a few dudes who play video games on my TV and shed beard hair all over my rug while I try to make them rehearse."

I glanced over at the other two Dirty Curtains, who were plugging their instruments into amps and saying, "Testing, one two three," and, "Is this thing on?" and, "Cocksucker cocksucker cocksucker" into their mics.

"They seem like a real band to me," I said.

"I just don't want you to regret asking us to play on your big night," Vicky said. "We might suck. Are you prepared for people hearing us and, like, vomiting all over your dance floor?"

"Vicky," I said, resting my hands on her shoulders. "Repeat after me. *I deserve to be here.*"

"I deserve to be here," Vicky said, looking into my eyes.

"I don't care if anyone thinks I look stupid."

"I don't care if anyone thinks I look stupid," Vicky echoed quietly.

"Okay." I took my hands off her shoulders. "Do your stuff out there. Show no mercy."

Then Vicky went to help set up, while I went to the booth and put on my headphones. I cued up the Undertones' "Teenage Kicks." Then the clock hit ten, Mel opened the door, and the crowd came pouring in. The night had begun.

It felt different, DJing a party that was all my own. The whole success of the night rested on me. If I messed up, I didn't have Char there to save me. But there was something about it that I liked, too. Because if the night was a success, I didn't have Char there to take the credit. That was all mine.

And by midnight, I was ready to say it: the night was a success. The dance floor was full, a pulsating mass of bodies moving to every track I played. Char had talked about reading the crowd like you'd read a book, but tonight I had moved beyond even that. It felt like invisible veins and arteries ran between me and every person in that room, communicating information between us instantly and noiselessly. It wasn't like reading a story. It was like I was writing a story.

And *everyone* was there. I saw the Dirty Curtains, of course, flitting through the crowd, and Pippa, Pete, Flash Tommy, Emily Wallace and her friends, my dad.

Everyone was there, except for Char. His absence still hurt me. But it hurt less now than I had thought it would.

Shortly after midnight, Vicky showed up next to the DJ booth. "Ready?" she asked me. The Dirty Curtains were up on stage, Dave strapping his guitar over his shoulder and Harry adjusting his mic stand.

"So ready."

She flashed me a grin, then hopped up on the stage. I faded out the music, and Vicky shouted into the mic, "Ladies and gentlemen of Start, I have one question for you: *Are you ready to party?*"

"Woo!" a few people shouted, moving closer to the stage.

"Hit it!" Vicky said, and the Dirty Curtains began to play.

They were extraordinary.

I say this not as Vicky's friend, and not as the girl who booked the band to play, but as a DJ who has listened to thousands upon thousands of bands, who lives with earphones on, who attended her first live concert at the age of eight months because, as my father said, "Even infants like James Brown, right?" I've heard it all and I'm hard to impress.

But Vicky's band blew me away.

In a flapper-style dress and gold heels, she strutted around the stage like Tina Turner on steroids, her hair cascading down her back, her eyes flirting with the crowd, her voice never faltering. Behind her, the guys played their instruments madly, building a wall of sound for Vicky's vocals to rest on top of.

Everyone in the club pressed closer to the stage, and the cameras came out. The room filled with bright sparks of light.

Vicky marched to the front of the stage and held the mic up to her bright-red lips, almost like she was kissing it. The words came out of her like a cannon shot.

"Hey there. Yeah, you. You with the eyes.

Do you like what you see?

Do you like my chest?

Yeah, do you, do you?

Do I pass your test?

Yeah, do I, do I?

Do you like my hair?

Well, here's the thing, baby . . ."

Here she leaned forward, like she was about to tell the audience a secret, and she snapped out the last line:

"I don't care!"

The room filled with whoops and cheers as the Dirty Curtains slammed through the final chords of the song. When it was over, Harry was visibly covered in sweat, and Dave chugged about half a bottle of beer, his hand shaking. But Vicky looked as crisp as if she'd just emerged from a day at the spa.

"Hey, Start," she said into the mic, batting her false eyelashes. "We're the Dirty Curtains. And we like you."

"We like you, too!" shouted a voice from the back of the room.

Vicky chuckled. "Well, you're about to like us just a little bit more. Boys, let's go!"

Harry smacked his drumsticks together, and they were on to the next song.

I was so captivated by Vicky's performance that I didn't even notice Pippa approaching me until she was standing right next to me in the booth. She was wearing a black slip dress and a large hairclip with jewels and feathers. She had a cocktail in her hand, which made me suspect that whatever sort of anti-partying ethic her parents had tried to instill in her over the past few weeks hadn't worked that well.

"Hi, Pippa." I felt my heart beat faster.

"Hiya," Pippa replied, blinking rapidly. "Um, Vicky's doing great, isn't she?"

I nodded and waited for her to go on, because no way Pippa had come over here just to tell me that Vicky was "doing great"—which was, by the way, the understatement of the year.

"Look, Elise, I just wanted to say . . . well, thank you."

"For what?" I asked.

"For this." Pippa gestured around the room. "Thank you for giving Vicky the chance to play."

I shrugged. "I'm not doing her a favor or anything," I said. "She's incredibly talented. She deserves this."

"Obviously," Pippa agreed. "But people don't always get what they deserve." She shifted her weight from foot to foot. After a pause, she spoke again. "Vicky is my best friend. I'd do anything for her. Anyone who makes Vicky this happy is good with me. No matter what."

"Thank you," I said quietly. "And I'm sorry," I added, "about the whole Char thing."

"Oh." Pippa's cheeks flushed a little. "Yeah."

"But you know," I went on, hoping that Pippa could handle a little honesty, "it wasn't all my fault. Char kissed me first. I just kissed back."

Pippa's face drooped, like the idea of Char kissing me physically hurt her. "I know," she said. "I mean, I figured. I guess I told myself it was all your fault so that I could keep believing it wasn't what Char wanted. I think I just . . . wanted him to be something that he isn't."

"Me, too," I said. "But he isn't."

"But I really think," Pippa said, perking up, "that he *could be*. You know?"

"What?"

"Obviously Char made mistakes. And so did I, and so did you. But I just *know* that if I give him some time to think it through, and explain to him why he hurt me, he will be better next time."

"Seriously?" I said.

Pippa's eyes were bright with feverish intensity as she said, "Listen, Elise. I have met a million guys, and I have never felt about any of them the way that I feel about Char. Everything about him is perfect. I mean, except for some of the things he's done to me. But I honestly, *honestly* believe I can fix that part."

I said nothing. Because I didn't believe that at all. People are who they are and, try as you might, you cannot make them be what you want them to be.

Side by side, Pippa and I watched the rest of the Dirty Curtains' set together. Vicky had the audience in the palm of her hand. She shone brighter than any camera flash in the whole club.

When the last song drew to a close, the room burst into applause. Vicky pointed at me and shouted into her mic, "Thank you, DJ Elise, for booking us to play, and for being Glendale's hottest DJ!"

I blushed and rolled my eyes, but the applause somehow grew even louder as all eyes and cameras turned to me.

"We love you, Elise!" Vicky called.

The crowd picked up the cry. "We love you, Elise! We love you!"

I let this go on for another few seconds before I started up the turntables again and pressed play on the Pulp song "Common People." There was a collective shriek of excitement, and then the room exploded back into motion.

I looked out over the crowd and breathed in deeply. All this was mine.

In a way, Amelia Kindl had been right when she once said to me, "I saved your life." She was right, but not in the way she meant it. When she saw the suicide note on Elise Dembowski's Super-Secret Diary and called my father, she set into motion the chain of events that led to me being in the DJ booth tonight. And that, in a way, had saved my life.

I was playing the Justice vs. Simian song "We Are Your Friends," and everyone was jumping and flailing and singing along—"Because we are your friends, you'll never be alone again, well come on!"—when Harry approached the DJ booth. "Hey!" he yelled up to me. "Is it okay if I . . . ?"

"Of course!" I waved him up.

He climbed in next to me. "You are doing such a good job," he blurted out at the same time that I said, "You guys rocked!"

We both laughed.

"Seriously, you were awesome," I said. "I had no idea the Dirty Curtains were so good."

"Me neither!" Harry beamed. "And you know what? There was this old dude in the audience, and he's in some famous seventies band, and he told Vicky he thinks the Dirty Curtains could really be going places, and he wants to introduce us to his manager! Is that insane or what?"

I cracked up. I couldn't help myself. I looked across the bar to my dad, who was chatting with the bartender. "You're right," I said to Harry. "That's insane."

"Okay, now let's talk about how this is the best party I have ever been to in my entire life," Harry said. "Like, even better than my seventh birthday party when my mom bought me a Star Wars cake and we played Pin the Light Saber on the Jedi. Okay, just kidding, that was actually my thirteenth birthday."

I laughed again. "Hey, Harry," I said, and then I stopped.

"Yes, Elise?"

I swallowed. "Do you want to go to a way less exciting party tomorrow night?"

"With you?" Harry asked.

"Yeah. It's called the Glendale High Freshman/Sophomore Summer Formal. It's in the school gym."

"Yeah," he said. "I'll totally go to that with you."

We looked at each other and smiled. We were still looking at each other when the sound cut out.

I registered the shock on Harry's face an instant before I realized that the music had stopped. Frantic, I fumbled with the computer, the mixer, the wires, everything, trying to figure out what had gone wrong. I couldn't find the problem. I didn't know. Char had been right: I was too young, too inexperienced, and of course I had screwed this up. And he wasn't here; there was nobody to rescue me from silence.

Only there was no silence.

Everyone in that room kept singing, as though the music was still with them—no, more than singing, *screaming* really, insistent, off-tune, beautiful.

"Because we! are! your friends! you'll never be alone again! Well, come on! Well, come on! Well, come on! Well, come on!"

Their hands were in the air, raised toward me, heads thrown back, a spinning collection of lights and sound and people. An instant later, I figured out which wire I had knocked out. I re-plugged it and the song kicked back in, exactly in time with the singing crowd. And they all went nuts.

"Because we are your friends, you'll never be alone again!"

And for the first time in my life, I knew that was true.

I caught my breath, took a big gulp of water, and smiled. My party raged on.

You think it's so easy to change yourself. You think it's so easy, but it's not. True, things don't stay the same forever: couches are replaced, boys leave, you discover a song, your body becomes forever scarred. And with each of these moments you change and change again, your true self spinning, shifting positions—but always at last it returns to you, like a dancer on the floor. Because throughout it all, you are still, always, *you*: beautiful and bruised, known and unknowable. And isn't that—just you— enough?

ACKNOWLEDGMENTS

I am lucky to have so many supportive friends in my life, and it is thanks to their combined efforts that *This Song Will Save Your Life* came into being.

Thanks first and foremost to Joy Peskin, who is not only a friend to me, but also an extraordinary mentor, inspiration, teacher, and editor, too. I have been so fortunate to get to work with you over the years.

To the whole of Foundry Literary + Media, especially my agent, Stephen Barbara, for the devotion with which you take care of my career, and of me.

To the entire team at Farrar Straus Giroux, for welcoming me with such enthusiasm. Special thanks to Angie Chen, whose editorial insight is matched only by her talent with a pair of knitting needles; Elizabeth H. Clark, for the gorgeous cover design; and Kathryn Little and Molly Brouillette, for their energy and creativity.

To my copy editor and best parade-going friend, Kate Ritchey. *There are no grammatical errors in this book*. And if there are, that's my fault, not Kate's.

To my writing partner, Rebecca Serle, for dreaming big, and for daring me to dream even bigger.

To Katie Hanson, for sharing with me such a wonderful home for a writer to create.

To my parents, Amy Sales and Michael Sales, for, well, basically everything.

To all the DJs who have knowingly or unknowingly helped change my life. Special thanks to New York nightlife legend and international scenester, DJing skills consultant, and the voice of our generation, DJ VH1 (aka Brendan Sullivan). And to DJ Brian Blackout (aka Brian Pennington) for his kindness, ingenuity, sense of humor, and unwavering support.

To the book *How to DJ Right: The Art and Science of Playing Records*, by Frank Broughten and Bill Brewster, for showing me how to write about DJing right.

To my favorite dance-floor partners, including but not limited to Emily Haydock, Emily Heddleson, Kendra Levin, and Allison Smith.

Finally, thanks to all the dance parties that inspired and informed this novel, especially these: from Bristol, Ramshackle and Klub Kute; from New York City, Motherf*cker and Mondo; and from Boston, the Pill and, of course, Start.

BONUS MATERIALS

ELISE'S TOP SONGS TO PLAY AT START

Some of the songs you're most likely to hear at Start,
or at an indie dance party near you.

"The Boy with the Arab Strap," by Belle and Sebastian

"Girls and Boys," by Blur

"Cannonball," by the Breeders

"Dancing in the Dark," by Bruce Springsteen

"Train in Vain," by the Clash

"It's Friday, I'm in Love," by the Cure

"Just Like Heaven," by the Cure

"A Letter to Elise," by the Cure

"Lights & Music," by Cut Copy

"Modern Love," by David Bowie

"Just Can't Get Enough," Depeche Mode

"Come On Eileen," by Dexy's Midnight Runners

"Connection," by Elastica

"A Little Respect," by Erasure

"Ready for the Floor," by Hot Chip

"Town Called Malice," by the Jam

"Maple Leaves," by Jens Lekman

"Head On," by the Jesus and Mary Chain

"Love Will Tear Us Apart," by Joy Division

"D.A.N.C.E.," by Justice

"We Are Your Friends," by Justice vs. Simian

"All These Things That I've Done," by the Killers

"Victoria," by the Kinks

"Daft Punk Is Playing at My House," by LCD Soundsystem

"North American Scum," by LCD Soundsystem

"Deceptacon," by Le Tigre

"You! Me! Dancing!" by Los Campesinos

"Time to Pretend," by MGMT

"Bizarre Love Triangle," by New Order

"Blue Monday," by New Order

"Temptation," by New Order

"Smells Like Teen Spirit," by Nirvana

"Young Folks," by Peter, Bjorn and John

"1901," by Phoenix

"Debaser," by the Pixies

"Rocks," by Primal Scream

"Common People," by Pulp

"Mis-Shapes," by Pulp

"Whoo! Alright—Yeah . . . Uh Huh," by the Rapture

"Get Off of My Cloud," by the Rolling Stones

"Panic," by the Smiths

"This Charming Man," by the Smiths

"Elephant Stone," by the Stone Roses

"You Only Live Once," by the Strokes

"Beautiful Ones," by Suede

"Once in a Lifetime," by the Talking Heads

"Born Slippy NUXX," by Underworld

"Rock & Roll," by the Velvet Underground

"Bitter Sweet Symphony," by the Verve

"Baba O'Riley," by the Who

ELISE'S TOP TEN SONGS
FOR WALKING AT NIGHT

The only things you need are good walking shoes
and good headphones.

"Maybe You Can Owe Me," by Architecture in Helsinki

"Anthems for a Seventeen Year Old Girl," by Broken Social Scene

"Hey Jealousy," by Gin Blossoms

"Tonight the Streets Are Ours," by Richard Hawley

"Tourist," by RAC

"Vapour Trail," by Ride

"With Arms Outstretched," by Rilo Kiley

"Tonight I Have to Leave It," by the Shout Out Louds

"1979," by the Smashing Pumpkins

"The City," by Patrick Wolf

ELISE'S TOP TEN SONGS FOR STUDYING

A hot chocolate, a textbook, and this playlist—
you're all set for a night at your desk.

"Would You Say Stop?" by Acid House Kings

"I Didn't See It Coming," by Belle & Sebastian

"So Here We Are," by Bloc Party

"The Sweetest Thing," by Camera Obscura

"I'd Rather Dance with You," by Kings of Convenience

"Roadrunner," by the Modern Lovers

"In the Aeroplane Over the Sea," by Neutral Milk Hotel

"Such Great Heights," by the Postal Service
"Ladies and Gentlemen We Are Floating in Space," by Spiritualized
"Mersey Paradise," by the Stone Roses

ELISE'S TOP TEN SONGS
FOR THE DIRTY CURTAINS TO COVER

Vicky would totally rock these.

"Dancing with Myself," by Billy Idol
"Kiss Me Deadly," by Lita Ford
"Damaged Goods," by Gang of Four
"Standing in the Way of Control," by the Gossip
"How Will I Know," by Whitney Houston
"Bad Reputation," by Joan Jett
"Heartbeats," by the Knife
"When You Were Mine," by Cyndi Lauper
"Teenage Kicks," by the Undertones
"Maps," by Yeah Yeah Yeahs

ELISE'S TOP TEN DANCE PARTY OLDIES

*Classics—teenagers have been dancing to these songs
for half a century and they still feel fresh.*

"Quarter to Three," by Gary U.S. Bonds
"Papa's Got a Brand New Bag," by James Brown
"Do You Love Me," by the Contours
"Keep on Dancing," by the Gentrys

"Rave On," by Buddy Holly

"Twist and Shout," by the Isley Brothers

"Tossin' and Turnin'," by Bobby Lewis

"You Can't Hurry Love," by the Supremes

"(Your Love Keeps Lifting Me) Higher and Higher," by Jackie Wilson

"Uptight (Everything's Alright)," by Stevie Wonder

ELISE'S TOP TEN BREAKUP SONGS

For when you need to feel a little less alone.

"Evaporated," by Ben Folds Five

"This Modern Love," by Bloc Party

"Hallelujah," by Jeff Buckley

"Country Mile," by Camera Obscura

"Fight Test," by the Flaming Lips

"Someone Great," by LCD Soundsystem

"I Don't Want to Get Over You," by the Magnetic Fields

"Ceremony," by New Order

"I Know It's Over," by the Smiths

"Your Ex-Lover Is Dead," by Stars

DISCUSSION QUESTIONS

1. The opening line of the book is "You think it's so easy to change yourself." Do you think it's easy—or even possible—to change yourself? Why or why not?

2. Do you understand why Elise didn't tell her parents about the fake blog? Do you think they could have helped if they had known?

3. Char teaches Elise to "read the crowd" when she's picking songs. Do you think this lesson extends beyond DJing? In what ways is it possible to give people what they want and what they don't yet know they want?

4. Why do you think Elise called Amelia after she cut herself? What do you think she wanted Amelia to do, and why do you think she was so upset when Amelia called 911? What would you have done if you were Amelia?

5. Why do you think Elise fit in at Start when she had never really fit in anywhere else before?

6. How do you think Elise's feelings about Chava and Sally change over the course of the book, if at all?

7. Do you think Elise should have told her father about Start? Might he have understood, because he's a musician? Why or why not?

8. Even though Elise is hurt by Char in the end, do you think he did more good for her than bad? Why or why not?

9. Do you think Elise did anything wrong by getting together with Char while her friend Pippa had feelings for him? Is a boy or girl "off-limits" when your friend likes him or her?

10. Why do you think Elise destroyed Alex's poetry castle? Elise said she did it "to protect her. Like a big sister should." What was Elise trying to protect Alex from?

11. In the end, Elise makes friends and gains acceptance, just like she always wanted. But does she do this by changing herself, or becoming a truer version of herself?

A CONVERSATION WITH LEILA SALES
AND HER EDITOR, JOY PESKIN

"You think it's so easy to change yourself. You think it's so easy, but it's not." Leila Sales, this is a killer first line. Did you ever try to change yourself when you were a teenager? If so, in what way, and was the change successful?

I am not a person who likes change very much, so I never went on a full-fledged self-reinvention campaign like Elise did. But, of course, there were times I tried to make myself different in order to fit in.

For example, for many years, I refused to wear jeans. My rationale was that I might want to turn a cartwheel at a moment's notice, and jeans were too restrictive. In sixth grade, I guess my classmates were vaguely snide about how I was still wearing leggings "like a baby," or whatever, but I didn't pay much attention.

Then I showed up for the first day of seventh grade and noticed that *everybody* was wearing jeans. Every single girl in my entire middle school, except me. Maybe they always had, and I'd just never noticed enough to care before. So I decided that I, too, would wear jeans.

The problem was that I owned only one pair, and my parents didn't have time to take me shopping until the weekend, so for the entire first week of seventh grade, I wore the same pants, which actually resulted in *more* teasing than I would have gotten for wearing a different pair of leggings each day.

I don't know what to take away from that whole experience except that it is really hard to change yourself, and to change how people perceive you when they already have an idea in their minds about who you are.

Incidentally, I have now gone full circle and as an adult, I almost never wear jeans. I am 100% about the leggings. I'm sorry, jeans just *are* uncomfortable. I was right about that part.

Elise feels like she was born to be unpopular. Were you popular when you were her age? Don't try to play modest by saying you were "bookish," or "neither popular nor unpopular, but kind of in the middle." Tell us the honest truth.

Well, I guess I kind of gave away the answer to this question with my jeans story above! Look, I was unpopular up until the end of ninth grade, maybe early tenth grade. In eighth grade, I used to play a game with myself to see how many hours it would take until one of my classmates spoke to me directly, and sometimes an entire school day would go by and nobody would have said a word to me.

I moved to a small, all-girls school for high school (which later would be the inspiration for my novel *Mostly Good Girls*), and that made a huge difference. My new classmates were generally more accepting of girls who liked to read books and answer questions in class—many of them were those girls themselves. I never became popular in the queen bee/homecoming court/coed parties every weekend/teen movie sort of way. But eventually, I developed a group of girls who I really connected with, and they remain some of my closest friends to this day.

It sticks with you, though. I am in my early thirties now, and I have so many really amazing friends whom I love to death, and still sometimes I worry that I'm unpopular, even though, like, what does "unpopular" even mean when you are an adult? It's crazy how pernicious those teenage experiences are, and how those rejections can still affect your self-perception long after they are relevant.

We went back and forth on titles for this book before we ended up with *This Song Will Save Your Life*, which I really love by the way. So I'll ask it: Do you think a song can save someone's life, or perhaps more to the point, do you think music can help us through hard times?

Titling books is so hard! None of my books have been published with the titles that I'd initially given them. I forget whether it was me or you who ultimately came up with *This Song Will Save Your Life*, but I love it now.

Absolutely, I think music can get us through hard times. I remember when I was sixteen, I was going through some really hard stuff, when it just felt like everyone had turned against me, and I listened to the Matchbox Twenty album *Mad Season* over and over and over again because I felt like that band *got* me. It seemed like all of those songs could have been written about me, specifically, and about the heartbreaking experience that I was going through. That album saved me, as have so many other songs since then, because it made me realize that I'm not alone. Other people have gone through loss and pain, and they have emerged intact to create art about it, and you can, too.

You and I have often discussed our experiences as only children, and yet you really nailed the sibling relationships in this book. I particularly like the dynamic between Elise and Alex that develops around Alex's poetry castle. How did you get the sibling stuff so right?

I love being an only child, but both the protagonists of my first two novels were only children, and so I was like, "Okay, Leila, *somebody* has to have a sibling." I don't really know what that's like, though, having brothers and sisters, so the way I got around it was by giving Elise half-siblings who are much younger than she is. That way I felt like I'd "branched out" as a writer (e.g., into someone who writes about siblings), while still having Elise be the only child of her father and mother, like me!

I think I may like Char more than you do, in part because I think his lesson to Elise about how to give people a mix of what they know they already like and what they don't know they like yet is perfect for both DJing and life in general. Did you draw Char purely from imagination, or do you know a Char-esque DJ or two in real life?

Oh, I don't dislike Char! I would make out with him, I think. I mean, not *now*, since I am way too old for him and that's creepy. But when I was his age, I would have been into him.

Like all my characters, Char is an amalgamation of many people I've known over the course of my life, both male and female, both DJs and non-DJs, and then also some characteristics that I invented just for him. I borrowed the poster in his room and his tattoo and his dance moves, small pieces like that, from various people I've known. But no one I know in real life *is* Char. As an author, you need characters to be fictional, because otherwise they would never do what you need them to do!

I have known lots of DJs in my life, and the way that Char talks about music is based on them. I love listening to music and going out dancing. I don't know how to use turntables myself, but when I was in college I used to show up to parties with mix CDs in my coat pockets and slip them into the stereo when the hosts weren't looking, so clearly I have some hidden DJ aspirations.

"That's what I learned about myself on the first day of my sophomore year of high school: I didn't really want to die. I never had. All I ever wanted was attention." Powerful stuff, and perhaps the most powerful line in the book (if you ask me). I realize this is kind of a broad question, but why do you think we—as children, as teens, as adults, as humans—want attention? And more specifically, why do you think Elise wants attention? What does she hope getting people's attention will do for her?

Attention is validating, isn't it? If somebody pays attention to you, it's like proof that *you matter*. And if a *lot* of people pay attention to you and if they seem like important people, then that must be proof that you *really* matter.

Of course, we know this isn't rational. You matter regardless of who pays attention to you, and your opinions are legitimate even if no one wants to hear them, and your art can be meaningful even if nobody wants to look at it. You should never put other people in charge of deciding how much your life is worth. But that's hard to achieve. At the start of the book, Elise hasn't gotten there yet. So I think she wants attention to prove to herself that she is worth it.

How do you feel about the response you've received to the book? Have you heard from readers who relate to Elise in one way or another?

I've received some extraordinary emails and letters from readers. People who say that they've felt the same as Elise, or that they too have considered suicide, or that they wish they could find their passion, like Elise does with DJing, or that they *have* found a passion, and it's saved them. These notes from readers mean so much to me, and I never quite know how to express that to them. I just think of the books and movies and songs that have supported me over the years—like I was saying earlier about that Matchbox Twenty album in high school—and it feels astonishing that I have created a work that can help somebody else. It's the best feeling in the world.

Over the course of the book, Elise finds a passion, and a talent, for DJing. Where did you find your passion and talent—in high school music, theater, field hockey, basket weaving, writing, or something else?

Yeah, totally, how did you know I was a champion basket weaver? (Okay, not really.) Yes, writing has always been an important part of my life. I competed in debate in high school and college, which I loved. I did gymnastics until I was seventeen years old, and it's still hard to believe that someone who practiced for as many years as I did was still as bad as I was, but I was passionate about it nonetheless. In college, I started doing improv and sketch comedy, and that was maybe my favorite activity of all. All of those were opportunities for me to connect with other people, to have teammates who were rooting for me, and it felt like the exact opposite of eighth-grade Leila going all day without speaking to anyone.

This is a really important question, and I can't believe we've never

discussed it. Where did you get the idea for the line, "We sent rappers to the gallows on Friday"?

Like so many lines in my books: I have no clue. We have family friends with the last name Gallos, so that must be how I came up with the Gallos/gallows thing. As for the wrappers/rappers part—who knows? I have never actually heard of mummy conventions, but presumably they could exist? They sound like a thing that would exist.

Let's close out with a lightning round of Best Song For . . . a game I have just created.

Best song for getting over a breakup: "Someone Great," by LCD Soundsystem. "Fight Test," by the Flaming Lips. "Your Ex-Lover Is Dead," by Stars. Actually, I guess none of those will help you get over a breakup, but they will make you feel like you're not alone in your heartbreak.

Best song for a day you need to feel brave: "We Are Golden," by Mika.

Best song for a day when you feel on top of the world: "Time to Pretend," by MGMT. I listen to that song every time something good happens in my writing career, and it never lets me down!

HE SEEMED LIKE THE PERFECT GUY.
UNTIL THEY MET.

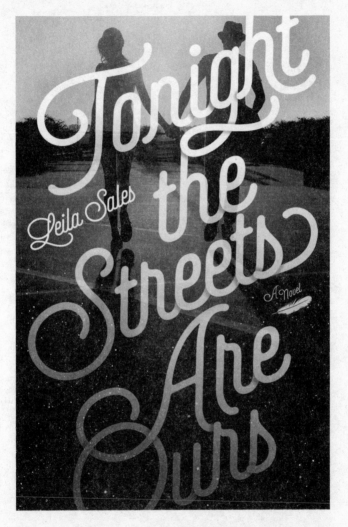

CAN ONE CRAZY NIGHT CHANGE YOU
FOREVER?

Part One

WELCOME.

Like all stories, the one you are about to read is a love story.
If it wasn't, what would be the point?

EVERYTHING FALLS APART.

"You can find your own way home," Arden says to Lindsey, her voice shaking with rage.

"Home . . . to Maryland?" Lindsey asks.

The three strangers sitting on mildewing couches beside Lindsey look on impassively. The mannequin's head, which hangs from a noose in the center of the room, sways gently back and forth, like it's making eye contact with Arden, then Lindsey, then back again.

Arden hesitates. "I mean, if you need my help . . ." she begins, but it's too late. Lindsey shakes her head. *No.* "Okay, then," Arden says. "You're on your own. Just how you wanted it."

"What's her *problem?*" The girl with a ring pierced through the center of her nose asks Lindsey, sneering at Arden.

Arden has almost never heard anybody speak about her in that tone of voice. Her stomach twists, and she swallows hard, looking to the boy by her side for support. He nods, and that gives her the courage she needs.

"I'm over this," Arden says to Lindsey. "Good luck finding your way out of here."

She turns and walks away, her legs trembling with every step. She focuses directly in front of her, navigating through the press of bodies and random sculptures of fairies and trees.

"Arden, wait!" she hears Lindsey call behind her, and she turns. But that must have just been her imagination crying out, because Lindsey is still sitting on the couch, talking to the pierced-nose girl, as if everything is normal. As if she doesn't even care that Arden is leaving her.

So Arden squares her shoulders. And she keeps walking away.

LET'S GO BACK IN TIME.

Two months before that night, back when Arden and Lindsey were still inseparable, when the only septum piercing Arden had ever seen was on punk rockers on TV and the only mannequins she'd encountered had been modeling clothes in store windows, shortly before the end of the school day on a Friday in February, Arden was summoned to the principal's office.

A runner showed up at her Spanish class and briefly consulted with Señor Stephanolpoulos, and Arden paid no attention because when the principal needed someone, it never had anything to do with her. Instead she took this break in the class to try to make sense of her notes, which were supposed to illuminate the future tense, but which in practice just said things like, "Irregular verbs . . . something," and, "Add 'i' or 'e' to end of words FIRST PERSON ONLY (??)"

Spanish was not Arden's strong suit.

"Arden." Señor Stephanolpoulos beckoned her. "You're needed in Principal Vanderpool's office."

There were a few "Oooh"s from her classmates, but halfhearted ones; none of them seriously believed that Arden Huntley, of all people, would be in trouble serious enough that it would warrant a visit to the principal.

"I'll take notes for you," whispered Arden's friend Naomi. Arden smiled her thanks. Naomi's notes tended to be word-for-word transcripts of teachers' lectures in stunningly legible purple-penned handwriting.

Arden lifted her bag and followed the runner out of the classroom, through a series of halls, and downstairs. Cumberland was one of those towns where land was at the opposite of a premium. It was in northwestern Maryland, so far west it was almost West Virginia, so far north it was almost Pennsylvania, a solid two-hour drive from the nearest big city (which was Pittsburgh), in a corner of the world that should have been called something like MaryVirgiPenn, but wasn't. All Cumberland *had* was land. As a result, the high school was sprawling, mega-mallsized—and the principal's office was at the other end of it.

Maybe Arden should have been nervous on that long walk to the principal, but she wasn't. She suspected this had something to do with her mother, and as such, she flat-out refused to care.

Eventually they reached Vanderpool's office, and the runner left her under the watchful eye of Mr. Winchell, the principal's geriatric secretary. Arden waited on a plastic, too-small chair that seemed better suited to an elementary school than to Allegany High.

When she thought Mr. Winchell wasn't watching, Arden slid her cell phone out of her bag and texted Lindsey. GOT CALLED INTO VAN'S OFFICE. WTF.

A minute later, Lindsey texted back. Arden knew that Lindsey should be in Earth Studies right now, so either she was cutting, or she was texting in the middle of class, both of which seemed like plausible Lindsey behaviors.

OH SHIT, was Lindsey's reply, and that gave Arden her first inkling that perhaps her best friend knew more than she herself did about why the principal wanted her. But before Arden could ask what, exactly, "oh shit" meant, Mr. Winchell snapped, "No telephones!" in the triumphant fashion of a man who has missed his true calling as a prison warden.

After another ten minutes of waiting, Arden was brought in to see the principal. Mr. Vanderpool was a preposterously tall human—so tall that it was easy not to notice how bald he was unless he was seated—who seemed awkward whenever confronted with actual teenagers rather than school board members or faculty. He rarely wandered the hallways and never showed his face in the cafeteria; his one interaction with the student body as a whole was during assembly, when he would stand on the stage and address them en masse, from afar. He had a seemingly endless collection of novelty neckties, which was either the one area of his life where he gave himself permission to entertain whimsy, or was his sad attempt at appearing "kid-friendly." Arden wasn't totally sure that Mr. Vanderpool knew who she was, as this was their first proper conversation in her nearly three years at his school.

"Arden Huntley," he said once she was seated in his office, on the other side of his desk. "Do you want to tell me why you're here?"

Arden blinked at him. "You called me here, Principal Vanderpool."

He looked pained. "I am aware of that. Do you want to tell me *why* I called you here?"

Arden really wished that Lindsey had said something a little more useful than "oh shit."

"Um, I don't know," Arden told the principal.

He cleared his throat and reached into a drawer in his desk. What he pulled out was a small plastic bag filled with some brownish flakes. "Does this look familiar?" he asked Arden.

"No?"

He sighed. "Arden, we found this bag of drugs in your locker today."

"What were you doing in my locker?" Arden blurted out, even though that was, perhaps, not her most pressing question.

"Routine random locker checks," Mr. Vanderpool replied. "But what I'd like to know is, what was *this*"—here he shook the baggie—"doing in your locker?"

Now Arden knew exactly what Lindsey's text message had meant, and she knew the answer to the principal's question, as well.

She and Lindsey shared lockers, as they shared pretty much everything. Thanks to stupid school bureaucracy and geography, they had been assigned lockers on opposite ends of the building from each other, and from where most of their classes and activities were. So Lindsey usually used the one that was officially Arden's, because it was closer to the gym, while Arden usually stored her stuff in Lindsey's, which was right by the theater and library. They had always known each other's combinations, to school lockers and to everything else, and Arden had seen nothing but benefits to this sort of sharing.

But that was before Lindsey, apparently, stashed a bag of pot in her locker.

Arden knew that Lindsey got high sometimes: weekends, parties, whatever. People did that—not *Arden*, but people, fine. But how could Lindsey have been so dumb, so thoughtless and foolhardy, as to bring it into school? Their school had a zero tolerance policy, a minimum three-day suspension for any student found in possession of any sort of drugs, no matter what kind, no matter what the quantity—though if they were worse drugs, in higher quantities, you risked a longer suspension or even expulsion. Everybody knew this.

But the worst part, for Lindsey, was that getting caught with drugs meant you were immediately kicked off all sports teams for the rest of the year. No way around it. And Lindsey *lived* for the school track team. She loved running roughly as much as Arden hated it. Not only that, but being recruited for track was basically Lindsey's only hope for getting accepted into a good college. She didn't have a whole lot else going for her. This was not, by the way, Arden's opinion. This was the opinion of countless guidance counselors, teachers, and Lindsey's own parents.

Arden knew what would happen if she explained exactly how that bag of marijuana wound up in her locker. Lindsey would lose it all. Over one casual, stupid decision, and one massive helping of bad luck. That sounded about par for the course, for Lindsey.

But fortunately, Arden didn't play any sports.